NETHERWORLD
FAE

A
NEST
OF
LIES

USA TODAY BESTSELLING AUTHOR
LEXI C. FOSS

This is a work of fiction. Names, characters, places, and incidents are either the product of the author's imagination or are used fictitiously, and any resemblance to actual persons, living or dead, business establishments, events, or locales is entirely coincidental.

A Nest of Lies

Editing by: Outthink Editing, LLC

Proofreading by: Katie Schmahl & Jean Bachen

Cover Design: Cover By Sanja Balan of Sanja's Covers

Title Page, Background Art & Chapter Headers by: Anna Spries

Illustrated Map by: Ricky Gunawan

Published by: Ninja Newt Publishing, LLC

Digital Edition

ISBN: 978-1-68530-408-9

Print Edition

ISBN: 978-1-68530-409-6

AI Disclaimer: This book does not contain any elements of AI content. All art was designed by real artists, and all of the words were written by the author.

For anyone struggling right now, please know that you're not alone. Writing is my mental escape, and the Netherworld Kingdom has provided me with a safe place to hide. So I hope you can find solace, understanding, and security in my fantasy realm, too.

Happy reading.

A NEST
LIES
of

A NETHERWORLD FAE NOVEL

ABOUT A NEST OF LIES

I'm being hunted by all of Mythos Fae kind.
Why?
Because I'm about to go into my first heat.

For years, I've just been Serapina the human.
Now, I'm Sera the Mythos Fae Omega.
And apparently I harbor millennia's worth of secrets inside
my soul.

So not only am I trying to discover the memories hidden
somewhere within my mind, but I'm also on the run…
With three irresistible fae.

Hades, the God of Death.
Morpheus, the God of Dreams.
Maliki, the Enforcer of Death.

I'm pretty sure their presence is going to inspire my heat to
overtake me sooner rather than later.
Which will leave me a mindless, vulnerable mess.

Can I trust my new guardians to protect me?
Or am I going to find myself twisted up in a nest of lies?

I'd better unravel the threads soon.
Because the feral Alphas are not the only ones
hunting me…
The truth is coming.
And it might just destroy us all.

Author's Note: *A Nest of Lies* is book two of the Netherworld Fae trilogy and ends on a cliffhanger.

WELCOME BACK TO THE NETHERWORLD KINGDOM

A Nest of Lies picks up right where *Bride of Death* left off, making this book two of the trilogy.

Things are about to heat up.

And the plot… is going to get twisted.

I hope you're ready for a chase. Because our unmated Omega heroine just became the prize in a primal mating hunt.

> *Better run fast, sweet mystery.*
> *The Alphas are coming.*
> *And they all want to knot you.*

Below are some themes you may find in *A Nest of Lies*:

✔ This is a Hades and Persephone retelling with a "why choose" twist (will our tortured hero learn how to properly share "his mate"?)

✔ No MM, but there are group scenes/play

✔ Consent between the heroine and her mates

✔ Psychotic Hero (Maliki)

✔ Celibate Hero (Hades) — But he likes to watch…

✔ Hero who loves CNC and sleep play (Morpheus)

✔ No Other Woman or Other Man Drama (No Cheating)

✔ Pregnancy/Breeding

✔ Primal Energy

✔ Possessive Over The Top Alpha Males

✔ Touch Her and Die Vibes

✔ Alpha/Omega Dynamics

✔ Knotting, Nesting, Purring & Growling (because yes, please…)

Enjoy! <3

NETHERWORLD FAE KINGDOM

NETHERWORLD MOUNTAINS

CORPSE FAE CRYPT

FAIRY CATACOMBS

CREEK OF THE DEAD

NETHERWORLD VILLAGE

NETHERWORLD MOUNTAINS

DEATH'S PALACE

NETHERWORLD COURTYARD

TUNNEL TO MORPHEUS KINGDOM

DEATH'S DEN

NETHERWORLD MOUNTAINS

BLOOD RIVER

DEATH FAE CASTLE

SOUL YARDS

NETHERWORLD MOUNTAINS

MORPHEUS
PROLOGUE

I STARE AT THE MIRROR, WONDERING WHAT SERAPINA WILL dream about tonight. A twisted part of me hopes she'll think of me. But I suspect the honor will go to Hades.

Again.

It's always him, his history with her soul surpassing my softer claim.

Sighing, I turn away from the ornately decorated wall and step out onto my balcony to take in the blood moon glowing in the sky.

It's particularly dark tonight, suggesting an ominous presence to come. Whether that's an omen for me or for the beings of my kingdom, I don't truly know.

So much has changed here these last few hundred years. The Ghouls and Strigoi who call this land home still revere me as their God, but their plights have become… unmanageable.

Too many chaotic dreams. Not enough mortal feed. A waning blood supply. Dead kings. Or rather, a single dead king.

A corruptible mess who deserved his fate, to be sure. But it's left the kingdom without a proper ruler.

Alas, it's not my responsibility to fix it.

No, my attention is wrapped up in a beautiful, blonde human and her troubled Omega soul.

She's on a date with Hades.

Not by choice, but by force.

"Idiot," I mutter, wanting to wring my cousin's neck for his possessive behavior. He refuses to believe that Serapina is innocent, that she doesn't harbor the memories of her soul. And likely never will.

That's not how reincarnation works.

Or how it should work, anyway.

Of course, our kind has never truly been reincarnated until recently. So the rules are… unclear.

I just hope Serapina isn't erased by Persephone's memories. As much as I adore and miss my soulmate, this new version of her is… enthralling.

Serapina is strong. Independent. Smart. She asks questions and doesn't shy away from hard answers, even though I'm sure she wants to hide and forget everything she's learned.

She's also so beautiful that it hurts me to look at her. Because all I want to do is thread my fingers through her silky hair and pull her in for a claiming kiss.

I close my eyes, imagining doing just that.

Which is an easy fantasy to create, as I've been daydreaming about the gorgeous little human since the day I realized she existed.

"One day soon," I vow in a whisper. "I'm going to cherish you the way you deserve, sweetheart. With my hands, my tongue, my *knot*. And then you'll dream of me. Always."

Perhaps with Hades and Maliki, too.

That's fine.

I simply want—

Electricity flows through my veins like lightning fire, causing my eyes to open in an instant.

It's a bolt of *need*. A flare of pure, unadulterated *lust*.

"Fuck," I breathe, my knees nearly giving out beneath me. "*Fuck*."

That sensation came from an Omega, one who is freshly awakening. And in need of an Alpha to satisfy her needs.

Because she's unclaimed.

I haven't felt this flare in eons, this intrinsic call one that has my inner beast roaring with desire and a need to *hunt*.

"Serapina," I breathe, realizing that the source of that sensation came from my little dreamer. My intended. *My soulmate.*

She's about to go into heat. Perhaps not right this second, but soon.

And that sensual summoning of hers just alerted all of Alpha kind to her presence.

Not only that, but her powerful call provided her exact location, too.

In the Netherworld Kingdom.

"Run," I breathe, misting to the balcony outside of her rooms in Death's Palace. "*Run!*"

However, before I can even finish shouting the demand, my soulmate is already gone.

Hades has her, I realize, sensing Serapina with ease, thanks to my connection to her spirit.

But then I frown when I ascertain where he's taken her.

It's a place our kind isn't supposed to go anymore. Not after what happened a few thousand years ago.

Although, I know Hades keeps a place there. I've visited before. But not in a very long while.

Hmm, I hum, latching onto their combined essences as I engage my misting ability once more. *To the Human Realm we go, then...*

SERA

A Few Seconds Earlier

So this is what bliss feels like, I marvel, lost in a cloud of wondrous gratification. *When can I experience it again?*

Maliki is between my thighs, but his mouth is no longer providing pleasure. He's staring at Hades. My fiancé. Husband. *Soulmate.*

My lashes flutter as I try to understand what's happening. Hades told Maliki to please me. But now he's radiating violent intent.

Is he going to kill Maliki for touching me?

Oh, I hope not.

I told him not to. I said this was *my* choice. Was this all a test? A way to punish me for my soul's betrayal?

Does he think I betrayed him… by letting Maliki pleasure me?

"Hades—"

He snatches Maliki's coat from the bed and drapes it over me, then he yanks me up into his arms.

I stiffen. "What are—"

The world blurs, causing my eyes to go wide in the darkness. I cling to his shoulders, my euphoria melting into terror.

His purr ignites in response, the rumble seeming to echo through every inch of my being. "You're safe, Serapina," he whispers against my ear.

Safe? I repeat, dizzy from the rapidly changing sensations in my body. *Safe from what? You?* I don't understand what he's doing.

I can *feel* the violence in his aura. It's at odds with the soothing vibrations coming from his chest.

Stars… My mind is telling me to scream, but my body refuses the action, some intrinsic part of me too calmed by this Alpha's purr.

It's like I have no control over my reactions, my being enslaved to the God of Death's commanding presence.

This is not okay, I decide. *I am my own person. I do not…*

The mental rant trails off as a world of color appears around us. My eyes round as I take in the expanse of water, the sight of which I've never seen in person.

However, I recognize what I'm seeing. *An ocean.*

My lips part.

Then my mind is immediately distracted by the warmth shining down upon me.

The sun. I instantly look right up at it, which is the absolute wrong thing to do, as I've spent the last year in the darkness of the Netherworld Kingdom. My brief visit to Morpheus's palace in the Mythos Fae Realm was not nearly long enough to reacquaint myself with such intense solar power.

Nor should one ever look directly at the sun.

But I'm not exactly feeling like myself right now.

Hades reminds me of his presence, his purr intensifying as he says, "Stay here and don't move. I need to go back and help Maliki."

What?

My heels—because, oh yeah, I'm naked yet still wearing four-inch heels—touch the sand.

And Hades disappears.

"Oh!" My knees wobble, and my ridiculous shoes send me sprawling onto my side.

Where I just lie for a moment as I try to figure out what in the thorns just happened.

I—

A whooshing sound has me sitting bolt upright. Black dots still decorate my vision, thanks to my previous glance upward, but I train my squinted gaze on the source of that rumbling roar.

Waves.

Ocean.

Deep blue waters.

It's all I can see.

As well as the sand I'm currently sitting in.

Stars. Looking down, I run my fingers through the unique texture and note that it's not unlike the Netherworld Courtyard dirt. Only, it's pale in color.

Because it's sand.

Or I assume it is, anyway, since I appear to be on a beach. *By. The. Ocean.*

My legs scramble beneath me as I try to stand again, only for the heels to dig into the earth and practically melt into the ground.

Growling, I plop back down, then wince because I'm still naked. The jacket Hades wrapped me in is sprawled out beside me, the fabric having slipped off during one of my falls. I'm not even sure when. But it doesn't matter because I am now covered in sand.

"Pricks," I mutter. "One problem at a time."

I focus on the heels first, the straps impossibly difficult.

"Why does anyone wear these?" I ask no one in particular. "They're impractical. Nonfunctional. And *why are there straps?!*" I yank on it, irritated by the hook.

I am not an inept individual.

"I will master this shoe," I tell myself.

"Well, feel free to take your time," a silky voice replies, causing me to freeze. "I'm rather enjoying the show."

A shadow blocks the sun, allowing me to look up.

Right into a pair of striking blue-green irises. "Morpheus," I breathe.

"God of Dreams," he replies, his gaze running over me. "And a dream you indeed are, my heart."

I'm pretty sure I stop breathing.

Not only am I naked, but he also caught me having a pep talk over a pair of shoes.

And he called me *my heart.*

That's new.

I… I think I would relish it more in any other situation. Alas, I'm currently on fire. And it has nothing to do with the hot sun.

"Would you like some assistance?" he asks softly, crouching before me. "I imagine walking in the sand is difficult with those sinfully sexy heels on."

I swallow, my shoulders dropping.

"This really can't get any more embarrassing, can it?" I mumble, more to myself than to him.

"*Embarrassing* isn't the term I would use," he murmurs, his exposed forearms bracing on his thighs.

He's dressed like Maliki was back in my bedroom—in a

button-down shirt with the sleeves rolled to the elbows and a pair of dark slacks.

The only difference is that Morpheus's shirt is white. Maliki's was black. *Is he even still wearing it? And where is he, anyway?*

Hades said he was going back to help Maliki.

Help him with what?

"*Arousing*, perhaps," Morpheus goes on, drawing my focus back to where he's crouching before me. "*Adorable* works, too." He smiles. "Want to give me your foot, little dreamer?"

I stare at him and decide, *Why not?* As I already said, I'm fairly certain this can't get any more embarrassing.

He may find it *arousing* and *adorable*, but I don't.

I feel meek again. Ridiculous. *Small*.

How did I go from enjoying the best pleasure of my life to falling onto a sandy beach framed by cliffs and a vast ocean?

"Where even am I?" I marvel, glancing around as I lean back on my palms and give Morpheus my foot.

"Mykonos," he says, the word foreign to me. I don't know if he's answering my question or saying something random.

With Morpheus, it's hard to say. He loves imparting information, though. And I appreciate that trait about him.

However, I don't appreciate how deftly he unfastens my heel.

He's barely touched me, and poof, the strap is unhooked.

I glare as he pulls the shoe away like it was the easiest task in the world.

"Practice makes perfect," he tells me as he gently sets

my foot down. Rather than ask for the other, he simply takes hold of my opposite limb and repeats the action.

Except he doesn't release me right away like last time. Instead, he leans in and presses a kiss to my ankle before freeing me, then reaches over for Maliki's jacket and holds it out for me to take.

"How about a shower?" he asks after I bundle myself up in the coat. "I always need one after playing in the sand."

I blink at him. "Where would I shower? In the ocean?"

He glances back over his shoulder, his crouched form blocking my view. "Oceans are fun and all, but they don't help much with the sand. Actually, I think it's worse because then you're wet and it sticks."

I squirm, his comment about being *wet* reminding me of the slickness between my thighs. *The sand is already sticking*, I think, wincing. "A shower sounds... yes. I would like that. But, uh, where if not the ocean?"

He gestures with his chin behind me. "In Hades's house. If you can even call it that. More like a fucking cave. But last I checked, it has running water."

"And when was the last time you *checked*?" a cultured tone interjects, the words precise and underlined with a quiet fury.

Swallowing, I readjust Maliki's jacket around myself, suddenly relieved that it fits me like a blanket.

All these men are huge compared to me. I've always been shorter and smaller, but they make me feel even more inferior somehow.

Meek, I mock with a mental snort, intentionally using it again. *Stars, I really loathe that word.*

"Mykonos?" Maliki's voice has me spinning in the sand to search for him. "Really?"

I gape at the large gash across his face and scramble up from my seated position to try to run toward him.

And promptly trip.

Hades catches me by the hip, his brow furrowing. "Did you give her wine?" he asks.

"She's never walked in the sand before, Hades," Morpheus replies. "Give our Omega some grace."

"She's not *our* Omega. She is *my* Omega," Hades corrects him. "And why are you here, Morpheus?"

I push away from Hades and try to carefully navigate toward Maliki. My "mate's" possessiveness can wait. "Are you okay?" I ask Maliki, reaching for him.

He smirks down at me. "I'm fine, trouble. Just got in Ossa's way, is all."

My hand hovers over the jagged mark on his cheek. The blood is still oozing from the fresh cut.

"Ossa did this?" I ask, shivering as I think about Hades's pet guard—a three-headed wolf beast with three names. Ossa, I gathered, is a female. Mort and Howl are her... brothers, I guess?

Maliki nods. "Ossa's positively feral when she's pissed off. I tried to move, but I wasn't fast enough." He turns thoughtful. "Though, it may have also been intentional. With her, it's hard to say."

"Why was she feeling feral?" I ask slowly. Then I frown. "Does it have something to do with why we're here? In Myko-ah-nos?"

Pretty sure I didn't get the name right.

But I tried.

"Why are we here, again?" I ask, aware that Hades just made a similar inquiry of Morpheus. But I think our questions actually hold different meanings. "What happen—"

"Gods, I love the Human Realm." Reaper's voice travels to my ears, making me look for my sister's mate.

And did he just say *Human Realm?*

"But couldn't we have hit up New York City instead?" he goes on as he appears in a cloud of smoke, his Death Fae heritage seeming to cling to his skin as he fully materializes right next to the water. "I could go for a pizza."

"You could always go for pizza," Flame mutters as he appears with him, the Corpse Fae looking oddly deformed, like he's engaged his deadly traits.

Orcus and my sister arrive next. He's in full beast mode, his black wings spread wide. When I spy the baby bundle in his arms, I instantly understand why. His protective instincts have been triggered.

Why? What has happened? And why are we in the Human Realm?

"Sera!" my sister yells the moment she sees me and starts scrambling across the sand with about as much success as I did moments ago.

Reaper swoops in to grab her, his arms cradling her as he shadows himself across the small space to gently deposit her in front of me and Maliki.

"I always knew I liked you," Morpheus murmurs.

"Everyone likes me," Reaper says. "I'm fucking amazing."

Alina ignores him and throws her arms around me. I return the hug as a storm of emotion overwhelms me.

So much has happened over the last... week? Few days? Years?

Stars, I don't even know.

"Lina," I whisper, using the nickname I've had for her since we were kids.

She squeezes me tighter. "It's going to be okay. The

Alphas won't find you here. And you're not marrying or mating *anyone* without consent."

That last part seems clearly directed at Hades, but I'm hung up on the comment before the marriage one. "Alphas are looking for me?"

"*Hunting* is a more accurate term, sunshine," Reaper drawls, the nickname one he gave me early on in our acquaintance. The Death Fae has a lot of quirks. But he treats my sister like a queen, so I accept his bizarre proclivities and focus on the term he just gave me.

"Hunting?" I echo, not liking the sound of that at all.

Reaper grins. "Yep. You're an unclaimed Omega and about to go into her first heat. From what I understand, you're a walking beacon for Alpha chaos. And I am fucking here for it."

A blade appears in his hand as Alina slowly releases me, her gaze searching my face as I struggle to process what Reaper is saying.

"You know me," he goes on with a charming smile. "I love a good bloodbath. So let's make it rain."

MALIKI

Shock and confusion flicker through Sera's beautiful features, her blue eyes locked on Reaper.

"Don't scare my sister," Alina chides.

Reaper frowns down at her. "I'm telling her about a party. Why would that scare her?"

"You're talking about a *massacre*," she corrects him.

"Yes. Also known as a feast of souls, thus a *party*. I can bring you some Alpha hearts, if you like?" He gives her a hopeful expression. "Would that please you?"

Sera's expression tells me that this sort of gift would *not* please her at all.

That's fine.

I would much rather *pleasure* her in other ways.

Such as with my tongue between her thighs.

Styx, I can still taste her. Less than an hour ago, I was

feasting on the most divine pussy I've ever tasted, and now I can't wait to do it again. With or without Hades's permission.

Because I won't be asking. I'll be taking instead.

He should have known there would be consequences to letting me play with his wife.

She's mine now.

A statement I declare without words as I sweep her up into my arms and turn toward Hades's cavern. My beauty needs a shower and to be properly cared for.

She also needs to understand what's happening.

"Hades," I say, glancing back at him. "Come with us."

He arches a brow at my command. As a God, he makes the rules. But I'm not in an obedient mood.

I was happy between Sera's legs, enjoying her pleasure. And now we're all in the Human Realm, hiding from a bunch of crazed Mythos Fae Alphas.

Why?

I have no fucking idea. All Hades told me was to expect company, then he grabbed Sera and disappeared without a word, thus leaving me to greet the incoming Alphas.

Fortunately, he returned before too many of them appeared, and quickly misted me here.

One word could have saved him the trouble. But no. He didn't give me a location at all. Just vanished.

Perhaps he reacted without thinking. I don't know because he hasn't explained himself yet.

But he will be elaborating soon.

Preferably inside the cavern.

Maybe while Sera takes a bath.

Hades must see something in my expression because he doesn't question me. Instead, he simply looks at Morpheus, heaves an irritated sigh—likely because he's annoyed that the God of Dreams is here—and steps toward me.

I take that as confirmation to lead. "We'll talk once we're inside," I promise Sera.

Her brow crinkles as she looks around. "Inside where?" she asks me. "No, forget that. Why does Reaper think I'm about to go into my first heat?"

"Because you are," Hades says as he reaches my side.

"That doesn't mean you can just knot my sister," Alina states, following us as well. "I know you think she's yours, but she's not. She's my sister—"

"She's not," Hades interjects. "You're not related by blood at all. And further, you should know that Alphas are possessive. We don't like it when our Omegas mention another Alpha's *knot*." He looks pointedly at Orcus. "Teach her."

Then he moves with purpose toward his front entrance, the rock instantly transforming into a sheer material that grants him entry.

Sera's lips part at the sight while her sister sputters behind us.

"Do you want that Alpha's heart?" Reaper offers her softly. "Because I will happily kill him for you, pet."

I don't stick around to hear Alina's reply and instead follow Hades inside, which causes Sera to gasp in my arms. She instantly lifts herself to look over my shoulder.

Which is when I realize she can't see through the enchantment.

Right.

Because the cave-like entrance is riddled with magic, one that masks Hades's cavern as an impenetrable landscape. All Sera would have been able to see was a beach framed by massive white cliffs.

And we just walked through one of those cliffs.

"It's a spell that protects Hades's hiding place in this realm," I explain as I follow him down a rocky corridor.

"Humans can't see the entrance. We also just crossed through one of those veils like in Death's Palace, so we're heading to Hades's personal wing."

Which means Morpheus and the others won't be able to follow us. But I don't add that part as it should already be implied.

Hades is very particular about whom he allows into his space. I'm pretty sure Sera understands that already.

He leads us into a modern kitchen with dark marble countertops and an enchanted refrigerator.

"That's no ordinary fridge," I tell Sera as I gesture to the appliance with my chin. "You just touch the handle, and inside, it'll create whatever you desire. Then you simply open the door and take out your meal of choice."

The contraption—along with this entire cavern and all the magical wards surrounding it—was created by Hades and his powerful manifestation ability.

But I don't tell Serapina that part. It's not my place to explain Hades's gifts to her.

The God in question glances back at me with an arched brow. "Are we giving a tour?"

"Are we staying here long?" I counter.

His jaw tightens, and he resumes walking without acknowledging or responding to my query.

It's not like Hades to keep me in the dark. Not when it involves one of my tasks, anyway.

But I'm feeling oddly out of my element here.

Orcus arriving with his mate-circle suggests that some sort of plan was triggered—a plan I'm not familiar with.

Which indicates that I wasn't factored into whatever is happening right now.

As for Morpheus, either his penchant for eavesdropping paid off, or he showed up here because he's connected to Sera's soul.

What I care about more is *why* we are here. As well as the comments regarding Sera's heat.

I assume Sera feels similarly. Perhaps even more so.

So as we enter Hades's loft area—one that leads to his bedroom—I say, "Sera needs answers, Hades. And so do I."

He doesn't acknowledge my demand, just continues toward his room.

And into the adjoining bathroom.

My gaze narrows when he opens a bespelled cabinet to pull out two fresh towels. When he sets them on the double-sink counter, he turns toward me and says, "Bathe Serapina. We'll talk when I return."

Hades vanishes before I can question him. "Cryptic arse," I mutter.

"I don't understand anything that's happening," Sera whispers. "I'm going into heat? We're in the Human Realm? Alphas are *hunting* me?" She phrases everything as a question, her eyes rounding more and more with each inquiry.

"You're not the only one who is confused," I admit, irritated. Not with her, of course. But with Hades.

"Perhaps I can be of assistance," Morpheus offers from the doorway behind me.

My eyebrows shoot upward. "How did you make it through the wards?"

He merely smiles. "I'm a God, Maliki. You would be amazed by what I can do."

The innuendo lacing those words is not lost on me.

But this isn't the time or the place to issue a sensual retort.

"If you can pass through the barriers that easily, then other Alphas can, too, yes?"

He shrugs. "Perhaps, yes. But why would they bother?"

"Because they're hunting Sera?" I prompt.

"Ah, true. So if you're planning to bathe Sera with your tongue, I wouldn't recommend it. That would be akin to shooting off a flare in the sky. But so long as you keep her libido in check, as it is now, we should be fine."

I stare at him.

He stares back, his brow beginning to furrow. "You don't know, do you?"

"Know what?" I demand.

Morpheus sighs and runs his fingers through his long silver-white hair, then leans against the door frame as he slides his hands into the pockets of his slacks. "One would think that losing a mate would leave behind some sort of impact—a lesson, if you will. But Hades's arrogance truly is extraordinary, is it not?"

I assume that's a rhetorical question, so I don't acknowledge the question and instead face him fully as I repeat, "Know what?"

Sera gives Morpheus her attention as well, her body tensing in my arms. "Please answer him," she says softly. "I want to know, too."

The way Morpheus's expression softens as he looks at Sera tells me how much power she wields over the God of Dreams. He practically melts in response to her attention.

Which is interesting to observe.

Hades doesn't react that way.

Yet I know he feels deeply for his soulmate.

But how does he feel about Sera? I wonder. *Does he finally realize she isn't Persephone, but a human with his Omega's soul inside her?*

I never really considered the repercussions of that distinction before. However, now I'm wondering what he might do to try to free his soulmate from her human confines.

Will he hurt Sera if it means saving Persephone?

Are they even two separate entities? Or will they join?

With Morpheus, I have no doubt he sees them as the same individual. He sees *Sera*. And that may make him more of an ally than I previously believed.

At some point, Sera started to mean more to me than I realized. I'm protecting her because I want to, not because I have to. So if anyone—Hades included—attempts to harm her, I won't hesitate to retaliate.

And it seems Morpheus may be inclined to react similarly.

"I'm not sure what happened during or after your dinner, little dreamer, but given the state I found you in on that beach, I'm inclined to believe you experienced an orgasm."

Her cheeks redden, the flush seeming to creep down her neck to disappear beneath my suit jacket. "A glorious one," I murmur, not because I want to embarrass her, but because I want to praise her.

"Hmm, I can imagine," Morpheus muses. "And by the pride radiating off you, Maliki, I can detail that fantasy just a tad bit more within my mind. Well done."

My jaw tightens as I look back at him. "Get to the point, Morpheus." I may have started this tangent by complimenting Sera, but I won't allow him to derail us further.

"My point is, that *glorious* orgasm awoke her inner Omega," he says. "And that inner Omega essentially broadcast her presence to every Mythos Fae Alpha in existence."

Sera swallows, her lips parting as though she wants to say something yet can't find the words.

"Think of it like a mating call," Morpheus goes on before I can comment, his gaze locking on me. "Serapina's

20

inner Omega basically told my kind that not only is she about to go into heat, but she's also unclaimed. Hence the Alpha suitors descending upon the Netherworld Kingdom right now."

My nostrils flare at the implications of what he's saying. Hades cautioned me about Alpha powers and potential complications. But he made it sound like a one-off scenario and primarily focused on Morpheus.

Why didn't he mention this as a possible outcome?

"Once they realize she's gone, they'll begin the real hunt." Morpheus's gaze goes to Sera. "Which, sadly, means no more orgasms for you, little dreamer. Your pleasure will call them right to you. And we can't risk that. Not while you're unmated."

Her lips part again, but no words come out. However, her eyes tell me she more than understood what Morpheus just said.

"I can fix this problem, if you like," he offers in a purr-like murmur, his blue-green eyes practically glittering as he stares at her. "But we can discuss that more after you take a shower." He regards me with a quick look. "Do you want to help her with that, or shall I?"

Sera gapes between us, her mouth finally closing into a firm line. "I know how to take a shower."

Morpheus arches a brow at her. "Oh?"

Her eyes narrow. "I may be a little... overwhelmed at the moment, but I'm more than capable of washing myself."

He cocks his head. "You're sure?" He glances at my arms and then back up at her. "Because you don't seem all that adept at standing right now. And you could barely walk on the beach."

She scowls, which has my lips twitching at the sides.

Because I suddenly realize what Morpheus is doing—

he's goading her. Mere minutes ago, outside, he told Hades to give Sera grace for not knowing how to traverse the sand.

Now he's using the whole incident as a way to tease her, perhaps to distract her from the situation he just revealed.

She's being hunted because her orgasm served as a beacon to the Mythos Fae Realm.

I'm not clear on whether or not they can track her here, but I'll wait to ask Morpheus that question.

Sera's comfort comes first. And part of that comfort is buoyed in strength. Which means she needs to feel more confident in her surroundings and in her ability to take care of herself.

From what I've observed of Sera, being able to handle situations on her own is important to her.

Fortunately, I can help with that.

However, before I can even try, Morpheus asks, "Do you even know how the shower works?"

His words confirm what I already determined—he's toying with her. Morpheus claimed outside that he's been here before, and even if he hasn't been in this specific room, he can no doubt sense the manifestation magic littering these walls.

Because he, too, possesses a talent similar to Hades's. All Alphas do. What varies between them are the worlds they command.

However, Morpheus absolutely knows that the shower operates in the same fashion as the kitchen appliances— they are all magically enchanted to provide whatever the user wants. So for the shower, all Sera needs to do is stand under the showerhead, and it'll heat or cool to her unvoiced preferences.

"I know how to turn on water," Sera snaps. "I'm not helpless, Morpheus."

"Says the woman still clinging to Maliki like a security blanket," the God of Dreams drawls.

Her nails dig into my shoulders like claws.

"All right, trouble," I interject before she can bite Morpheus's head off. While I would enjoy watching that unfold, I don't think now is the right time. "How about you go take a shower while Morpheus and I conjure up some food, yeah?"

She has to be hungry, as she never ate dinner with Hades. Instead, we skipped straight to dessert, whereby *I* ate *her*.

And I want a chance to ask Morpheus some questions.

Questions I would ask Hades if I knew where he went.

Though, right now, I'm not sure he would give me the answers I need. Such as why everyone else seemed to know to meet here... *except me.*

Clearing my throat, I shove my annoyance aside and focus on setting Sera down.

"Seems to be standing just fine to me," I tell Morpheus, my hands on Sera's hips as I wait for her to find her balance. It takes her a moment—something I know the God of Dreams notices since his eyes are roaming over her torso—but he thankfully doesn't comment on it.

Instead, he says, "Let us know if you can't figure out the shower."

"I'll figure it out," she returns, determination emboldening her tone.

Amused, I dip my head down and press a kiss to her neck, then draw my lips up to her ear. "Then let me know if you want company instead," I whisper. "I'll happily join you in the shower anytime, trouble."

She gasps, and I give her hips a squeeze, then release her and turn toward Morpheus.

"Let's go make a mess in the kitchen," I tell him.

It'll piss off Hades.

Just like my insinuative comments to Sera will as well.

Because I meant every word.

She's mine to play with now. His fault, not mine. And I might just decide to keep her.

For good.

HADES

I EXPECT THE PUNCH A SECOND BEFORE IT LANDS, THE HIT sending me spiraling to the side as my brother appears before me in a wave of full Alpha fury.

Sighing, I roll to my back and stare up at Orcus's furious form. "I'll give you that hit, as it's deserved," I tell him. "The next one—"

His foot collides with my abdomen, propelling me across the sandy earth.

I halt the movement by slamming my palms against the ground and shoving myself upward to stand.

Orcus is there in a flash, his black wings beating at his back as his dark eyes glow red. "The first one was for upsetting my mate," he tells me. "The second was for endangering Thea. And this—" His fist flies toward my face again, but I catch it.

Only to feel pain echo up my spine as a Death Fae appears behind me and drives a dagger into my lower back. "Is for upsetting our pet," Reaper says, finishing Orcus's statement.

I growl and mist out from between the two insane males.

"I was going to say for not communicating and thereby jeopardizing our mate-circle," Orcus tells Reaper conversationally, his wings disappearing along with his temper. "Are you going to give Alina that bloody dagger as a gift?"

"Do you think she'll like it?" Reaper asks, his expression radiating adoration and hope. "Or do I need to stab him again?"

My jaw clenches, my torso pulsing with agony, thanks to the Death Fae's unanticipated attack.

Very few beings are suicidal enough to try to attack a God. It's what first intrigued me about Maliki, so I suppose I can understand why Orcus chose Reaper for his mate-circle.

Pressing my palm to my back to prod the already healing wound, I glare at my brother and his friend and interrupt their conversation by saying, "We need to strengthen the wards." The words are for Orcus. "You'll be doing more of the work now."

He folds his thick arms. "The Alphas won't come here."

"They will if they sense Serapina's presence."

His dark brow arches upward. "Serapina?" he repeats. "Not *Persephone?*"

"I don't have time for one of your lectures right now, brother. Nor do I have time to teach you and Reaper a lesson in power. We need wards. *Now.*" Because I'm not risking my Omega's life over this bullshit.

Orcus may be right about our kind avoiding this realm, but all it will take is a single pleasurable moment, and the Alphas will descend upon this world and ravage it in their quest to hunt Serapina down.

She's an unmated Omega.

One who is about to go into heat.

Thanks to Maliki's skilled tongue.

Fuck, I can picture him between her thighs. It's a distraction I don't need right now, yet I let it fuel my movements as I head down the beach along the rocky cliffs.

"Handle the sea wards," I tell my brother over my shoulder. It's not a request but a demand. He went into Alpha mode, thus calling out his wings. Saves me from having to do the same.

He ignores me, his focus on Reaper again as the Death Fae asks, "Pepperoni and sausage?"

"You can't be serious," my brother mutters.

"So that's a yes, then?"

Orcus's resulting sigh reaches me even though I'm more than twenty feet away from them now. "Just don't take too long."

"Well, I'll try. But I want to get our pet a few different options for our visit."

"This isn't a vacation, Reaper. And you know she prefers veggies on the pizza."

"I'm very aware of what our mate likes," Reaper says back to him, a hint of offense in his tone as I begin calling magic to my fingertips.

It would be so easy to redirect the deadly enchantment to hit him in the ass, causing him to spiral down into my lethal playground. But I sort of need him alive right now, in case we need to fight.

"I meant that I'm going to get her a few varieties to

try," he goes on. "Proper Italian, New York style, Chicago deep dish, you know. So I'll be back… soonish."

"Hold on, Reaper. You can't—"

I glance back and watch as the Death Fae vanishes.

Orcus blinks at the space Reaper just occupied, then growls. "Fucking lunatic."

"Indeed," I agree. "Now will you focus on the water wards?"

The look he gives me says he would prefer punching me again instead.

"I gave you two free hits," I remind him. "Three, if you count Reaper stabbing me in the literal back. Do not expect me to be any more understanding or accommodating than I've already been, *little brother*."

He was right to be angry with me over endangering his mate and child, but I didn't realize an orgasm would set off Serapina's mating call.

In hindsight, I suppose it makes sense that pleasure would be the key to awakening her inner Omega. However, I wasn't anticipating my mate broadcasting herself as *unclaimed* to the whole of Mythos Fae kind.

The fact that she could even emit such a signal confirms that she's not my Persephone.

Oh, she possesses my mate's soul… But Serapina is very much her own person.

Which leads me to wonder what will happen during her estrus.

Will she join with Persephone? Or is she merely a reincarnation of my mate?

Everything about this situation is unprecedented, leaving me conflicted about how to proceed.

I could claim her; she's technically already mine. However, I… I don't know if Serapina will accept me as hers.

And I need her consent to proceed.

My bite would tame her by force, but it would break her spirit. Hurt her. Make her hate me more than she probably already does.

So no, that's not an option at all.

Fuck.

I shake my head, needing a clear mind to concentrate on my task.

Manifestation magic comes from the soul, which means I can't think about my mate right now. Otherwise, I'll lose myself to a series of questions that I may or may not be able to answer.

Swallowing, I draw my hand through the air and imagine a barrier spell, one meant to sound alarms inside my cavern should an unexpected presence arrive.

Specifically, an uninvited *Alpha* presence.

As Morpheus is already here, I'm forced to include his essence in the framework of my creation. If I don't, the sirens will blare until I physically remove him.

So he can stay.

For now, I think, growling to myself.

I loathe the fact that he followed us here, not just because he's an irritant that refuses to fuck off, but because it further proves his connection to my mate's soul.

However, he mentioned he's been here before, too. Something I wasn't aware of until I overheard him commenting to Sera about running water.

There's no way he knew I intended to bring her here, though. I have homes all over the realms. Yet, with how fast he discovered us, I know he didn't check any other locations first.

And the only person who knew about this emergency meet-up location was my brother, who I'm certain would never share that detail with another Alpha. Especially our cousin.

Thus, there's only one way my cousin knew where to go—his spiritual link to my Persephone. And I fucking despise seeing proof of his connection to *my* Omega.

I've known for millennia that he fancied her as his mate, but I've ignored his claim.

This, however, I can't ignore. Nor will I ever be able to forget it.

My jaw clenches as I finish the barrier spell, the magic tangible despite being invisible in nature. That's part of what makes it a successful enchantment.

Misting a mile away, I craft a similar ward, just in case anyone tries to sneak up on us by foot. A rare choice, given our abilities, but an Alpha on the hunt can be quite clever.

The next layer of power includes a masking charm, one that should cloak our presence here on the island. There are some beings who will easily see through my design—or sense the manifestation magic itself—but not many Alphas can weave their way through my deadly labyrinths.

Because my energy is underlain by death. Which is a bit of a contradiction in theory, but creates a lethal combination of effects.

Therefore, tampering with my spells or trying to fracture them... *kills*.

Or that's the layer of protection I add to my creation, anyway.

Orcus is likely doing the same, his magic similar to mine, as he's my brother. Only, his source of power is different from mine. Less potent and not nearly as deadly.

He can access my death world, but the souls there bow to me as their God and view Orcus as more of a prince. He's able to wield control and issue demands, while I'm the one they pray to and revere like one would a king.

Hence my role in the Netherworld Kingdom.

My dynamic with Orcus is complicated and unique. However, it works.

Something that becomes evident as we meet on the beach outside of the cavern once more. He manifested half of it ages ago, just as I took the other side, the two of us hollowing out the cliffside with our joint powers to create a safe haven for us to enjoy in this realm.

I'm about to thank him when Reaper appears and hands Orcus a stack of pizza boxes. "Ran out of hands," the Death Fae says before blinking out of existence once more.

Orcus sighs heavily. "Restraint is not one of Reaper's strengths."

"Clearly," I deadpan, thinking about the blood drying against my lower back. The wound has already healed, but the residual mess is proving to be uncomfortable.

A shower will be needed upon my return.

I wonder if Serapina has finished bathing, I think, picturing her delectable form in my shower. Wet. Naked. *Writhing.*

It's an enchanting image, one that has my knot pulsing with intent.

Alas, I can't play with my Omega here. It's not protected enough. One orgasm will alert all of Mythos Fae Alpha kind, and they'll ravage this world with a vengeance.

Not to mention the fact that said Omega probably doesn't want to play with me. Only Maliki.

Hmm.

My fantasy shifts to visions of him licking her sweet little pussy, the mewls she made when she came, the way his lips glistened with her slick.

Fuck, I need to see that again.

And soon.

Once our Omega is safe. Once I have her consent. Once I make her mine... again.

If she'll have me.

Clearing my throat, I shove that errant thought from my mind and focus on my brother. "Tell Reaper he owes me a suit." Then I grab a pizza box from the top. "And please give Alina my apologies. However, I meant what I said, Orcus. You need to teach her Alpha etiquette."

Our kind is possessive. Mentioning another male's knot —especially in front of an Alpha mate—is a good way to inspire a brawl.

"Also, if Mykonos is breached, we'll need to separate," I add, not giving him a chance to comment. "I don't want to know where you'll take Thea and Alina, just in case." Nor would I be sharing where I intended to take Serapina.

It's the best way to ensure the safety of our Omegas.

While Alina may be claimed and therefore won't emit any mating calls whilst in heat, the Alphas of our world have gone feral over the last few millennia. They'll stop at nothing to *take*.

Which puts Alina at risk by being in close proximity to an unmarked Omega on the vestiges of an estrus.

Orcus nods, telling me he understands.

He'll put his mate-circle first, as he should.

I'll do the same for Serapina.

And Maliki, I think, considering my best friend. *Yes, Maliki, too.*

Because it seems clear my mate cares about him. That makes him even more important to me than he already was.

"Thanks for dinner," I conclude, about to disappear.

"Be kind, Hades," Orcus says softly. "And remember our roots."

I stare at my brother. "I told you I'm not in the mood for a lecture."

"Neither was I, yet you chose to tell me *twice* that I need to teach my Omega. So I'm giving you advice on how to treat yours. She doesn't know you. And once upon a time, neither did Persephone. Try to remember that when handling your intended." With that profound statement, he vanishes.

As does the box of pizza I was just holding.

I frown, irritated by both his words and his actions.

Apparently, I'll need to manifest a pizza in the kitchen like a normal Alpha.

That's fine. It would have been cold after my shower anyway.

Or maybe I'll send Morpheus to Italy, I decide. *If he's going to stay here, he might as well be useful.*

Energy surrounds me as I engage my misting ability, my mind set on sending my cousin on an errand, when a flicker of blue causes me to still.

It's barely perceptible and in the corner of my vision, but as I slowly turn toward it, the color becomes more vivid.

My eyebrow arches, a rare emotion stealing through me—*surprise.*

I felt it earlier when I first heard of this little soul and his link to my mate.

And I feel it again now as Pip—the name Serapina has apparently given him—wavers in the in-between, his fiery eyes peering at me with tiny nervous flickers.

"You've come to guard your ward?" I guess.

He cants his head at the term, like he's not sure he understands.

"Serapina," I say slowly.

Her name causes his glowing orbs to crease into what

appears to be a smile right before he executes an odd little twirl.

"I assume that's a yes," I murmur.

He nods and starts toward my cavern.

I step into his path, which causes him to backpedal. He's smart to do so. While I may be in corporeal form, I command the in-between. That makes me impenetrable in both realities, no matter what form I choose to take.

"It's dangerous here," I tell the lost soul. "You can't let anyone other than us see you. Do you understand?"

Pip glances around the vacant beach.

"I'm talking about the human visitors," I elaborate. "There may not be any right now, but they do frequent this cove in their yachts."

Twin flames blink at me.

"They won't be kind if they see you," I go on. "They won't understand what you are, and they will fear you. So don't interact with them."

I've had this conversation with Ossa, Howl, and Mort before. Of course, they ignored me. Hence, the legend about a three-headed creature named Cerberus was born. No idea which mortal coined that title for my beloved familiar, but he or she is long dead.

"You must stay hidden," I reiterate, then look him over. "Actually, you might be quite useful out here, if you want a job."

Pip drifts a little closer, his eyes widening with what I presume is an indication of interest.

So I tell him what I would like him to do.

And watch as his chest puffs up with purpose at the request to essentially guard the coastline.

By the time I'm finished elaborating, he's nodding eagerly.

I smile. "Serapina is lucky to have you."

He executes another twirl.

Then he bows and scurries off to protect his ward while lurking in the in-between.

His existence is another layer of proof that Serapina isn't Persephone.

Because my Omega would never have a soul as a familiar. She adored life too much for that.

Which leaves me with several lingering thoughts as I start toward my cavern.

This Omega may have my mate's soul, but she isn't anything like my Persephone.

So…

What kind of Omega is Serapina?

Who is she as a person?

Will she even let me get to know her after how I've treated her?

I suppose there's only one way to find out.

But first, I need a shower and some new clothes. Then I'll find my Omega.

And we'll do what we should have done from the beginning—*we'll talk.*

SERA

I GLARE AT THE MARBLED WALL, SEARCHING FOR A KNOB OR a button or *something* to turn the shower on.

But no.

It's just *rock*.

Growling, I look up at the showerhead. "Turn. On."

Of course, it doesn't listen.

Why would it do what I demand?

"Ugh." I am *not* going to walk out of this room to ask for help. It will defeat the purpose of saying I could do this myself. "You are not going to show me up." The words are for the spout over my head. "Same goes for you," I say to another one at the opposite end of this giant space. "I mean, who even needs a shower this big?"

At least seven people my size could fit in here.

It's ridiculous.

As is the lack of a knob!

"Maybe I should have taken Maliki up on his offer," I

growl under my breath. Then I shiver because that *offer* is all I can think about.

Well, aside from the malfunctioning shower.

"I'll happily join you in the shower anytime, trouble."

My thighs clench as his words play through my mind, his deep baritone reminding me of other sinful things he said to me back in Death's Palace.

In bed.

While between my spread legs.

"Fuck, Sera. I've never seen such a needy pussy."

"You're so wet, sweet girl."

I squirm, the sensations he awoke below seeming to be more intense now than before.

It's insane. I have no idea why I'm feeling so needy. So pent up. *So ready for more.*

Hades just whisked me off to a place in the *Human Realm* that I can't pronounce. I should be focused on that. I *was* focused on that.

Until Morpheus taunted me about this shower.

And Maliki whispered an idea that I can't seem to stop thinking about.

What would he look like naked? I wonder. *Would the water turn on for him?*

Stars, I like the notion of him being in here with me. Even if he just chose to go shirtless. Because then I could touch his damp skin, revel in his heat while the shower rained down upon us both.

It's a decadent fantasy, one that nearly makes me forget my purpose here.

Which is to take a shower.

Something I can't do without water.

I huff at the ceiling, then step out of the shower to check my surroundings… *again.*

How much time have I wasted in this bathroom? I wonder.

Once again finding nothing of use, I snap, "Why is this so difficult?"

"Why is what so difficult?" a cultured tone asks, causing me to spin around with a surprised yelp.

Hades stands in the bathroom, his commanding presence making me want to shrink backward into the marbled walls.

"Serapina?" he prompts when I don't immediately reply. "Why haven't you showered?"

My teeth clench. I can't answer him. If I do, I have no doubt he'll ridicule me for not knowing how his fancy shower works.

Or worse, accuse me of playing a game.

Maybe I'm not being fair. Or perhaps it's exhaustion and confusion making me want to lash out. Regardless, I'm not replying to his question.

"Why do you care?" I demand, feeling defensive. "I thought you had things to do." Isn't that why he disappeared? Too busy for a tour? To answer any questions? To explain why we're in the Human Realm?

That haughty eyebrow of his arches, making me want to wipe that smug look right off his too-handsome face.

If the shower worked properly, I would be tempted to spray him right in the—

Water bursts to life overhead as a geyser shoots off in Hades's direction, drenching him from head to toe.

My lips part in shock.

Hades shouts something I can't hear over the rushing water, his arms coming up to try to halt the harsh flow.

Now you decide to turn on? I think, gaping at the shower enclosure. *You're not even putting water where it belongs!*

Instead of staying inside the glass, it's getting all over the bathroom.

Well. Primarily all over *Hades*.

But still… this isn't what a shower is meant to do.

Though, it is kind of amusing to watch it soak the God of Death's suit.

His expression, however, is thunderous, and has me hoping the shower stops assaulting him soon so he—

Everything shuts off in a whoosh of silence, leaving only the sound of dripping in its wake.

A dripping that originates from Hades's clothes.

He growls.

And I take a step back.

"What the Styx is going on in here?" Maliki demands as he materializes near the door.

"An excellent question, indeed," Hades mutters as he unfastens his suit jacket. "I told you to bathe our Omega. Yet somehow *I* am the one taking an impromptu shower whilst clothed."

He pulls the fabric from his shoulders and allows it to fall to the floor with a loud *plop*.

Maliki glances between us, his gaze running over me in a slow caress. "You haven't showered yet?" he asks, his brow furrowing.

"It's malfunctioning," I grit out, gesturing to the glass and then to Hades. "Obviously."

"The shower can't malfunction," Maliki says slowly. "It's desire-based."

I blink at him. "It's what?"

"Desire-based," Hades echoes, like I have a hearing problem.

He's unbuttoning his black vest now, the soaked clothing sticking to his muscular physique and somehow making him all the more intimidating.

Yet I can't stop myself from snapping, "I heard Maliki just fine, thank you. I'm trying to understand what *desire-based* means."

That arrogant eyebrow of his wings upward again, making me wish the water was flow—

The shower springs to life to drench him again, causing my eyes to widen.

Because oh.

Ohhh.

I think I… I think I understand now.

Maybe.

My lips curl down as I think about the water shutting off.

It does.

And Hades growls again.

Oops, I think. *But why didn't it turn on before when I told it to?* I wonder, my frown deepening as I look at the enclosure. "I swear it wasn't working five minutes ago."

"Maybe you didn't desire a shower then?" Morpheus's voice has me spinning toward the door to find him leaning against the frame, his long legs crossed at the ankles and his hands in his pockets. "I believe Maliki offered to join you right before we left. Perhaps I'm wrong, but that's the kind of promise that inspires daydreams, yes?"

I blink at him, my cheeks heating.

Because he's right.

I was fantasizing about Maliki being in the shower with me.

Stars, this is embarrassing.

My gaze starts to fall to the ground but snags on the mirror… where I see my reflection. My *very naked* reflection.

"Oh!" I jump toward the counter to snatch a towel.

I've been just standing here, not even realizing that all three *clothed* men were talking to me while I wore nothing.

"A bit late for that, little dreamer," Morpheus murmurs. "Your gorgeous silhouette is forever embedded in my mind." He flashes me a charming smile. "I shall enjoy thinking of you later."

"Enough," Hades interjects, his possessive fury a whiplash to my senses. "Leave, Morpheus, before I escort you out."

"Hades—"

"You, too, Maliki," Hades says, a low rumble in his tone. "I want a moment alone with Serapina."

I tug the towel tighter around myself, wishing it were more of a shield than a piece of cloth.

Maliki and Morpheus don't immediately move, causing the God of Death to growl, "That wasn't a request."

The God of Dreams pulls his hands out of his pockets and lifts them in surrender. "Fine. But I'm not leaving the cavern." He steps backward into the bedroom. "If you need me, little dreamer, just say my name. I'll be back in a mist."

With that, he disappears.

But Maliki remains. "We didn't tell her how the shower works."

"Clearly," Hades grinds out.

"So don't punish her for something she knew nothing about," Maliki adds. "She's innocent, Hades. Remember that."

He vanishes into smoke before Hades can respond, leaving me to face the God of Death alone.

I swallow. "I… I'm sorry?" I phrase it as a question because I'm not sure if that's what he wants to hear, or if I even need to apologize.

His grunt tells me he either doesn't accept my words or doesn't want to hear them.

So I just… stop talking.

And freeze.

Because he just dropped his tie on the floor and now he's working on the buttons of his shirt.

Inch by inch, he exposes a strip of golden skin. He's pale, yet touched by a slight tan that seems to define the planes of his muscular torso, allowing me to see every dip and line of his too-perfect physique.

When his shirt falls to the floor with another wet *plop*, I shiver.

His chest and abdomen are on complete display now.

He has tattoos.

Not like Maliki's, though.

No, Hades's tattoos are more defined. Permanent. And they don't *writhe* like smoke.

Instead, they're darker, almost a solid black.

And depicting a crown on the right side of his chest.

A crown decorated with petals.

There are more flowers on his bicep, along with skulls, creating an alluring scene of life and death.

My fingers itch to trace the intricate designs.

But Hades is still moving, his hands unfastening his belt and drawing down his zipper.

My eyes widen as he kicks off his soaked shoes and tugs down his dress pants, leaving him in a pair of tight black boxers and socks.

The latter of which he bends down to remove.

"Come here, Serapina," he says as he steps into the shower in just the single undergarment.

"I… I don't think…" I clear my throat, my mouth still dry. "Hades—"

"Please?" he says softly, glancing back at me. "I'm not going to punish you, little soulmate. I just want to take care of you."

I blink at him, his tone and expression not at all what I've come to expect from the real Hades. Instead, he's talking to me like the version in my dreams. The Hades I long to see every time I close my eyes at night.

The water comes on, this time the way it should—by flowing down in the enclosure rather than spraying outside of it—and Hades holds out his hand. "I don't want to make you uncomfortable, Serapina. I simply want to help."

I stare at him and then down at his unwavering palm.

Can I trust him?

Probably not.

But I'm exhausted. And I... I really do want to take a shower.

He's also already seen me naked. *Stars, he watched as Maliki kissed me between my thighs.*

I shiver, recalling how it felt to be watched.

I liked it. Perhaps a little too much. And now, I just... Oh, I simply want to relax. Maybe eat and sleep. However, I need to wash all the sand off first. It's sticking to my legs. *Because I'm still wet... down there.*

My cheeks heat at the thought, my throat once again trying to swallow.

This is ridiculous, I tell myself. *He's seen me without clothes already. And he's kind of my mate. So. What does it matter?*

I release the towel and take a step forward.

Hades holds my gaze, his hand still steady before him.

Releasing a breath, I start toward him and nearly slide across the wet tiled floor. Hades is on me in an instant, his palms grabbing my hips to ensure I don't fall.

Which sends me right into his bare chest.

Warmth immediately surrounds me, as does the scent of a chilly winter night. *Right before a snowfall,* I think, inhaling deeply as I close my eyes. *Stars, I miss this fragrance.*

I used to step outside of the greenhouse with a freshly cut rose and indulge in this exact aroma.

How is it possible for him to smell like this? I wonder, dizzy. *Why is it so comforting?*

His purr rumbles to life, adding to my tranquility. I sigh, lost to his touch. His magnitude. His masculine presence.

Gone are my concerns and fears.

And all that's left is a sense of peace unlike any I've ever known.

I'm only vaguely aware of him pulling me into the shower, his hands roaming up my sides to my back and into my hair. It feels so good, so *freeing.*

For a moment, I just... exist. In solace. In kindness. In a warm state of security.

Because I feel safe.

I shouldn't. Deep down, I know that. Hades thinks I'm Persephone, that I betrayed him in the worst way imaginable.

Except...

"You're using my name," I say, my voice a whisper. "My *real* name."

Serapina.

He referred to me as such before, too. But I haven't had a chance to comment on it. And I'm just groggy enough to do it now.

"Why?" I ask.

His fingers comb through my hair again, only he knots them at the ends to tilt my head back. I startle as I meet his intense gaze, his dark orbs seeming to radiate a dozen emotions at the same time, making him impossible to read.

I shiver, despite the warm water, and fight the urge to touch him. His purr is soft and soothing, the sound emanating from his chest and inspiring so many competing desires within me.

To rest my palm on his tattoo.

To curl into him and soak up his strength.

To simply *submit*.

It's a heady need, one that worsens my dizziness. I don't want to give in to the wills of my body, not while my mind is still radiating warnings about the Alpha who is currently touching me.

"You possess my mate's soul," Hades says, his grip tightening in my hair as his opposite palm goes to my lower back.

He pulls me closer, which is when I realize I was swaying, and his hold is all that's keeping me in place.

"As you've learned, she betrayed me," he goes on. "And given that betrayal, I assumed she was playing a dangerous game, one meant to hurt me even more than she already has." He cants his head to the side. "It's hard for me to believe that I may have been wrong in my assumptions. Almost as hard as it was to accept what she did to me."

I swallow, my eyelids growing heavy.

It's his purr, I realize. *Or maybe it's him.*

"But watching you fall apart proved to me that you're not my Persephone at all," he adds, his low voice sliding around me in a silky caress.

One that seems to tighten like a noose around my neck as the meaning behind his words begins to register.

"Watching you fall apart proved to me that you're not my Persephone…"

He's talking about when Maliki pleasured me. *My orgasm.*

My eyelashes flutter. "Is… is that why…?" I can't formulate the question I want to ask. Not because I don't want to know the answer, but because I'm just not quite sure what I want to know.

"Morpheus suggested I kiss you," he says. "He told me that would be the best way to test my mate—because an

Omega is a slave to her Alpha's touch. And your kind can't fake pleasure."

Some of the fog begins to leave me as I continue to process his comments.

But he's not done.

"It's an intrinsic response to your needs. Omegas are made to take an Alpha's knot. It's how we bond. So the best way to test you was to see how you reacted to another man's touch," he murmurs, his grip tightening as he leans in to run his nose against mine. "And the way you responded to Maliki told me everything I needed to know, *Serapina*."

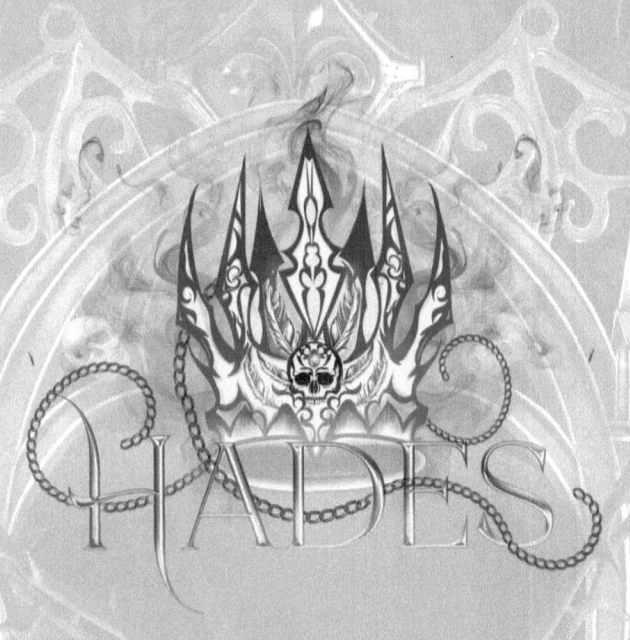

HADES

THE WAY SERAPINA STIFFENS IN MY ARMS TELLS ME THAT I've done something wrong.

She was relaxed. *Content.* I dare to even believe that she temporarily felt *safe*.

But I've ruined that somehow.

Something she proceeds to prove by pressing a palm to my chest to push me away. "Stop purring," she demands, making me frown. "*Just. Stop.*"

I do what she commands, though I can't help asking, "Why?" Because it's a strange request for an Omega to make. An Alpha's purr is meant to soothe, which she seems to need. She's upset and tired, and rightly overwhelmed. I simply want to help.

"Because you're making me dizzy," she says, her hands going to her head. "I feel fuzzy, and I need to think."

I frown. "My purr makes you dizzy?" That doesn't

seem right. But then, nothing about my Omega is what it should be.

From her strange estrous cycle to her reactions to me as her Alpha mate, everything is different. *She* is different.

My frown deepens as another thought nags at me. *Orcus was right.* He told me that Serapina wasn't Persephone, and he knew that after only a few minutes in her presence. He advised me to do the same, but I refused.

And now I realize his advice was given with true purpose.

Everything about Serapina is unique, including the fire in her gaze now as she looks up at me and meets my stare directly.

"You told Maliki his life depended on how much I enjoyed his pleasure." She utters the words slowly, like she's trying to ensure she understands. "You... you forced him to please me, just so you could determine if I've been lying. Because my word wasn't good enough."

"That's not quite—"

"You put me in a vulnerable position," she goes on. "Forced him to give me my first..." She clears her throat, her expression contorting with an emotion I don't like.

Pain.

Fury.

Sadness.

"I'm not Persephone," she grits out. "I've never lied to you. Yet you feel it's your right to betray me—*hurt me*—because I harbor Persephone's soul. You're punishing me for her sins. And I think, no, I *know*, I can accept that. But to punish Maliki, too?" She takes a step back and shakes her head. "That's not fair."

I move toward her, the water meeting my back as I shield her from the overhead spray. She cowers—*fucking cowers*—and shrinks back against the wall.

48

I nearly growl in frustration. This has all gone horribly wrong.

Morpheus's previous comments start to beat through my skull, his reminders that we don't treat Omegas this way. His chastisements about not talking to Serapina. His demands that I *fix* this.

Yet all I've done is make this worse.

When Serapina's gaze falls to the marbled floor of the shower, I wince.

"Serapina, I'm not going—"

"Stars, is that *blood*?" she asks, her eyes widening.

"What?" I glance down, my frown returning. "Oh. Yes. Dried blood." I try to look over my shoulder, which is an idiotic move since I can't see my lower back. But I'm feeling very out of sorts at the moment. Very un-Alpha-like, too.

Clearing my throat, I shake my head and try to regain control of the situation.

This is my soulmate. I... I can, no, I will, fix this.

"Reaper stabbed me," I explain, wanting to be forthcoming and choosing this as a way to be truthful with her. To try to *talk* to her. "I forgot about it, as it's already healed, but that's actually why I came in to shower—to wash off the blood."

She gapes up at me. "Oh, fae, is Reaper okay?"

And I'm frowning again. "Is Reaper okay?" I echo back at her. Did she not understand what I said? "*He* stabbed *me*." There. That should be clearer.

"Yes, I heard that part. Is he okay?"

My brow furrows. "You're worried about Reaper? When I'm the one who was wounded?" That doesn't make any sense.

"Did you punish him?" she asks, her soft tone holding a note of caution to it, one that has me realizing her concern is founded on her perception of me. Of what I've done to her. Of what she believes I did to Maliki.

Fuck. "No," I snap and move away from her to run my fingers through my hair.

I knew things between us were distorted and wrong. But this? It's far worse than I realized.

And it's all my fault.

I whisper a curse and step beneath the spray, letting it wash over me as I try to figure out how to recover from this.

Movement causes my focus to return to Serapina as she starts to tiptoe around me.

"Please don't leave," I say, suddenly feeling more exhausted than I have in a very long time. "I didn't punish Reaper, nor was I punishing Maliki. Actually, if anything, I was *rewarding* Maliki by letting him touch you."

Because I knew he wanted to. And he needed me to essentially demand he do so in order to feel *allowed* to act on his desires.

"I would never force Maliki to do something he didn't want to do. Actually, I'm fairly certain I can't force him to do a damn thing. He may respect me as his friend, but he has no problem telling me to fuck off when I overstep."

In fact, I'm pretty sure he's been doing that a lot over the last year where Serapina is concerned.

"He likes you," I go on. "And for months he's been saying you're not pretending or lying. I stubbornly believed my mate had deceived him just as she'd done to me. So I chose to engage her—*you*—in a game. One I now realize has caused significant harm."

Serapina slowly turns to face me, her gaze guarded.

It's a look that physically undoes me.

Because I've earned that expression. And I fucking hate what I've done.

She's an Omega. She deserves to be cherished. Yet all I've done is frighten her and make her think the worst of me.

"It's not an excuse, but I truly believed you were Persephone and merely pretending not to remember me." The words come out bitter because I'm still struggling to accept that I was wrong, that my soulmate isn't actually staring back at me right now.

But the proof is irrefutable.

She's not Persephone.

However, she *is* my soulmate.

Which means she deserves to understand my motives and what I originally intended to do.

"I was trying to punish Persephone in my own way," I admit. "That's why I re-created our engagement announcement and even went as far as to plan a replica of our first wedding. It was meant to remind her of who we once were, while the environment around us showed her who we had become—as a result of her deception."

I've had millennia to prepare for her return. Never did I consider that the version of her wouldn't be the one I once knew.

"I've been hunting her soul for over two thousand years," I confide softly. "I knew she wasn't truly gone. I felt her. Sensed her in every breath. Knew she was somewhere I couldn't touch. And when I finally found her—found *you* —with Demeter, I assumed you were a reincarnated version of my mate, all memories intact."

It was an intelligent assumption.

But a wrong one.

"This is all unprecedented, Serapina." I run my fingers through my hair. "You're mine. I feel in my heart and soul that you are my mate. Yet that mating call you unleashed earlier says otherwise." It should have been impossible. However, that's exactly what happened.

Which provided even more proof that Serapina may possess my mate's soul, but she isn't Persephone. *And she isn't truly mine, either.*

A fact I'm refusing to accept.

Because it makes no sense.

I feel our connection thriving between us. Though, I don't think she feels anything at all.

Except fear. And maybe disgust.

She thought I meant to punish Maliki by forcing him to please her. Then she showed concern for Reaper...

Fuck, this female doesn't understand me at all.

My jaw ticks. "I—"

"Morpheus said," she starts, interrupting what I was about to say. "Oh, sorry. I, er, I thought you were done. Never mind."

"If anyone needs to apologize here, it's me, Serapina. I realize I've not been the best communicator and I've failed you in a lot of ways, but despite what you've witnessed, I do know how to be a good Alpha." Of course, it's going to take me some time to prove that to her.

But I have to start somewhere.

May as well begin with this.

"What did Morpheus say?" It has to be one of the hardest questions I've ever asked anyone. Because I don't truly want to know what my cousin said to my mate. However, it matters to Serapina, and therefore, it matters to me.

"He said I basically informed the Alphas that I'm unclaimed, but I don't understand how I did that. Was it... because I moaned?" Her cheeks turn red, but she doesn't look away from me as she adds, "When I climaxed, I mean?"

Her words evoke a memory of said climax, causing my knot to pulse in response.

Because *fuck*. She was stunning. Unique. *New*.

It almost felt wrong to react to her in such a way. She's mine... and yet... *not*.

I haven't touched anyone in over two thousand years. Persephone was my everything, my *life*. Now her soul is standing before me as someone I don't know.

Is it wrong to crave Serapina? To watch her come undone again, all while knowing she's not my Persephone?

I swallow, unsure of how to feel about this growing conundrum.

So I focus on what she just asked me instead.

And do my job as her Alpha.

"Your aura emitted a call to all of Alpha kind in this dimension," I explain. "It wasn't a sound or anything you actively did. It was your Omega soul crying out for a mate. Because you're going to go into heat soon and you're going to need a knot."

She looks a little unsteady. "Okay. And what... what does that actually mean? Morpheus said the Alphas were hunting me. Did they hunt Alina, too?"

I take a step toward her as she sways. "How about this," I say slowly. "I'll explain everything, answer all your questions, while I wash your hair, okay?" I really just want a reason to touch her, to try to *calm* her. It's an intrinsic need, one driven by my inner beast.

She's an Omega in distress.

All I want to do is purr for her, but she told me not to.

"Please," I add, feeling a little desperate. "I know I haven't earned the right to touch you, but it should help a little."

"Help what?" she asks, her voice quiet. "I don't even understand what's happening."

"Your inner Omega is awakening," I tell her. "This happens when an Omega is ready to take a mate and procreate. But your situation is unpredictable and rare. And, honestly, it's also *unknown*."

Because the only two beings in existence with answers are Demeter and Persephone. The former isn't talking. And the latter, well, she doesn't remember.

Knowing that serves as a kick to my heart. I thought I'd found my mate, that she was playing some sort of deceitful game for months, only to realize that this isn't Persephone.

It's Serapina.

She stares up at me with big blue eyes, so different from the dark ones I used to look into, and blinks long blonde lashes when I cup her cheek.

"We're going to protect you," I promise her. "Maliki and I, I mean. Maybe my cousin, too. Regardless, I need you to know you're safe. Those Alphas can't touch you here."

Her nose scrunches. "You mean your brother, right? Orcus?"

"Well, him, too. But no. I was referring to Morpheus. He's my cousin."

The way her eyes widen tells me she didn't know that detail.

Which only makes me feel worse.

Because there is so much she doesn't know. I made far too many assumptions where Serapina is concerned.

"We're going to need to start over," I tell her, sighing. "If that's even possible." I run my thumb along her cheekbone, my gaze holding hers. "Hi. My name is Hades. And I'm your intended mate."

SERA

I GAZE UP AT HADES, UTTERLY AT A LOSS FOR HOW TO respond.

Starting over doesn't feel possible, just like he said.

"If I'm your mate, then why did my 'inner Omega' send out a signal saying otherwise?" I ask him, focusing on that part of our conversation instead of his reintroduction.

Though, truly, it was the first time he's ever actually introduced himself to me.

Other than the first night we met when he gave me his name—after I asked for it. And I thought that was a dream, not reality, for thirteen months.

His jaw clenches a little, the only indication that he's not thrilled by my question. "Your soul is mated to mine," he says. "But you, *Serapina*, the physical entity, are unmarked."

I frown at that. "Okay, then mark me. I'm supposed to be yours, right?" Wouldn't that solve everything? No more hunt?

His dark eyes narrow. "When I mark you, Omega, it won't be under some misguided obligation on your part," he replies, his accent thickening as his voice deepens. "I'll claim you because you want me to, not because you need me to."

My brow furrows. "So this requires my consent? But declaring our intended marriage didn't?" I can't help the sarcastic lilt underscoring my words. Because this doesn't really make any sense. "What's the difference?"

"I thought my Omega was playing a game with me, so I arranged a reenactment of our first mating ceremony. And in my mind, I wasn't actually forcing you to do anything at all. I was playing with my mate. As I've said, I now realize my mistake."

Patience radiates from his tone, despite him basically repeating what he's already said. Even his touch is gentle.

Like the Hades in my dreams.

I blink and shake my head, needing to clear it again. It's not just his purr that makes me dizzy; it's *him*. His presence. His scent. *His abs.*

It's then that I realize my palms are on his torso.

No idea when I placed them there. Maybe when he cupped my cheek? Perhaps a second ago?

I… I don't know.

But this too perfect of a male specimen is making me feel insane.

Is this part of my heat? This irresistible urge to caress him and be near him?

He said touching me would help me.

Not sure this is *helpful*.

"I need to talk to my sister," I blurt out. Alina went through this. She can guide me. Maybe. Or… Or no. I really don't want to ask her about any of this.

I…

I huff a breath. "Never mind. I would rather you just mark me so I don't have to worry about being hunted," I mutter. "Was Alina hunted?" I ask in the next instant. "You didn't answer my question."

Instead, he talked about washing my hair.

Which derailed my focus.

"I want you to explain to me what Morpheus meant when he said the Alphas were hunting me," I tell Hades directly. "And please answer my question about Alina. Is she even still here?" My eyes widen. "Is Reaper okay?" Because Hades also never really answered that, either. Just gave me an emphatic *no* when I asked if he punished Reaper.

That doesn't mean much.

He could have killed him, for all I know.

Reaper stabbed Hades.

I step to the side and try to walk around Hades to see his back, but he moves with me.

"Alina wasn't hunted because she went into heat in another dimension. And I'm guessing Orcus claimed her quickly, too." He turns in a circle as I continue to try to figure out where Reaper stabbed him.

Maybe I've lost my mind, but this seems important.

Or perhaps it's just a necessary distraction.

"The Alphas are hunting you because you sent out a beacon saying you needed a knot," he goes on, basically reiterating what I already knew.

Which, yeah. Okay. I asked a redundant question. But this is a lot.

"Yes, your sister is still here. She's in Orcus's wing with his mate-circle." He steps into my path before I can circle him again, his palm suddenly on my neck. "And I'm not sure why you're obsessed with Reaper's well-being when he can take care of himself, but he's fine."

57

"He stabbed you."

"Yes, he did. Perhaps you should ask if I'm okay instead?" he suggests, his eyebrow rising.

"You're clearly fine," I return.

"Am I?" he asks, still gazing down at me with that arrogantly arched brow. "I just found out my mate's soul is inside a stranger. One I've treated horribly as a result of my need for revenge. And now that Omega is about to go into heat, yet I can't properly help her without potentially hurting her. So instead, I'm going to risk everything to protect her. Because that's what a good Alpha does."

He releases me so abruptly that I nearly fall.

Which, of course, ends with him catching my hip to steady me.

"I'm going to wash your hair now," he tells me. "Then I'm going to wash myself. And afterward, we'll go eat, as I'm sure you're starving."

A denial graces my lips right as my stomach growls.

Oh, I think. *I guess I am hungry.*

And tired, too.

When was the last time I slept or ate?

What day is it even?

I don't have the energy to figure it out. I'm suddenly exhausted. Depleted. *Done.*

Hades must take my silence as acquiescence because he starts combing his fingers through my hair.

When the familiar scent of roses reaches me, I close my eyes and let the aroma mingle with his wintry cologne.

Memories assault me of standing outside the greenhouse on a cold morning.

Only, the vision shifts to one from my dreams of Hades holding me in a garden surrounded by fiery orange flowers.

It's an image from one of my earlier dreams,

reminding me of why I first took a rose outside. I was trying to re-create the fragrance from my fantasy.

Is it normal to smell something so beautiful while one sleeps? I wonder. *Or is my dream actually something else entirely?*

Hades told me the roses I picked were similar to fire lilies, at least in terms of scent.

Are those what blossomed around us in my dreams?

I've never smelled a live fire lily, only the decaying ones Pip often leaves on my pillow.

I wasn't even sure of the species due to the black petals and leaves, but he wrote it down for me one day.

Then Hades mentioned that it was Persephone's favorite flower.

Is that a coincidence?

"Serapina?" Hades murmurs, the question in his voice suggesting this isn't the first time he's said my name.

I open my eyes and find him standing in front of me, his hair dripping onto his muscular shoulders.

He's intimidating. Large. Ridiculously handsome. Yet watching me with a guarded gaze, like he's afraid I'll somehow hurt him.

It's strange. Utterly impossible. Yet his nervousness is almost tangible.

"Do you want the soap bar, or can I touch you?" he asks.

I swallow. I should probably take the soap bar and tell him to leave me alone. To give me space. To just... *go away*.

But I really don't want any of that.

I've been trying to take care of myself for months. I'm not sure if I've even begun to succeed. But I need a break. I simply want to let someone else take control, even if it's just for a few stolen moments.

Lifting my palm, I press it to the crown tattoo on his

chest and close my eyes again. "You win for now, Hades. I don't have energy for anything else."

He releases a rumble that sounds more like a growl than a purr. "We're not playing a game, Omega."

"Says the Alpha who demanded I marry him because he hates my soul," I mutter.

His palm is on my nape again in a flash, and I'm suddenly up against a wall.

No. *Between* two walls. One made of marble and the other all hot, hard *man*. "I do not *hate* your soul, Serapina. I *love* your soul. Persephone may have betrayed me in the worst way, but she is still mine. And I could never *hate* my Omega."

I shiver, my gaze glued to his as he stares me down.

"The games Persephone and I played were complicated," he goes on. "But what's happening between you and me is not a battle or a game or any other passing amusement."

His palm moves to my throat, giving it a subtle squeeze.

"*This* is intense, Serapina. It's serious. I fucked up, and I'm going to fix it. And if I can't, then you'll choose who sees you through your heat. All while I'll be forced to watch and guard. Because I won't let anyone hurt you, Omega. You're mine to cherish and mine to protect. But you're not mine to knot. Not until I earn your trust."

With that, he steps backward and holds out the soap.

"Take it and finish washing yourself while I find you something to wear."

My limbs obey on autopilot, my hand meeting his in a touch that's far too brief.

He moves away from me, rinses himself off, and leaves without looking back at me.

I watch every movement, take in the defined planes of his form, then realize he never once took off his boxers.

Yet I saw the outline there, too. His massive size. Stars, it was just as intimidating as the rest of him.

All while I stood here... completely naked.

I blink. It's not like nudity is new to me. There were certain requirements in Nightingale Village that made me rather acquainted with the concept.

But Hades never once made me feel uncomfortable about my nude state.

Just about everything else, I think, looking down at the soap in my hand.

I don't have the energy to think about everything he's said, so I just focus on finishing my shower. I'm pretty sure he thoroughly washed my hair since it feels refreshed and soft. So I don't bother with anything other than cleansing my body. Then I step out of the shower and jump when it magically shuts off.

"Stars," I whisper. I'm in the Human Realm and still surrounded by magic.

As evidenced by the neatly folded warm towel that appears on the counter in front of me. The one I dropped on the floor before has disappeared, too.

"Okay." I'm not even going to question it. I'm just going to accept the fluffy haven, dry myself off, and...

And face Hades, I think, sighing.

He said he was getting me clothes.

Maybe his closet magics things into existence, too.

Wrapping the towel around myself, I run my fingers through my damp hair and head toward the bedroom, just as I hear Hades demand, "Why are you here?"

I freeze, thinking he's talking to me for a moment.

But Morpheus answers with "I let you lead last time. And we all know how that ended. So I won't be doing that again because, unlike you, I refuse to make the same mistakes as I did two thousand years ago."

"I'm not repeating my mistakes," Hades says, the calm tone he used with me in the shower nowhere to be heard. "That's evidenced by Maliki being here."

"Funny, that," Maliki drawls. "It seems everyone else knew to meet here except for me. So why am I here, again?"

I slip out of the bathroom and see Hades clench his jaw, his focus on Maliki. "The only one who knew to meet here in an emergency was Orcus."

"And you didn't feel it was important to let your hired babysitter know to bring his charge here in the case of an emergency as well?" Maliki asks.

I frown at him referring to himself as a *babysitter* and me as a *charge*.

Hades glares at him. "I wasn't anticipating the need. Orcus and I agreed on this location many moons ago."

"Before Serapina," Morpheus murmurs. When Hades shifts his narrowed gaze toward the God of Dreams, Morpheus holds his hands up and adds, "Sometimes clarifications help when asking for forgiveness."

"You have nothing to do with this conversation, and you certainly have no business being here. So why don't you kindly fuck off?" Hades suggests.

Morpheus simply smiles. "No."

"She's not your Omega."

Morpheus cants his head. "Oh? Is she yours?"

Hades steps up to him, and a chilling energy sweeps through the room. "Careful, *Cousin*."

"I'm done being *careful*," Morpheus returns, his smile slipping as power whips around him.

My eyes widen. "Okay, that's enough," I say, over all of this. "I'm tired. I'm hungry. And most importantly, *I* belong to *me*. Sera. Human. Mine. Whatever. I'm not anyone else's anything. I am just... *me*. Now, can I please have a shirt or something? Because I... I want food. I want some sleep. And..." I trail off, uncertain of what else I want. I'm pretty sure I'm just being repetitive at this point.

But I'm done with today.

Done with the possessive shenanigans.

Done with Hades's heavy words.

Done with concepts of being hunted. And going into heat. And...

"Hold on," I say, aware that I'm rambling and not really caring. "*When* am I going into heat?" Because no one has really explained that yet. "And while I'm asking questions, I know a knot ties an Alpha to an Omega. But, uh, *how* does it do that?"

Because Morpheus didn't explain that part. Just told me the purpose of a knot.

I also understand the concept of a heat and the purpose of it—thanks somewhat to Alina. But I don't know exactly what it entails.

Though, it's... it's kind of obvious what the outcome will be.

Which, naturally, has my lips parting as I think about *that* part. "Oh, fae, you're going to get me pregnant..." My eyes widen and I step backward. "Ohhhh, no. No, no, no." I clutch my towel like it's a shield. "I am *not* ready for that."

Or any of it really.

I just want a snack.

And a nap.

I press my hand to my head, and suddenly Maliki is in front of me. Not sure how or when he arrived, but his hands are on my arms and he's pulling me into a much-needed hug.

"I've got you, trouble," he murmurs against my ear.

"How about we kick the Alphas out, enjoy a meal, and snuggle, yeah?"

I nod. Because that sounds like a really nice plan. "Yes, please."

"You're kicking me out of my own room?" Hades asks, sounding incredulous.

"You're a God. Manifest a bed or a couch or something in the other room," Maliki tells him. "And you... we'll keep talking soon. But right now, Sera is my priority."

"As she should be," Morpheus replies.

"Keep talking about what?" Hades demands.

"Ask Morpheus," Maliki suggests. "But preferably in the other room. Or, Styx, another realm would be fine, too. Just fucking go." His arms tighten around me, and I sink into his protection, loopily pleased by his warmth and his familiar leathery scent.

I practically bury my nose against his chest and inhale.

He's wearing a T-shirt. I don't know how or when he changed. But I don't care. It smells like him and I like it.

Silence descends around us, then Maliki chuckles. "Morpheus just grabbed Hades and misted him somewhere. Kind of wish I could follow with some popcorn." He kisses the top of my head. "However, I'll settle for enjoying some pizza with you in Hades's bed instead."

My brow furrows. "Pizza?" My nose twitches. "As in... human pizza? Like with the pepperonis?"

He loosens his hold and pulls back to look down at me. "So you're a fan of it?"

I nod a little. "Reaper made me try it last year. It's... it's really good."

"It's amazing," he corrects me. "And he dropped off the best kinds for us to try. I ended up tossing everything I created in the kitchen as a result. But it's delicious." He drops one of his arms, then starts walking me toward the bed. "How about you get changed and I'll go grab the food? Then we'll make a mess in Hades's sheets."

My cheeks heat at his words. "A mess?"

His lips curl. "With crumbs, trouble. But if you're open to another kind of mess…" He lets that comment linger, then leans in to press his lips to my ear. "Morpheus says no orgasms. But sometimes delayed gratification is fun." He nips my earlobe. "We'll discuss it more… after you eat."

MORPHEUS

Maliki shadows across the room to our Omega and gathers her in his arms, his instincts proving his worth as a member of this mate-circle.

Unfortunately, the same cannot be said about my cousin.

Hades's possessiveness is going to put Serapina at risk.

And I just can't allow that.

Grabbing his arm, I mist us out of the cavern and to the secluded beach outside. The sun is beginning to set in this realm, which means we should be free to fly soon, if needed.

I release Hades as soon as my leather shoes touch the sand and mist ten feet away to avoid his incoming fist. "Our Omega needs to eat and sleep," I tell him sternly.

"She's not—"

"No, Hades. It's my turn to speak. We both know the only reason I was able to trace Serapina here is because I'm linked to her soul. You've never wanted to accept it before, but you have to now."

The way his jaw flexes tells me he's not only aware of this but has already thought about it, too.

"The only reason I didn't fight for Persephone in the beginning was because I didn't want to force her to choose. But she would have had to because you would never be willing to share. So I protected her sanity by staying away. And it's my biggest regret in life. Because had I been there, I may have been able to save her from Demeter's influence."

It hasn't been proved, but I strongly suspect Persephone was manipulated into helping her mother.

Had I been involved in the mate-circle, I may have picked up on a clue as to what was happening.

Or perhaps I would have missed it entirely.

But at least I would *know* my part in it all. Instead, I've been an outsider to my own affairs, and I'll never know if I could have helped or not.

However, I won't be making that mistake again.

"I can't stay away from her this time," I inform Hades. "I don't want her to have to choose between us. But if you demand that a decision be made, I will fight for her. Hard. And, dear Cousin, after all you've put our mate through… I think I'll win."

What I don't admit aloud is that I know it will be a shallow victory. Forcing Serapina to choose is a loss in itself. I won't be the one to demand that choice. It'll be Hades.

And that will be his inevitable downfall.

Omegas are not meant to mate only one Alpha.

They're meant to take a mate-circle. To be protected. Worshipped. Properly cared for.

I failed Persephone.

I refuse to fail Serapina. I won't lose her, either.

Hades says nothing, just stares me down with an intensity I both admire and despise.

"You know I'm an ally," I tell him, a note of irritation threading through my tone. "I'm powerful. I'm trustworthy. I'm fucking family, Hades. If anything, *you* have proved to be an enemy in this situation. Not me. But I'm still willing to work with you. Because I am putting our Omega's needs and desires first. Can you say the same?"

"I haven't forcibly removed you from my beach yet," he replies flatly. "That implies effort on my part."

I simply look at him. He's not necessarily wrong, but if this is the furthest he's willing to bend, then we're absolutely going to battle one another.

His eyes narrow, his jaw tightening again as he shifts his focus to the waves rolling over the sand. "I hate that you followed us here."

My eyebrow arches. "You can't be surprised that I did."

"I'm not," he admits. "But I still hate it."

"Because it proves what she means to me." I don't phrase it as a question, but as a statement.

He grunts in response, neither confirming nor denying my words. However, we both know she's my soulmate, too. He's just never wanted to accept that fact.

And now he's being forced to face fate.

"I'm not leaving," I reiterate. "She's *ours*, Hades. Mine, yours, and Maliki's."

That last part grabs the God of Death's attention, his eyes burning as he glares back at me. "Be very careful, Morpheus."

I smile. "Or what?"

"Or I may begin to assume that you're interested in more than just my Omega."

"Maybe I am." It's a taunt. A dare, really. A way to push my cousin's buttons and force him to consider everything—*and everyone*—that he will lose if he chooses to go to war over Serapina.

Because I suspect she won't be the only one to pick me in the fight.

Maliki might, too.

Not for me, but for *her*.

That's the heart of all of this—our world centers around Serapina Everheart. Yet Hades wants it to revolve around him and his Omega.

But that's not how this works. Not anymore, anyway.

"If Serapina wants Maliki, then so do I," I add. "Because marked or not, we both know an Omega can undo another Alpha's claim."

Hades's jaw now resembles granite from clenching his teeth so hard.

But I'm not done.

He needs to be pushed. And I'm the right one for the task. Which ironically is what makes me an ideal candidate for his mate-circle.

"Does Maliki even realize that you've claimed him?" I press, aware that the enforcer has no idea what Hades has done to him. "Do you plan to tell him?"

"My dealings with Maliki are not your concern."

"They will be soon," I murmur, a notable threat lingering in my tone. "As I said, an Omega can undo an Alpha's claim. And it seems to me that *our* Serapina has already chosen *our* enforcer."

Hades's hands fist at his sides as he takes a bold step toward me. "Stop pushing me, Morpheus."

"No," I answer simply. "You need a good shove, Cousin. I've been patient. *Very fucking patient.* And I'm done catering to your ego. Because I'm not your subordinate. I'm your equal. A fellow Alpha. Your bloody ally. Now it's time you pay me the respect I deserve."

I hit him with a wave of power, one that changes the landscape around us into his infamous death world. Only, this is *my* illusion. *I* am the one in control here. Not him.

He growls my name in warning.

I ignore him and say, "All I want is what's best for Serapina. I won't take her from you. I won't hurt her in any way. I'm here to protect her. So do not tell me to leave. And stop questioning my intentions. I've been up-front with you from the very beginning. She's just as much mine as she is yours."

Hades takes another step forward, his eyes alight with barely restrained fury.

I feint a mist to his left, my control over his vision forcing him to think I'm right beside him when, in reality, I haven't actually moved.

"As far as Maliki goes, you've set it up for Serapina to claim him first. Which is what makes him equally mine because, like it or not, I'm in Serapina's orbit now. I'm courting her. And if she decides to have me, too, then Maliki and I will form a mate-circle around her—with or without you."

Hades's fist flies at my illusion's face, so I mist the creation to his opposite side.

"Fighting me won't fix this," I go on. "Work with me instead, Hades. Let me prove to you how much of an ally I can be."

"I don't need you as an ally," he returns flatly.

I'm about to reply when the world shifts, my illusion

fading away into smoke as I suddenly find my throat gripped by Hades's palm.

"You're right about us being equals," he says as he materializes fully in front of me. "You're wrong to assume that I want to work with you in any capacity."

Now my jaw is the one that clenches.

Because he's cut off my air supply, thus making it impossible to reply.

So I manifest another version of myself and have the illusion do the talking for me. "Wanting to and needing to are very different phrases," my replica says.

Hades's gaze narrows even more, and his fist flies out to punch my illusion in the face while his opposite hand releases my throat. "*I know*," he growls, taking a step back. "That doesn't mean I accept any of this."

I massage my neck, my vocal cords still feeling constricted from his residual touch.

So my illusion responds for me with "Unfortunately, fate isn't giving you much of a choice."

He grunts at that and turns away from me, his fingers combing through his dark hair as he begins to pace.

I retract my power, the image of me disappearing as the beach comes into full view once more.

Hades continues to walk an angry path back and forth by the water while I wait for my throat to heal. When I'm seconds away from being able to speak again, he says, "I need to check on the Netherworld."

My eyebrow arches. "Oh?"

I assume his word choice of "need" is purposeful. Because, yes, he really should ensure his kingdom is all right. Just as he *needs* to work with me. Both obligations, and for somewhat related reasons. Yet entirely different ones, too.

"Ossa," he says, his voice seeming to carry on the wind

as he appears to ignore my presence. Though, I'm aware he murmured the name aloud on purpose. Because he could have called his beast to him with his mind rather than his voice.

I take a step back just as a three-headed monstrosity appears on the beach, the paws pounding across the sand as Hades's creature adheres to his every command.

"You know the rules here," he says conversationally, his focus on the one with silver eyes and a matching collar around the fluffy neck. "Keep your brothers in line."

Ossa dips her head, while Howl and Mort both loll their tongues to the side, like they think the order is a joke.

"Guard our Omega with your life," he says, and I know he's referring to *his* Omega that he's sharing with *his* creature.

But I choose to believe he means *our* as in *Hades's and my* Omega. Because she is indeed *ours*.

"And, Pip," Hades goes on, calling the little soul over to him. "Alert Maliki of any issues first, then come find me in the Netherworld. Understood?"

The little soul gives a salute and proceeds to march off with a purpose, his cloak stomping in the wind beneath his invisible feet.

Howl glances at the cloaked figure with interest, but Ossa snaps at him. I assume she's telling the playful head to focus instead of considering a chaotic game of chase.

Mort cocks his head as well, and Ossa growls.

Hades sighs in response and looks at me. "We had better make this quick. I don't know how successful this guarding mission will be."

"We?" I echo.

"Yes, *we*," he replies. "You wanted to prove yourself as an ally, right? Cleaning up the Netherworld seems like a good place to start." Then he disappears.

My lips twitch. This isn't what I meant at all, and he knows it. But I'm not about to turn down an opportunity to show off my talents. Especially when it means punching some old Alpha enemies. If I get to "accidentally" hit Hades a few times in the process, all the more fun.

I mist back to his palace, ready for a bloody good time.

And instead come face-to-face with the Hell Fae King.

I glance around, looking for Hades, and find him nowhere to be seen. *Typical.*

"Morpheus," Typhos Lucifer says, his long hair billowing on an invisible breeze as he turns toward me with fury swimming in his dark blue eyes. "Care to tell me what the fuck is going on in my realm?"

I sigh. Hades clearly set me up. *Should have seen that coming*, I mentally mutter to myself.

Then I focus on the furious Hell Fae King and reply, "An Omega has awakened, and with that comes... a wave of feral Alpha aggression."

When it's clear he needs more of an explanation, I start from the beginning.

All while cursing Hades in my mind.

He told me he wanted me to prove myself as an ally by helping him clean up the Netherworld Kingdom. I naïvely assumed *helping him* meant *working with him*.

Seems he meant for me to do the work for him instead.

Well played, Cousin. Well played...

MALIKI

SERA LOUNGES IN A BUTTON-DOWN SHIRT THAT LOOKS FAR too sexy on her. She's wearing it like a dress, the black fabric reaching her knees. And the only thing I can think about is unfastening it to expose the sweet figure beneath.

Fuck.

I should not be hard right now. But I am. *Too fucking hard.*

Because she's off-limits to me. *Again.* Yet all I want to do is grab her and truly kiss her. Then explore every inch of her with my tongue and make her fall apart beneath me.

But apparently, that will cause her inner Omega to light up like a beacon to all of Alpha kind and alert them to her presence here.

I nearly growl in frustration.

74

Morpheus caught me up in the kitchen, telling me how Sera's Omega woke up, thanks to my talented hands—his words, which he promptly changed to *talented tongue* after observing my reaction. After a beat of silence, he gave me a smile and asked, "How did she taste, Enforcer?"

When I didn't answer, his smile only widened.

"I suppose I'll find out soon enough," he said before going on to explain the signal her Omega gave off and what it means for all of Alpha kind.

Basically, he told me what I already gathered—Sera is an unclaimed Omega who is about to go into heat. When that heat will occur is a mystery, but Morpheus expects it will come on quickly.

"Leading up to it will be quite fun for you," he told me earlier.

I arched a brow. "For me?"

He smiled again, his grin revealing twin dimples. "You've awakened a feral need that can only be satisfied by a knot. Yet I suspect you might be the only one she'll let touch her for now, which means the privilege falls to you to give her pleasure. And she's going to be beautifully insatiable." His blue-green eyes slid over me. "Your shadows may become quite useful."

I didn't ask him what he meant. Because I already understood.

My shadows provide sensation. They can also create textures and shapes.

Not many know that about me. Either Morpheus was making a guess, or he's watched me before.

I'm willing to bet it's the latter.

He's the God of Dreams. It only seems natural that he would be a voyeur.

Or maybe that's an Alpha trait.

Styx knows how much Hades likes to watch.

Though, I'm the one *watching* right now as Sera brings a piece of pizza up to her delectable mouth. She's on her third helping, something I find remarkable given her small stature. But she was clearly hungry. And the little moans she's emitting tell me how much she's enjoying her meal.

My lips twitch as a pepperoni slides off the cheese… then I groan when she catches it with her tongue. "Shadows, trouble," I breathe. "Are you trying to kill me over here?"

She frowns as she chews her food.

Then swallows.

And *fuck*, now I'm imagining something else sliding down her pretty throat. Something warm and maybe a little salty. Something *euphoric*.

"What did I do?" she asks, the picture of innocence.

Oh, how I would love to teach her a lesson in seduction right now. Fist my fingers in her hair and yank her back over the arm of the chair and feed her my cock.

Then lean over, tug up that sinful shirt to expose her slick pussy, and *feast*.

"Maliki?" she whispers, her big blue eyes blinking. "You're… glaring at me."

"No, trouble, I'm admiring you," I correct her, my voice gruffer than intended. But I don't bother clearing my throat. "You're eating that pizza in a way that's making me want to eat you."

Her cheeks pinken, her full lips forming a surprised little O.

Which doesn't help matters at all. Because now all I want to do is press my tip to her mouth, force those lips to widen for me, and demand that she *suck*.

I lean forward in my chair, a proposal lingering on my tongue, only for a loud knock to disturb the moment.

My eyes narrow at the door, and Sera freezes. "Keep

eating, trouble," I tell her as I stand. "In fact, I want that slice gone before I sit back down."

Because otherwise I'm going to act on my urges.

I've never claimed to be a good man. Actually, I'm fairly certain I've claimed the opposite.

If her orgasm sets off a signal, I can just… shadow her elsewhere.

Not a fantastic plan.

But it's one I consider heartily as I walk toward the bedroom door.

Except the being waiting in the hallway has me reconsidering all my ideas and reevaluating my will to live. Because Hades's dark gaze holds a note of fury that very rarely ends well for the object of his ire.

Which appears to be me since he's glowering in my direction.

I lean against the door frame and lift a brow. "Yes?" I drawl, not willing to bow to his mood.

He's the one who told me to please *his wife*. Not my fault if he's having regrets over it.

Because now that I've tasted her, I'm not all that inclined to stop.

"I need to mist back to the Netherworld Kingdom," he tells me, his voice low. "Morpheus is meeting me there. I just wanted to let you know that you're in charge of protecting our Omega."

"Our?" I repeat, my eyebrow winging higher.

"I'm not here to debate semantics. I'm here to give you a task—*guard*." He takes a step back. "My beast is roaming the beach with Pip. If there's an issue, Pip will notify you."

I stare at him, waiting for more. "Is that it? You're not going to tell me what to do if there's a problem?"

He shrugs. "I trust you."

"So I can take her wherever I want?" I push, curious as to why I'm being given so much freedom and faith.

Sure, Hades usually lets me manage my own assignments. But Sera is no ordinary assignment.

"Yes" is all he says. No elaboration. No context. Just an affirmative.

"Okay."

"Okay," he echoes. "But be very careful, Maliki. No matter where you go, I'll know. And trust me when I say I will follow you. Always."

With that cryptic load of Styx, he disappears.

My jaw ticks. "Arse."

Shutting the door, I return to find Sera standing with her hands twisting in front of her. "Everything okay?" she asks.

"No," I reply, leaning back against the paneled wood behind me and sliding my hands into my pockets. "You're still looking far too edible in that shirt."

She glances down and frowns. "You gave this to me to wear."

"Yes. And now I'm having regrets."

Her brow furrows more, then she slowly looks back up at me. "I see." Her features smooth over, and a new side of her awakens, one that has me instantly intrigued. Because I can see the shift in her face, the way her lashes lower coyly as she asks, "Would you prefer I wear nothing?"

Mmm, she's flirting now.

I like this.

I like it a lot.

"Honestly?" I take in the dark fabric and her exposed lower limbs. "No." I push off the door and saunter toward her. "Having the shirt on gives me something to play with, sweet mystery." I grab the fabric in my fist and yank her toward me, just so she knows what I mean. "It also gives me something to remove."

I lean down and brush my lips over hers.

"Or maybe it's the barrier I need," I go on. "Because Morpheus says I can't make you come again. Not yet. Even though you're apparently going to beg me to do so."

He gave me a few important highlights regarding an Omega's heat, how they lose their minds with lust and demand satisfaction.

But it's so much deeper than that.

They need to be full of *seed*.

Worshipped by their mates.

Driven to climax over and over until they pass out.

Only for it to begin anew the moment the Omega wakes.

Shadows, I want that.

With Sera.

Except it's not time yet.

"Now that her sexual spirit has risen, she's going to become more... explorative," Morpheus warned me in the kitchen. "Be prepared to guide her. She'll need your expertise."

He didn't elaborate on what that means, but the way Sera is melting against me now tells me all I need to know.

She's not mine to please. Not mine to cherish. Not mine to kiss.

But death it, I don't bloody care about anything other than *her*. Her wants. Her needs. Her *desire*.

My grip on her shirt tightens, my opposite hand going to her hair. "Do you want to play, trouble?" I ask, my lips so fucking close to hers that it physically hurts not to close the distance between us. However, we have to discuss this first.

Because there are limits to what we can do.

We're safe here so long as her inner Omega doesn't send off another flare.

Sera presses her palms to my shirt, her nails digging into my pectoral muscles through the thin fabric. "I want you to kiss me, Maliki," she whispers. "*Really* kiss me."

"I believe I already did that, mystery," I murmur. "I *thoroughly* kissed you."

She shakes her head. "I mean on my mouth."

I know that's what she meant, but I couldn't help teasing her.

"Will you please be my first real kiss?" she asks, and the question has me realizing all over again how innocent the female is.

It's not usually a characteristic I desire, but with her... it just fits.

She's a Goddess.

A being of impossibilities.

A woman who redefines the meaning of temptation.

And she wants me to kiss her.

Who am I to say no?

Tightening my grip on her shirt and in her hair, I close the gap between us and firmly press my lips to hers. She shivers against me, her body seeming to melt into mine.

It's a chaste embrace.

One that belies the tension building inside me. The feral hunger. The intrinsic *need*.

But this is about her and her fantasies.

I want to make every dream of hers come true.

Only, her *moan* destroys my best intentions.

It's a soft hum, one that echoes around us and dismantles every ounce of self-control I possess.

Because I need to hear that sound again.

Styx, I need to taste it. Own it. *Embolden* it.

My hand leaves her shirt and goes to her hip, my other

palm sliding down to her nape, as I pull her flush against me.

Then I deepen our embrace by parting her plump lips with my tongue.

And groan as she clutches me with her hands. Almost like she's afraid I might let her go.

But I'm pretty sure she's stuck with me now.

I've never felt this way about anyone. Maybe it's the forbidden aspect. However, I fear it's something so much darker than that. So much more intense.

I feel caught in her web.

Ensnared by her beauty and enthralled by her sincerity.

Captivated by her strength and lost to her needs.

I simply never want to leave. Never want this to end. Just want to indulge in her... for as long as I live.

Which may only be hours if Hades finds out what I've done.

But this kiss is worth facing his wrath.

Because this kiss makes her *mine*.

Something I solidify with my tongue. It's a whispered vow, one I'm sure she doesn't understand. Though, I don't fucking care. She'll learn.

And if she doesn't accept my claim, then I'll protect her from afar. Ensure her happiness. Worship her in my own way.

Sera's arms slide around my neck, her perfect lips dancing with mine as I teach her what I like. Introduce her to my kiss. Possess her with my *tongue*.

She moans again, arching into me and practically begging me to lift her into my arms.

So I do and carry her to the bed, where I nestle her into the silky sheets, all while worshipping her with my mouth.

Her fingers thread through my hair as she holds me to her, and my little mystery tries to take control.

It's cute.

Alluring.

Downright *enchanting*.

So I let her lead for a moment, give her time to play with my tongue and explore my mouth the way she wants to.

She shudders in response, her nails scraping my scalp before drawing down to my neck and over my shirt. "I want this off," she says against my mouth.

"Yeah?" I reply. "Then take it off, trouble."

Her resulting pout is endearing. But the way she narrows her eyes is hot as fuck.

It's a sensual juxtaposition that has me far too eager to see where this goes.

Which is a problem since I can't actually fuck her.

Or even make her come.

Not without putting her—and everyone else here—at risk.

Styxxx, I groan to myself, so fucking irritated by this situation.

Because I have to stop. *We* have to stop.

And naturally, my girl is taking off my shirt—because I told her to—just as I'm realizing that this can't go much further.

I asked her to play. But I'm beginning to understand that there can't be much *play* between us. Not if I want to stay in control.

She's too fucking alluring for her own good.

I shift to allow her to tug my shirt off over my head, then settle on top of her once more. "We can't go any further, trouble," I tell her.

She stares up at me, her pupils blown with desire.

"Why not?"

"Because I don't trust myself to hold back," I admit, my nose brushing hers. "Besides, we should probably get some rest."

It's been an intense day. Longer than a day, actually.

"But I want to kiss you more," she whispers.

I smile. "I want to kiss you, too." I lean down to demonstrate, my tongue leisurely dominating hers in a few languid strokes.

Strokes that turn into lingering caresses.

Shadows, she's addicting…

Her small palms run over my back and up to my shoulders, while my hands itch to explore her soft curves.

But I hold myself back and wrap my fingers around her neck instead. It reminds me that she's fragile. Vulnerable. Mine to protect.

She hums beneath me, the sound vibrating my palm as I continue to master her with my tongue.

Seconds turn into minutes. And I begin to realize that I could kiss this female for hours. Days. *Weeks*.

She's simply perfect.

And so fucking sweet.

"Styx, Sera," I breathe. "I feel like I could lose everything for you and not regret a second."

She trembles. "Please don't stop kissing me."

Now it's my turn to shudder. "All right, trouble." I press my lips to hers and give her what she wants.

All while holding myself back with my palm around her neck.

Time passes. The world shifts. It's just me and Sera until our kiss begins to slow.

And she gradually starts to relax beneath me as exhaustion takes hold of her.

This was something else Morpheus said would happen —her need to sleep.

"Omegas often rest for long periods before their heat," he told me earlier. "Because they won't be sleeping much during their estrus."

I didn't need to ask why an Omega wouldn't be sleeping much; I already knew.

And I sincerely hope to indulge in the experience myself.

With Sera.

I brush a kiss against her cheek, then lower my mouth to her ear. "Sleep well, trouble," I whisper. "I'll be here when you wake up."

I finally remove my palm from her neck and roll to my side, her smaller body moving with mine.

She nuzzles into my chest, almost as though she's seeking something from me. A purr, maybe. But I'm not an Alpha. I can't emit that low rumbling sound.

However, I can provide a different kind of vibration. A soothing one from my shadows.

Calling on my power, I pull my smoky ink to my torso and create a unique sensation, just for Sera.

And smile when she sighs with contentment.

Because I've calmed her. Protected her. *Pleased* her.

It's a heady feeling, one born of a strange sort of pride. I've always been good to my bed partners. But never in this way.

I've also never kissed a woman like I just kissed Sera. It always leads to more and ends climactically. Then the female leaves, and I sleep alone.

Only, I don't want that kind of ending with Sera.

I want this—her in my arms, sleeping against my chest, after kissing for eternity.

It's blissful, even with the ache radiating from below.

An ache that grows as Sera slides her leg through mine and presses her thigh to my hard cock.

I close my eyes and grit my teeth.

Then focus on the vibrations my tattoos are creating.

Because this is for Sera.

My sweet little mystery.

Hades might call her his *wife* and his *mate*. But to me, she's simply... *mine*.

HADES

"HOW NICE OF YOU TO RETURN," A DEEP VOICE DRAWLS AS I materialize in my palace den.

My jaw clenches for what has to be the thousandth time in the last few hours as I face the Hell Fae King.

I should have known he would be here waiting for me. While the Netherworld Kingdom is my home, it resides within the Hell Fae Realm.

A complicated conundrum that essentially means the fae here worship me while revering *him*—Typhos Lucifer— as their king.

It's a hierarchy that has worked for a very long time. He's even appointed his own lieutenants to run each of the different species of fae that reside within his wards.

However, he's always seen me as above all that, my Mythos Fae heritage affording me a leniency he has no choice but to give.

Only, I can tell by his expression now that he's not in a *lenient* mood. "I'm going to give you three minutes to express your frustration," I inform him. "Then I'm going to get to work."

I should have arrived an hour ago.

But I couldn't take myself away from Serapina and Maliki.

After initiating my mist, I lingered in the in-between. I shouldn't have. The longer I stayed, the harder it was to force myself to actually *leave*.

However, watching Maliki kiss Serapina literally froze me in the in-between. I couldn't tear my eyes off of them. And they were too caught up in each other to notice.

Was it wrong of me to observe them? Probably.

But it felt fucking *right*. Part of me wanted to throttle Maliki for daring to touch my Omega. Only, that part was drowned out by the side of me that wanted to tell him to go further. To strip her. Kiss every inch of her. *Fuck her.*

Maybe it's my millennia of watching him play that inspired these feelings.

Or maybe it's simply meant to be this way.

Regardless, I'm intrigued by the notion of sharing Serapina with my best friend. And there are very few things that interest me these days, making this a remarkable feat.

I also never thought I would want to share my mate with anyone.

But Maliki isn't just anyone. He's mine.

Not in a sexual way. Though, I do enjoy watching him fuck. So I suppose it is somewhat sexual. Just not in a traditional way.

"Are you even listening to me?" the Hell Fae King asks, his irritated tone interrupting my musings.

"Not really," I admit. "It's been a very tiring day."

"Oh? Has it been tiring for you?" he deadpans. "Because last I checked, this is your kingdom to protect. And you left your fae to face dozens of Alphas. *Alone*."

I sigh. "The fae weren't in any danger. All those Alphas desire is my mate, and she's no longer here."

"Yes, Morpheus brought me up to speed. That doesn't answer for your actions, though."

I stare at him. "If Camillia had an army of feral, Godlike beings after her, what would your priority be?"

He doesn't immediately respond. But he doesn't need to. Because we both know he would ensure his mate's safety before everyone and anything else.

"Camillia would help me handle the problem," he says after a beat. "She's my queen for a reason."

"Yes, well, my Omega is currently trapped in a human form," I tell him. "So until she blossoms into a Goddess, she needs to be protected."

He studies me for a moment. "Can you share your plans for her safety? So I know if I need to prepare for another attack on my gates?"

"She's nowhere near your realm right now" is all I tell him.

What I don't add is that if I have to bring her back here, it won't be to my palace. It'll be to a very different area of this kingdom, one no one can reach apart from me.

A space I built just for Persephone.

Which should fill me with excitement. Once upon a time, it did.

But now...

I nearly wince.

Everything has changed. My intentions. My plans. My *desires*.

Fuck. I rub a hand over my face and turn toward the

balcony framing my den. *One problem at a time,* I decide, focusing on the energy coming off my kingdom.

It's lively, which causes my lips to curl down. Because it's lacking my usual deathly glow.

In fact, it appears brighter than usual.

My steps hasten as I move through the open doors and walk to the edge of the terrace to peer into the valley below.

Blue flames meet my gaze, the sight of them expected. I can see the glow of lanterns in the courtyard, as well as from the Netherworld Village.

But the Creek of the Dead appears to be *moving.* Which is impossible. It's a ditch of skulls of bones. No liquid. No life. *No movement.*

My gaze narrows as I follow the trail up the cliff leading into the Netherworld Mountain. Walking with purpose around the edge of my balcony, I head toward the opposite side of my wing—in the direction of the rooms I gifted to Serapina.

Her exterior connects to mine since the whole palace is designed to suit my tastes, and my preference is to have my mate close by.

But my jaw tightens as I near her part of my wing. It's not far. Maybe a hundred yards or so away. And yet it feels as though I've entered a new realm.

I freeze as a butterfly—*a fucking butterfly*—skims my cheek.

Those do not exist in *my* kingdom.

This is the land of the dead. The Netherworld. We do not have *butterflies.*

Typhos moves to my side, his presence a nuisance that I want to swat at along with the fluttering creature. Instead, I walk forward and narrow my gaze as the garden I built for Persephone comes into view.

It used to be made of stone.

Now, it's bursting with lively activity.

And it's overlooking a *running waterfall* that's flowing into the Creek of the Dead.

"*What* is this?" I demand through my teeth.

"An upgrade," my cousin announces as he mists into view.

I'm about to echo his ridiculous words when another Alpha appears with him, one that has my hands curling into fists at my sides. "Ares," I say. "Shouldn't you be guarding a certain prison?"

The dark-haired male glances at me, the horns on his head glinting off the dual moons above.

Some Alphas have wings in beast form.

But not Ares.

His eyes still gleam a vibrant red like many others', but instead of forming feathery plumes at his back, he has two sets of horns. One that curls at the base of his scalp. And one on top of his head.

They're appropriate features that complement his harsher personality traits.

"You know, I was," he drawls. "Then I felt the most alluring presence—an Alpha brawl. And, well, you know how I feel about violence."

I nearly roll my eyes. Of course it was the battle that called to him, not my Omega's impending heat.

Ares has always been bloodthirsty, his temper legendary.

But he's the perfect one to manage and control Pandora's Box as a result.

However, if he's here, then... "Who is guarding the prisoners?"

He shrugs. "Triton."

My eyebrows rise.

"Don't bother," Morpheus interjects before I can comment on Ares's choice. "I've already said what you're thinking."

"And you dare to assume my thoughts?" I demand, irritated by the concept.

Morpheus merely grins. "I dare to do a lot of things, Cousin." He looks around the bustling garden. "Think Serapina will appreciate my manifestation?"

Ares snorts. "This just got boring."

"No one asked you to remain," Morpheus replies. "The Alpha hunt has already moved on, as should you."

"Yes," Typhos agrees, his domineering presence a dark shadow at my side. "Unless you want to remain for a lucrative discussion?"

Ares looks at the Hell Fae King. "I've told you before— I'm not interested in any deals."

Typhos lifts a shoulder. "Even Godlike creatures change their minds every once in a while." He glances at Morpheus when he voices those words, and I wonder what he's referring to.

The God of Wrath doesn't appear to share my interest as he merely says, "Right. Thanks for the good time, Death." He looks at my cousin. "See you for another round soon, Dreams."

With that, he vanishes, and I feel his presence disappear entirely from my kingdom.

I should have sensed him when I arrived, too, but my mind was still wandering and not entirely focused.

However, I'm paying attention now.

Which is how I realize this entire side of the palace has been completely reimagined. "You manifested several changes throughout my home," I say, my gaze narrowing at the one I know is responsible for these alterations.

"It was in shambles when I arrived," Morpheus replies.

"And as you left me to clean up the mess, I took certain liberties." He walks to the edge of the terrace balcony to look out over my kingdom. "The skeleton trees seem to approve."

I frown and follow his gaze down to the Netherworld Courtyard.

And see that my creations are sprouting purple dots on their skeletal limbs. *Flowers*, I realize, my gaze squinting at the morbid creation.

"You've defiled my kingdom," I say through my teeth.

"I've improved it," Morpheus replies. "But if you don't like the renovations, then perhaps you shouldn't have tasked me with handling the cleanup."

"As much as I'm enjoying this banter, can we discuss Onyx?" Typhos inserts.

My brow furrows. "What about him?" I ask, familiar with the one often referred to as the Corpse Fae King. He also happens to be Maliki's uncle. Not that Maliki seems to care about his royal bloodline. Ruling is the last thing my best friend has ever desired.

"He's dead," Typhos says dryly. "And I expect you to fix it since you're the reason he died."

I stare at him. "I didn't kill Onyx."

"No, your kind did that when rutting through this kingdom in search of Omega pussy," Typhos states flatly, his crude statement causing my hackles to rise.

"Do not speak about my mate like that."

"Do not assume my respect for you and your kind means I'll allow this chaos to happen again in *my* realm," he returns flatly. "You put *my* fae at risk. Forced *my* mate to come here and create a portal to *your* home realm. And therefore put *my* mate-circle at risk when we all arrived to help her."

"It was very impressive," Morpheus inserts unhelpfully.

"Azazel and Ajax also proved to be quite a force against our kind. I was both impressed and surprised by the display." He looks at the Hell Fae King. "You've done well for yourself, Typhos."

"I can't tell if you're being condescending or complimentary," Typhos responds. "And I'm not sure I care. What I do care about is reviving Onyx." His intense blue eyes capture mine. "Which *you* are going to help me with."

"Definitely the latter—a compliment," Morpheus murmurs. "And yes, Hades, it's your turn now. Have fun."

He disappears, leaving me growling in his wake. Because I have no doubt that he just went straight back to Mykonos.

Part of me wants to pursue him.

But the loyal side of me remains on the terrace.

Because I can't leave Onyx's soul to suffer in the death world. Not only is he an ally and a respected fae in my kingdom, but he's also important to Maliki.

Which makes him important to me.

"Any other casualties I should be aware of?" I ask Typhos, my gaze on the kingdom below rather than on the Hell Fae King.

There are several Corpse Fae standing in the Soul Yards with bowed heads. They look like ants from up here, but I can tell they're mourning.

Meanwhile, I see several other fae in the courtyard, staring at Morpheus's alterations. The purple flowers resemble specks to my enhanced vision, telling me they're much larger when standing before them.

Fucking Morpheus.

I'll fix his changes after I'm done visiting the death world.

"Two," Typhos says, giving me the names of the other

fae who perished while my kind stormed through the kingdom.

Honestly, I'm surprised there wasn't more physical damage.

Though, I suppose most of them focused on my palace and nothing else. Serapina's sweet Omega fragrance only bloomed here, not in any other parts of the village.

"How many Alphas ventured out of the palace?" I ask, curious.

"Less than a dozen," Typhos replies. "And I think they only did so to explore the kingdom. One of them was Ares."

I nod. "The more lucid of my kind, then."

"If you can call him lucid, then yes."

"*Psychotic* is probably a better term," I say, thinking aloud more than responding to his words. "Regardless, those few are the ones who pose a larger threat—because they're aware enough to hunt." I finally look at the Hell Fae King again. "I don't suppose you can identify the others for me?"

"I can and I will, after you bring back Onyx."

I grunt. "Always working in deals."

"It is what I do," he returns. "Now bring back my lieutenant."

I sigh.

What Typhos Lucifer doesn't realize is that I would save Onyx for free. But I don't feel like having that conversation right now.

I'm tired. Frustrated. And missing my mate. All while hating that Serapina is not actually mine.

So a visit with spirits may actually prove worthwhile.

Because I could use an outlet for my emotions.

And what better place to unleash my irritations than among an army of dead souls?

"I'll be back," I tell Typhos.

What I don't add is that he probably shouldn't waste his time waiting for me to return. Because it's going to take me a while to find the recently departed souls.

Instead, I simply mist to the plane born of my power.

The death world.

SERA

Mmm. Something smells really good. Like leather and man. Yet underlain with the sweet aroma of roses on a wintry morning.

And silk, I think, rolling in the soft texture. *Yes*.

I'm in a pillowy heaven.

Surrounded by the most alluring aromas.

Warmed by a masculine wall of energy.

I turn toward that presence and bury my nose against his chest. Yawn. And lose myself to my dreams.

Or I assume I do, anyway, because when I finally open my eyes, I'm alone in the massive bed. The cool sheets beside me suggest the man I was cuddled into left some time ago.

Maliki, I think, warm all over.

My lips seem to tingle at the memory of his kiss, my tongue suddenly craving another taste. Only, I feel like I've been asleep for years.

And I really want to take another shower as a result.

A strange desire, considering I just took one before falling asleep, but I give in to the need and roll out of the bed to go freshen myself up.

It's not until I'm standing in a towel post-shower—which, thankfully, worked as expected this time—that I realize I only have the button-down shirt to wear.

Twisting my lips to the side, I leave the bathroom and go to search for Maliki. Maybe he can help me find proper clothes.

Although, he's the one who gave me that shirt to wear. So maybe not.

I'll ask for Alina instead, I decide. It'll give me an excuse to check in with my sister, too.

Hades said she's here somewhere with her mates. Now that I'm less exhausted and thinking clearly, I realize I should probably have requested proof of—

I freeze in the kitchen when I find Maliki wagging a finger at Pip. "I told you not to touch that."

My little friend deflates, his shoulders curving down and causing his cloak to droop.

"Look, I know you mean well, but you can't handle these items without the gloves Morpheus manifested for you. So stop taking them off."

Pip's head bobs from side to side in a way that doesn't signify agreement, but something else.

"Don't mock me," Maliki chastises. "You know I'm right."

The little soul huffs.

"Yeah, gloves suck. But you can't make Sera breakfast without them. So do you want to learn or not?"

"He's teaching Pip how to properly make pancakes," a deep voice murmurs into my ear.

I spin around at the unexpected presence and come face-to-face with Morpheus's chiseled chest.

I blink a dozen or so times, my brain seeming to malfunction at the display of masculine beauty.

He's always wearing suits.

Yet right now, he's in a pair of gray sweatpants and nothing else.

"You have a tattoo," I sputter out, aware that I sound a little shrill. And maybe a tad bit ridiculous, too. Because obviously he knows he has a tattoo. It's a snake design in the center of his chest. "Is it moving?" I ask in the next breath, clearly unable to filter my words this morning.

Or evening.

Or today.

Or whenever it is.

I don't know.

But yeah, that snake is definitely moving. Kind of like Maliki's tattoos. "Oh, you have more on your arms," I realize aloud, my gaze dancing all over his flawless physique.

"What do you see when you look at them?" Morpheus asks softly.

I frown. "What do you mean?"

"What shape do they take on?" he rephrases.

"Uh, well, that one is a snake. Obviously." I clear my throat as I take in the adornments around it on his chest, as well as the decorations down his arms. "And flowers." My fingers lift of their own accord to trace one. "This looks like a rose."

Heat bathes my back as Maliki grabs my hip from behind. "A rose?" he repeats.

I nod, still caressing the intricate pattern. "Yes. And it feels alive."

A purr ignites in Morpheus's chest, drawing my focus back to the writhing snake. My fingers track the movement as I gently touch the slithering creature.

"It's beautiful," I whisper.

"The rose?" Morpheus asks.

"Yes. And the snake," I say, following the coiling path with my nail. "Snakes are useful guardians for the garden."

"And what do you see, Maliki?" Morpheus asks, causing my brow to crinkle.

"A suicidal Alpha attempting to seduce another God's Omega," Maliki drawls.

Morpheus smiles. "I love it when you flirt with me, Enforcer. But I'm trying to prove a point to our Serapina about my tattoos."

"What point?" I ask, mostly to distract myself from everything else they just said to one another.

Yet *our Serapina* echoes in my mind, which makes me shiver. A foreign part of me likes the sound of that. Perhaps a little too much.

"That my tattoos look different to everyone who sees them. So how do they appear to you, Ghost?" he asks, a taunting lilt in his tone.

"Like flames and skulls," Maliki answers. "No flowers or snakes for me. Just death and destruction."

"Hmm," Morpheus hums. "Should I take that as a threat or a promise of a good time?"

"Time will tell, I suppose," Maliki replies before brushing a kiss against my neck. "However, speaking of deadly objects, I have some pancakes to remake."

He gives my hip a squeeze and releases me.

Morpheus leans against the door frame, his blue-green eyes flickering with interest as he stares down at me. "Do you have any tattoos, little dreamer?"

A laugh bubbles out of me. "No. Pretty sure those are not a thing where I come from."

"Perhaps from your part of that world, no. But your universe is larger than you realize." He reaches out to tuck a damp strand of hair behind my ear. "Do you want some coffee?"

The abrupt topic change makes me frown. "Coffee?"

"Or clothes?" he offers, his gaze dipping down and reminding me that all I'm wearing is a towel.

"Oh. I, uh, yes. That's why I came out here." Then I was distracted by the shirtless men.

One is making breakfast with Pip.

The other is standing far too close to me now.

Yep.

I clear my throat. "Where can I find something to wear?"

"Is there a specific outfit you have in mind?" he asks.

"Maybe something from Alina?" I suggest. "Assuming she's here."

"She's here," he tells me. "But I can help you find your own clothes. Just tell me what you want to wear, and I'll make all your wishes come true."

I stare at him. "Why does that sound like a wicked promise?"

"Because you know I'll make those dreams come true, too," he murmurs, his lips curling into a sensual smile. "We can start there instead, if you like. I don't have to clothe you. I could simply"—his gaze skates down to where the towel is knitted against my chest—"disrobe you instead."

I swallow. "I really just want a tank top and some cotton pants."

His flirtatious amusement remains as he says, "All right. Follow me."

I'm about to when something crashes in the kitchen. "Pip!" Maliki shouts.

My ghost friend flies past me with a flaming sleeve, then disappears through the wall.

Maliki pinches the bridge of his nose and releases a

curse, while Morpheus chuckles. "You're the one who wanted to teach him how to cook. I was merely trying to assist with those gloves."

"Yes," Maliki grinds out. "Thank you for that."

I glance around. "Is he going to be all right?"

"He'll be fine," Morpheus promises. "He might need a new cloak, though." He waves his hand through the air, causing one to appear in his hand, the blue fabric the same color as Pip's eyes. Wandering into the kitchen, he passes Maliki and heads into an adjoining dining area that's set for a party of three.

I frown at it.

Pip doesn't eat.

So either the three males in my life were planning to eat without me, or… "Where's Hades?" I ask.

Morpheus lays the new cloak over a chair that doesn't have a place setting in front of it. "It's only been thirty-six hours, so he's probably still in the death world."

I blink at him. "What?"

"Closer to thirty-seven now," Maliki says as he flips a pancake. "I'm still shocked you slept that long."

"Wait, what?" I repeat.

"It's normal for an Omega on the verge of a first heat. I mean, not all rest like that, but I'm not surprised your soul demanded sleep. That just means your estrus is going to be even more enjoyable. And hopefully go on for a while, too." Morpheus grins sensually again. "I can only imagine how insatiable you'll be."

I… I don't know how to respond to that last part. So I focus on how long I apparently slept. And also what Morpheus said about Hades.

"Hades is in the death world?" I repeat. "Why? Is he okay?"

"As far as I know," Maliki responds and faces me. "If he weren't, Fleur would let me know."

I stare at him. "Fleur?" That name sounds feminine. Maybe because of the way he voiced it. "And who is Fleur?"

Maliki's lips curl. "She's the love of my life."

I gape at him. *The love of his life?* "And does the love of your life often let you sleep in other women's beds?" I demand, unable to hold back the question.

Because what in the thorns is going on here?

He kissed me for what felt like hours. Plus the other stuff we did.

And he has… *a love of his life?*

I want to scream.

Moments ago I was thinking about Morpheus's word choice. *Our Serapina.*

Sounds like I'm not Maliki's anything.

Because he has a Fleur.

Love of my life.

Ugh!

Maliki sets something down and gives me his full attention, his steps silent as he saunters toward me. "Fleur doesn't care who I play with so long as I eventually come home to her."

Play with, I repeat in my head as my eyes narrow at the too-sinful male. "Wow. What an amazing mate you are."

He palms my cheek, and I yank myself away from him.

Only to come up against a hard, masculine wall behind me. *Morpheus.*

"I'm not her mate," Maliki tells me.

"Oh. So just the love of her life, then?" I guess, torn between laughing and crying.

Fae, why does this hurt so much?

Maliki wasn't really mine either, right?

102

I belong to Hades. Or my soul does, anyway. I can't exactly be upset with Maliki for having another woman in his life.

But still. If she's the love—

"Yes," he says, interrupting my mental battle. "Similar, I imagine, to how Pip will feel about you, or perhaps already does."

My lashes flutter. "I... What?" I'm not following what he means.

"Fleur is my familiar," he murmurs, his lips curling again. "She's a cat. Well, she's more like a sphinx, I guess. But the size of a house cat."

I'm pretty sure my jaw is on the floor. "The love of your life is... your familiar."

"Yes." He cocks his head and gives me an innocent look. One that's far too forced to be genuine. "Why? Who did you think I meant?"

"I think what our enforcer is trying to say is that jealousy looks good on you, little dreamer," Morpheus whispers against my ear, his palm on my hip. "Now, do you still want some clothes, or do you prefer eating pancakes in a towel?"

"Jealousy?" I repeat. "I was not jealous."

Maliki smiles at me and leans in to brush his lips against mine. "You were and it was adorable," he says softly. "But you don't need to worry, trouble. I may like the concept of sharing you with Hades or Morpheus, but I'm not interested in anyone other than you."

He kisses me again before I can even respond to that.

Part of me wants to bite him, though. But the desire is chased away by his tongue.

I moan as he pulls me into him, then shiver when I realize Morpheus is still right behind me.

His hand is a brand against my hip just as Maliki's is a

claim against my throat. I'm not even sure when he grabbed me there, but it reminds me of last night. Or... or I guess two nights ago?

I slept for a day and a half?

Oh, it doesn't matter. Because Maliki is kissing me.

I wrap my arms around his neck and lose myself to his mouth. Only for a crashing sound to interrupt the moment.

Maliki releases me to investigate the sound. When Pip appears in the fresh cloak Morpheus created for him, I realize it was him knocking over a chair.

He gives me an apologetic look. Then bows at Morpheus, like he's thanking him.

"I don't think being a chef is in your future," Maliki informs my little soul.

Pip's eyes take on a big, sad quality.

"But I'll keep trying to teach you," Maliki rushes on to say. "Just promise you'll wear the gloves."

Pip bobs.

"And promise you won't touch the open flame on the stove," Maliki adds.

Another nod from Pip.

"Okay. Then you can help me take the food over to the table while Sera gets dressed."

Pip rushes forward.

"*Wear your gloves*," Maliki growls, causing Pip to freeze right before almost touching a plate. He slowly retracts his bony hand and scurries back to the table, where a pair of gloves is already waiting for him.

"Come on, little dreamer. Maliki and Pip will put the finishing touches on breakfast while I manifest a new wardrobe for you." He uses the hand on my hip to turn me around, then wraps his arm around my waist to pull me from the kitchen and down the hall.

When we enter a room that's different from the one I slept in, I realize he's taken me somewhere new. It's a smaller space with a single bed, presumably meant for a guest. "Is this where you slept?" I ask.

"No," he replies, releasing me and wandering off toward what I assume is a bathroom area. "I didn't sleep. I kept guard with Pip and the three-headed beast outside."

He disappears from view after crossing the threshold.

When he calls for me to follow, I do so cautiously.

Then startle when I find him in a closet full of tank tops and soft pants. No jeans. No dresses. Just comfortable clothes.

"I added some undergarments to the wardrobe there." He gestures to a dresser. "And shoes in boxes on the back wall." He looks at me. "If I've missed anything you desire, let me know and I'll manifest it."

He goes to leave me, and I echo, "Manifest it?" I'm sort of familiar with Alpha abilities because of Orcus. But I've never really asked how it works.

"Yes. My power tends to be a little extreme since I'm a natural dreamer, which makes me more fantasy focused. Just as Hades tends to be a little more lethal, given his penchant for death." He shrugs. "In the end, we're all similar. But I like to think my imagination affords me an edge."

"Oh." I'm not sure what else to say to that other than to agree that he might be right.

He smiles. "I'll be in the bedroom, waiting for you. Just yell if you need me." His gaze runs over me once more, then he walks away.

I'm left with a dizzy feeling that has me longing to follow him and learn more.

He's always teaching me. So patient and understanding.

And interested, I think, recalling the way he held me. The way he's spoken to me. The way he's simply been there for me.

What does it all mean? I want to ask him.

Maybe I will.

After breakfast.

Also after I have a chance to see my sister. Because she has to be worried about me. I need to tell her I'm okay. And maybe ask her some questions about Omega estrous cycles...

MORPHEUS

I stand with Maliki on the beach, watching as Serapina wanders off toward the water with Alina.

Flame is with them, his stance and expression guarded as he stares down the waves.

"Do you think he intends to pounce on the water if it touches his mate?" I ask conversationally, aware that Flame can shift into a black jaguar form.

Maliki grunts beside me. "Likely."

"Hmm," I hum, imagining the scene in my head. "It would be rather amusing."

Maliki doesn't reply, but I'm sure he's picturing the same scenario as me because his lips curl up on one side into a smirk.

"This is why we'll make a good mate-circle," I muse out loud. "We're similar, you and I."

The enforcer grunts again. "Similar implies we have a

lot in common, such as our likes and dislikes." He looks at me. "Aside from a mutual interest in Sera, I don't think we share a lot of hobbies or desires."

I consider that for a moment. "All right, then I would rephrase my assessment to state that we *complement* one another nicely. We both provide Sera with different qualities that allow for a more well-rounded experience."

He faces me. "Are you trying to convince me of our compatibility so I'll stand with you against Hades?"

"No. I don't need your help with my cousin. I'm merely pointing out that we have a strong foundation for our mate-circle." Which is important to me because our strength as a unit will ensure Serapina's protection.

But I don't add that last part out loud.

Instead, I meet his gaze and say, "I want what's best for Serapina. And I think that's you."

His gold irises flare, reminding me of the sun glittering off the ocean. It's only midmorning here, but it's summer, making the warmth intense despite the earlier hour.

Maliki seems to be radiating a similar heat.

"I won't betray Hades," he informs me.

"I'm not asking you to," I return. "I'm saying that Serapina's pleasure and happiness matter. Which makes you important to me. Because *you* please *her*."

He's about to respond when Reaper appears in a pair of track pants and nothing else. His silver-blue eyes instantly focus on Maliki as he coyly asks, "Want to play?"

The enforcer evaluates Reaper's attire and lack of shoes. "Last time we sparred, you tried to take out my heart."

Reaper gives him a dreamy smile. "That was a good idea, wasn't it?"

Maliki snorts. "You also drove a blade into my fucking thigh."

"Only because you sliced up my cheek." He points to his face. "Facial hits are a limit. I don't wish to upset my pet by ruining my finer features, even if it's temporary."

"You can't just decide on a limit in the middle of a sparring match," Maliki tells him. "You stated that there were no rules, so I responded in kind."

Reaper twists his lips, considering this. "All right. If we define the limits before we play, will you come dance with me?"

"You're not trying to fight Maliki again, are you, Reaper?" Alina calls from the water's edge.

Her question seems to startle Serapina, as she instantly turns around to stare at our little trio by the cliff. "They fight?" she asks. Though, I don't actually hear her voice, just see the movement of her lips. It's more of a whisper, I suppose.

"Yeah," Alina replies, her tone just as soft. "And it's usually bloody."

"I didn't ask him to fight. I asked him to play," Reaper says as he turns to saunter toward his mate. "Fighting implies violent intent. I merely want to make him bleed, pet. There's a difference."

Maliki grunts, clearly disagreeing. But I can tell by the intrigued glint in his golden orbs that he's going to accept the offer.

"Have some tension to work off, do you?" I drawl.

He glances at me. "Sera is a very active sleeper. Her favorite thing to do is slide her thigh between mine." He gives me a meaningful look as he adds, "So yes. I have a bit of tension to work off."

I smile. "I would offer to help you with that, but I suspect that's not your thing."

His eyes roam over me. "I'm currently craving

something a little more feminine in nature. But I wouldn't mind stabbing you, if you're offering."

I arch a brow. "Depends what you want to stab me with."

"Something sharp and laced with slug venom?" he suggests.

"That'll never happen," I return flatly. He fooled me once with that little trick. I won't be catching any of his daggers going forward. I'll simply mist.

He shrugs. "Then sparring with Reaper will have to do."

"If they're going to try to kill each other, then you're on guard duty," Flame says. "Because I'm going to go watch."

I look at him, curious as to whom he's talking to.

And realize he's staring right at me.

"You trust me to protect your mate?" I ask, surprised.

"Is there a reason I shouldn't trust you?" he counters, his dark brow arching and disappearing beneath his messily styled hair.

I consider his question seriously. "Serapina is the reason my heart beats," I inform him. "She's my primary priority, the one I'm willing to do anything for. That said, Alina is important to her, which makes her an equal priority in my eyes. So I believe that suggests you can trust me implicitly."

He nods. "Then you're on guard duty," he reiterates. "Once Thea wakes up, I imagine Orcus will join you."

I slide my hands into the pockets of my slacks and wander forward. I changed from my comfortable interior clothes into a white button-down shirt with khaki-colored dress pants for our beach walk.

A human might think I'm overdressed or perhaps warm with the heat of the sun, but I barely feel the sun.

Likely because I've created a light breeze around myself, one that teases the longer strands of my hair.

Serapina eyes me as I move, her focus going to my exposed forearms and then up to my neck where I've left two buttons undone.

The way she swallows tells me she appreciates the view.

I feel similarly about her tight black pants and blue tank top. Her blonde hair is pulled up in a messy bun, one I want to undo just so I can comb my fingers through her silky strands.

But it's her bare feet that I adore the most.

She refused to put on shoes, saying it would be easier to walk in the sand without footwear. I agreed with her assessment and left my feet bare, too.

It was my way of showing solidarity and proving that I accept her choices.

Maybe she doesn't see it that way. And that's fine. I'll continue to prove myself in every way I can, even with small gestures.

Like not wearing shoes, even though I almost always do when outside, including on a beach.

"I haven't actually agreed to spar yet," Maliki points out as I join the group by the waterfront. "Reaper needs to outline the rules first."

"No trying to kill each other," Alina inserts.

Reaper gives her an affronted look. "What? Why? Killing is part of the fun." He cocks his head. "You know how I feel about fun, pet. Would you really force me to make that a rule?"

She gapes at him. "Maliki is an ally."

"And what better way to test an ally's strength than to put him through his paces?" Reaper returns.

Alina just continues to stare at him.

"Don't worry," Maliki murmurs. "He can't kill me."

"I can," Reaper replies. "And I will."

Maliki chuckles. "Careful, Reaper, or I'll start to think you're trying to flirt with me. And I found out earlier today that Sera has a jealous side, so…"

Serapina's gaze narrows. "I do not."

"Okay, trouble," he agrees, wrapping his arm around her shoulders and giving her a squeeze.

She tries to squirm away from him, but he kisses the top of her head, and she almost instantly melts into his side.

Then seems to recall what he said and gives him a shove. "You can *flirt* with whoever you want," she tells him. "I'm not jealous."

His lips twitch. "The only one I want to flirt with is you, sweet mystery."

Her cheeks take on an adorable pink shade. "Go fight Reaper."

"Trying to get me killed?" he asks, arching a brow. "Or is this your way of punishing me for my comments about Fleur earlier?"

Serapina releases a little growl that has me instantly hard for her.

Dreams, I want more of that, please and thank you, I think.

Maliki pulls her in for a kiss, one that tells me he's feeling a similar way about that rumbling sound. When he slides his tongue into her mouth, I feel a pang in my heart. One that I suppose rivals Serapina's earlier feelings about Fleur.

Only mine is underscored in longing.

Because I want to be able to do that—to grab her and kiss her and make her mine with my mouth.

But I need her consent first.

I need to be her *choice*.

By the time Maliki releases her, she's drowsy with lust

and seemingly unaware of her audience until she meets my gaze. Her blue eyes widen, causing my lips to curl.

Maliki wraps his palm around her throat and whispers something in her ear that has her cheeks pinkening even more. I could have tried to listen, but I opted to give them their moment.

When his hand slides down her arm, she reaches out to him for support, and he brushes his lips against her cheek. "Will you mourn me if I die?" he asks softly, giving her a playful look.

She tries to respond but has to clear her throat to find her voice. "Don't kill each other," she finally manages to get out.

Alina nods.

And Reaper sighs dramatically. "It's like they don't want us to have any fun."

"I'm not worried," Maliki tells him. "I'm sure we'll get creative."

Reaper considers that for a moment. "So you're saying a boundary could serve as a challenge. Perhaps as a way to redefine said boundary?"

"You are a Death Fae," Maliki points out, his words seeming to hold a meaning that only Reaper is following. Because to everyone else, it feels like a deviation from the topic at hand. "And I'm a mutt."

"An abomination," Reaper corrects.

"Sure." Maliki shrugs. "But I have a sword."

"A very useful sword."

"Yes, except it doesn't cheat death."

"No, it doesn't." Reaper taps his chin. "Right, well, creativity can be intriguing. So I'm game."

Maliki nods. "Then we have our limits set."

Reaper holds out his hand. "Indeed we do."

The two shake on it, though I'm not quite sure what

limits they've actually defined other than to speak some gibberish about creativity, a sword, and defining their heritage.

"Seriously, no killing," Alina says.

"Oh, pet," Reaper drawls, then kisses her. "Maliki and I promise to behave."

Flame snorts.

And Reaper elbows him.

Then he waggles his brows at Maliki. "Ready?"

The enforcer lifts a shoulder and vanishes, leaving Reaper grinning like a lunatic in his wake before he follows suit.

Alina grabs Flame before he can shadow off as well. "If they hurt each other, I'm holding you accountable."

Flame gapes at her. "That is not fair at all, little panther. No one can control Reaper."

"Then you're going to try," she says as she goes up on her toes to reach his mouth with hers. "And when you succeed…" The words are a whisper against his mouth before she drags her lips to his ear, presumably to finish the statement.

Flame's violet eyes gleam with whatever she promises him. "Well, that seems fair," he murmurs before wrapping her up in a hug and giving her a kiss that has Alina squealing to be put down. He nips at her bottom lip. "Don't go in the water."

She rolls her eyes. "I already promised not to do that."

"Promise again."

"I promise not to go swimming alone," she says, causing him to nod, then frown.

"Wait, no. Say you promise you won't go swimming without one of your mates."

She growls.

He growls back.

And she clasps his face between her palms. "You'd better go check on Reaper before he tries to kill my sister's..." She trails off, like she just remembered said sister is standing right beside her. "Oh! Just go, Flame. I promise not to swim without you."

He grins. "Good girl," he praises her, then vanishes.

Her cheeks remind me a bit of Serapina's from moments ago. These two might not be related by blood, but they certainly blush similarly.

"Sorry," Alina whispers. "I don't know what you want me to call Maliki. But he certainly kissed you like... like a mate." She turns toward her sister and grabs her shoulders. "You didn't tell me you two were... I mean, I don't want to assume, I just..."

Serapina's cheeks are a bright red again, making my lips twitch right as she glances sideways at me.

Lifting my hands, I say, "I'll be just over there if either of you needs me." I point to a space in the sand—one I quickly manipulate into forming a lounge chair, a table, and a fruity drink. "Let me know if you need anything."

I take two steps before Serapina says, "Can I have one of those?"

I don't need to look at her to know she's talking about the little cocktail I whipped up. Hiding my grin, I form another set of lounge chairs about twenty feet away, plus a table with an array of drink options, and create twin umbrellas to help the Omegas hide from the sun.

"Wow," Alina breathes.

Looking back at her, I arch a brow. "Doesn't Orcus do this for you?" He's a fellow God, so I know he's more than capable of manifesting similar items.

"Yes, but I still haven't gotten used to it."

"Fair," I murmur before collapsing into my lounge chair and stretching out to bathe in the sun. "Let me know if you need anything else. Otherwise, I'll be napping over here."

It's a lie.

I'll be very much awake and listening for any signs of danger. But I'll do my best to give Serapina some alone time with Alina.

I'm sure she has questions.

And as much as I would love to respond to each and every one of those inquiries, there are just some things only another Omega can answer...

SERA

"So, where's Hades?" Alina asks me, her voice whisper-soft as she checks on Morpheus again with her eyes.

He said he would be *napping* over there.

I don't believe him.

But he does seem to be trying to give me and my sister some privacy, which I appreciate.

"Morpheus said he's in the death world," I tell Alina. "I guess he's trying to find King Onyx?" I phrase it as a question, as I don't really understand what happened other than what Morpheus mentioned during breakfast.

He told me there were a few casualties as a result of the Mythos Fae Alphas rutting through the Netherworld Kingdom in their search for me. And unfortunately, King Onyx was one of those casualties.

"Apparently, the Hell Fae King demanded that he retrieve the souls," I go on, my brow furrowing. "I don't know what that entails, but Morpheus mentioned it would not be a quick process."

Alina nods. "Erm, I suppose that's good. It gives you a break from his arrogant assumptions and means he can't force you to mate him."

I wince, aware from my sister's tone that she's not pleased at all by Hades's claim. However... "My soul is already mated to him," I say softly. "So I'm not sure if that qualifies as being *forced* since it's already, well, true."

She scowls. "*You* are not *his*. I don't care what he says. You're your own person."

"I am," I agree. "And I think he's starting to understand that part." Or that's how it felt after our discussion in the shower the other day. "He also said he wasn't going to mark me due to a *misguided obligation*," I add. "So I don't think you need to worry about him *forcing* a mating on me."

Her brow creases. "What did he mean by that? *Misguided obligation?*"

"I'm not sure," I admit. "But the Alphas are hunting me because I'm unclaimed, right? So I told him to just fix it. And that was his response."

Alina's frown intensifies. "Oh." Her nose crinkles. "Okay, well, I think that's good, then. He's saying he wants your consent."

I lift a shoulder. "I guess. But he had no trouble trying to force me to marry him." Though, he did say that was when he thought I possessed his mate's memories.

And it was a *game* to him.

"Well, I think he kind of apologized for that," I go on, my lips twisting for a beat. "Sort of. In his own way." Does Hades even apologize? I'm not sure. He seems a little too intimidating to actually voice the words.

But that's neither here nor there.

What I really want is to ask my sister about being an Omega, since apparently my *soul* has awakened.

Which has me wondering... "Do you really not remember anything from our previous life? Like, your soul's life, I mean?"

She blinks, the only indication that my abrupt subject change caught her off guard. But she quickly recovers as she shakes her head. "I have no memories apart from my own. Why? Are you starting to remember things?"

"I don't think so, no. Well, except..." I trail off, then shake my head.

Because I don't want to talk about my dreams with her. They're all about Hades and mostly sexual in nature. Which... doesn't really tell me much. Who knows if those fantasies are even true or if they were just my soul's way of trying to coax me back to him?

"Nothing relevant, I mean," I mutter. "I still feel like me, too. But they said I set off a beacon that signifies I'm about to go into heat. Did you do that?"

"Not that I know of," she says slowly. "But Orcus said it could be because I wasn't in the right dimension at the time. Or maybe because he had already started the process of claiming me. We're not really sure."

I swallow and nod. "And did you feel any different?" I ask.

"Uh, well, not until my heat actually hit. Up until then, all I felt was, er, *interested*, I guess."

"Interested?" I echo.

"You know... in Reaper, Orcus, and Flame." She blushes. "Sorry, that's... that's not appropriate."

I huff a breath. "In our former world, yeah. But you should hear some of the things the fae talk about at Death's Den." I learned a lot about what's *appropriate* in the fae world during my short time as a bartender. It often made me uncomfortable. But I'm thankful for the exposure. I think… I think in some way it helped prepare me for being on my own.

Except, I suppose, it was a waste of time.

Because I'll never be *on my own* as an Omega.

"But you really didn't feel any different otherwise?" I press, hung up on that aspect. Because part of me is hoping that *not feeling different* may mean Morpheus and Hades are wrong about my impending heat.

However, a little shake of my sister's head says it's a lost hope.

"Okay, then can you tell me what I should expect?" I ask. "Without sharing too much, I mean. I just… I want to know how to prepare. Or, I guess… What does going into heat actually mean?"

I understand the concept, but not what it'll do to me.

I'm about to clarify what I mean when Alina says, "It's both terrifying and amazing. You're going to basically lose your mind with… with *lust*. And your mates will see you through it."

My lips curl down. "Except I don't have any mates."

"Maybe not yet," she hedges. "But it seems like Maliki is interested." She peeks over at Morpheus—who still has his eyes closed—and whispers, "And maybe him, too."

I lean toward her. "So you approve of Morpheus more than Hades?" I ask, incredulous.

She frowns. "I never said I didn't approve of Hades. I just… I don't approve of him trying to force you into a marriage or mating."

Well, she's not wrong to feel that way. I didn't exactly approve either.

Sighing, I collapse into my chair and pick up one of the drinks on the table between us. It's pink and has a straw. I take a sip and find it's actually pretty good. Like a frosty strawberry drink.

Alina chooses one that's pale in color and has a pineapple wedged on top of it. The way her eyes round tells me she approves of the flavor, so we both swap without a word to try each other's drinks.

"What are these?" Alina asks, taking the question right out of my head.

"A strawberry daiquiri and a piña colada," Morpheus says, his voice holding a sleepy quality to it. "They're virgins, though, as I wasn't sure how Serapina would react to human alcohol."

I shiver as he says *virgins* because I'm definitely that. But I soon realize he meant the *drinks*. Which… okay. I don't understand that term being applied to a fruit smoothie, but maybe it's a faeism I haven't heard yet. I've only ever worked at Death's Den, and we certainly didn't serve fruit there.

"They're really good," Alina tells him. "Thank you."

His lips lift upward with a ghost of a smile. "Just let me know if you would like more." His grin disappears, and he pretends to sleep once more.

I study his profile, noting the way the sun plays off his defined features, and trail the rays down his muscular form. He's been very forthcoming with me, answering every question I ask, all while exuding a patience I respect and admire.

Very different from Hades. Even Maliki.

Yet all three of them make me feel safe in their own ways.

"Do you have any advice for my heat?" I ask Alina, my gaze still on Morpheus. "Anything I should prepare for?" I frown and look at her. "Is it going to hurt?"

"I, er…" She clears her throat. "Yes and no?"

My eyes widen.

"I mean, it'll probably be, erm, intense at first. But you'll end up enjoying it. A lot." Her cheeks flush. "Sorry, I don't... I don't know how to talk about this as well. Your mates, or, well, Maliki, maybe, would be better at explaining it?" She frowns. "Assuming Hades has told him. Um. Do you plan to...?"

I stare at my sister, unsure of what she's trying to ask me. "Do I plan to ask him about it?"

"About seeing you through it, yeah, that's what I'm asking. Or maybe you don't know yet. And that's fine. But I would... you should at least talk to him. Or them. Or..." She closes her eyes. "I'm not very good at this, am I?"

"Well, it's not like we've ever talked about sex before, so."

Her dark lashes flash open when I say *sex*. "*Serapina*."

"What? That's what we're talking about, right? I'm going to go into heat and have sex. And maybe get pregnant." My eyes widen again. "Oh, thorns. I'm going to have a baby!"

I palm my belly.

I realized this the other day.

But it... it still shocks me.

"I'm not ready." I don't want a family yet. Or I don't think I do, anyway. I don't even have mates. Or a *mate*, singular.

Except Hades. Kind of.

I frown. "Did Hades and Persephone have a baby?"

"No," Morpheus says softly, clearly listening to our conversation. Or maybe it's because I squealed the question so loudly that he chose to answer it. "Alphas can control procreation during a heat. It isn't easy, but it can be done."

"Persephone never wanted a child?" Alina asks, sounding surprised.

Morpheus angles his head toward her and lifts his hand to shield his eyes as he opens them to look at her. "Apparently not."

My sister stares at him. "Oh. I... I thought all Omegas valued the creation of life."

He glances at me before refocusing on her. "Some are not ready, as Serapina has mentioned. And a good Alpha knows how to respect an Omega's choice."

A tremble works through me at his words. *Morpheus is a good Alpha*, some part of me acknowledges. *A very good Alpha.*

He hasn't pressured me into anything at all, just treated me respectfully and with care.

"Alina," a deep voice murmurs as Orcus mists onto the beach with a very awake Thea in his arms. The little one takes one look at her mom and releases a bellow that has Orcus wincing. "Our daughter is hungry."

"And demanding food," Alina replies, clearly amused. She sets her drink to the side and stands. "Sorry, Sera. I—"

"It's okay," I interject as Thea grows louder. "Go take care of your precious one."

Alina was in the process of taking the baby into her arms when I spoke, but looks at me with intrigue.

It takes me a moment to realize why—my word choice. *Precious one.* I'm pretty sure I've never referred to my niece that way. But she is precious, even with her hungry cries.

Though now that my sister is holding her, the tiny bundle seems to be somewhat more content.

"I think she just wanted snuggles," I say, amused as Thea nuzzles into my sister. But then I note the way she's seeking with her mouth and chuckle. "Okay, no. She's definitely hungry."

Alina stares at me for a beat and then smiles. "I think you're more ready than you realize."

"For what?" I ask, confused.

"For your heat," she murmurs, then looks at Orcus. "Nest, please."

He gives her an indulgent smile and gathers her into his arms without question, the pair of them cradling their child between their chests. "Anything for you, little one."

They disappear without another word, and I'm suddenly reminded of why I chose to move out all those weeks ago. I wanted to give Alina privacy with her mates and their child. And I hated feeling like I was a distraction from what should matter most.

When Orcus starts to materialize again on the beach, I say, "I know. And tell her it's fine." This isn't the first time my sister has vanished without saying goodbye. So I'm used to him returning to voice my sister's apology. She doesn't mean to leave abruptly. She's just... otherwise engaged. "I understand, Orcus."

He finishes appearing and gives me a nod. But doesn't leave like he usually does. Instead, he looks at Morpheus.

"Hades won't like this."

"There are a lot of things Hades isn't going to like," Morpheus replies. "And those things are not your concern."

Orcus considers him for a moment. "Well. If he asks, I tried."

"I'll be sure he knows," Morpheus drawls.

Orcus starts to mist again but then returns to his corporeal state. "Are you okay being alone with Morpheus?" he asks me, like he just realized my opinion matters.

"If I weren't, I would have already said something," I tell him.

He winces. "Sorry, Sera. This…" He trails off and clears his throat. "This is new territory for all of us. Your sister loves you deeply, and I love her. Which means I love you, too, like you were my own sister. But Hades is also my brother."

"You don't need to explain yourself, Orcus. Just like Alina doesn't need to apologize every time she prioritizes Thea and all of you. I understand. And as I said, it's okay. So go back to my sister. You know how hungry she gets while feeding Thea."

His eyes round a little like I've just reminded him of a very important task.

Which I guess I have because Alina loves food.

"Thank you," he says, vanishing again.

I shake my head and chuckle a little. However, it's a humorless sound.

My sister has found happiness, and I'm pleased for her. Truly. Though, I can't help but feel a little jealous, too.

"She makes it look so easy," I whisper.

"Being a mom?" Morpheus asks, reminding me that he's still here.

"No. Just… everything. Finding her mates. Life. *Joy.*" I sigh. "Also being a mom, yes. But I more so mean being an Omega. She's fully embraced it. And I'm still not convinced I even am one."

He pushes off his lounger to join me beneath the umbrella and steals Alina's chair. Though, I suppose it's technically *his* chair since he created it.

Rather than lean back, he leaves his feet in the sand and balances his forearms on his thighs. "Are you unconvinced because you still feel human?"

"I *am* human," I reply.

He smiles. "Yes, for now. But you'll become a Goddess soon."

"When I go into heat."

"Exactly."

"And what will that mean for me, again?" I ask, aware that I've yet to receive much of a response to this. "I'll lose my mind with lust and… what? Beg for more kisses from Maliki?"

Morpheus's lips curl into a grin that makes me regret what I just said.

"Never mind," I insert quickly.

"Oh, no, little dreamer. We are going to discuss this."

"Nope." I roll off my chair and start walking. "Nope. Nope. No—"

His arms wrap around me from behind as he lifts me into the air and spins me around.

I shriek in response, and he continues his whirl.

"How about a swim?" he offers.

"*What?*"

"You know, the activity one often does in the water?"

"I thought we were going to…" Wait, no. I don't want to say that. If he's going to change the topic away from my heat, then why would I switch it back?

But a swim.

My eyes widen. "I don't know how to swim…"

"Then I'll teach you," he says, his tone suggesting it's the simplest thing in the world.

However, as the wave crashes against the sand, I seriously question his easy candor. "I don't think the ocean is a good place to learn, Morpheus."

"That's very true," he agrees, making me a little less nervous about his intentions.

Except then the world shifts around us.

And when our surroundings come back into view, I find myself staring at a secluded lagoon inside a cave.

"*This* is a much better place to learn," Morpheus murmurs. "And an excellent spot for an intimate conversation about your heat. So, shall we strip down and begin with an anatomy lesson before we swim?"

MORPHEUS

Serapina freezes in my arms, her nerves seeming to paralyze her limbs. I slowly release her and circle to face her. "Are you afraid of me or the water?" I ask cautiously, needing to know if I've pushed her too far.

Her nose scrunches as she looks up at me. "I'm not afraid of you or the water," she says. "I just… I'm nervous." She frowns. "And I don't want to be nervous. I want to be strong. Not timid. Not naïve. But adventurous. And… and you know what? Yes. I want to have an anatomy lesson. Explain what a knot is."

I arch a brow. "Explain it or show it?" I ask, intrigued by this bold side of her.

Her eyes widen. "You would show me?"

"I did just offer to provide an anatomy lesson, didn't I?"

She blinks. "Oh." She glances down and then back up.

"I... I actually would like to see a knot. If you... don't mind."

My lips curl. "An Omega asking to see her Alpha's knot is a fantasy, little dreamer. So I definitely don't mind at all. But I would ask that you lead in this exploration, as I don't want to make you uncomfortable."

Her blue irises pulse as she peers up at me. "Lead how?"

"Well, I'll take off my shirt. Then you can unbutton my pants. And we'll go from there, okay?"

She swallows, her pupils dilating. "Okay," she echoes, her gaze running over me with interest. "I... I accept." The way she squares her shoulders tells me she's trying to bolster her confidence.

"Good," I tell her, praising both her agreement and her obvious self-assurance. Then I reward her by making a show of removing my shirt, something her eyes confirm that she's enjoying as she watches me undress.

Though, even without her gaze, I would know she's interested.

Because her scent is suddenly all around me, causing me to inhale greedily.

Fuck. She smells like sin. Chocolate. Decadent nights lost in the sheets. My own personal dream come to life, right before me.

I want to kneel and beg for a taste.

Dine between her thighs.

Indulge in her *slick.*

But I force myself to remain steady, going as far as to fold my shirt before setting it on the ground. I went without an undershirt, so I'm naked from the waist up—something my Omega is currently admiring. "Your tattoos haven't changed for me."

"I imagine they won't," I reply. "They typically connect to an observer once and then never shift again."

Her pretty gaze returns to mine. "Is it a form of magic?"

"Yes. Illusionary magic."

She studies me. "Does that mean the tattoos are not actually real?"

I shrug. "Is anything real? Or do we all reside in a fantasy contrived by someone else? Maybe even one created by ourselves?" It's a hypothetical quandary, one I ponder often. "What matters is what we believe in," I go on. "And if you believe my tattoos exist, then they do."

She reaches out to touch my skin, her fingers tracing my pectoral muscle. "It feels real."

"*You* feel real," I tell her in a whisper. "Now the question is, will you make my fantasy come true?"

She bites her lower lip as she skates her attention down to my groin. "By removing your pants."

"That would be ideal, but I'll settle for you unbuttoning them instead."

She nods, seemingly to herself, and starts tracing a path down my torso. I shiver when her nail skims the muscular lines of my abdomen all the way to the light dusting of hair that guides her down to my groin.

Except Serapina pauses when she reaches the top of my pants, leaving me a little breathless with anticipation.

I'm so fucking glad I didn't wear a belt today. Otherwise, she might be inclined to stop. And I don't want anything to get in the way of her exploration.

Serapina visibly steels her resolve and pops open my button, then freezes like she can't believe she actually did that.

"Now the zipper," I encourage her. Only, she doesn't move, so I add, "I'm wearing boxer shorts, sweetheart. So you're not really exposing my knot yet, and you don't even have to if you don't want to."

I would never force her to do something she didn't desire to do. Push her limits, maybe. Seduce her, definitely. But I will never compel or force her to do anything.

She must believe me because she plays with my zipper —which has me swallowing a groan. Because *fuck*, that's hot. It's her touch coupled with the boldness flashing in her expression that has my knot pulsing in response.

Oh, I might not be naked when she finishes removing my pants, but there certainly won't be any question as to what a knot is once she reveals my tight boxer shorts.

Her eyes wander downward as she finishes unzipping my pants. "Now what?" she whispers.

"Whatever you want," I tell her. "You can push my pants down to the ground. Or you can turn around while I finish the job, then meet me in the water. Entirely up to you, Serapina."

She shivers, her gaze slowly returning to mine. "If I choose the water, will you be naked?"

"Would you like me to be naked?" I ask, my lips threatening to curl. I can tell she's nervous, though. So I don't allow myself to smile. I want to make her comfortable, not overwhelmed.

"I don't know," she admits. Then frowns and says, "Yes, I do. I want… I want to be adventurous."

"Then how about you turn around while I finish disrobing and get in the water. Afterward, I'll face the wall while you decide how many clothes you want to leave on, and we'll regroup in the lagoon."

Her brow furrows at the idea, and she glances around me at the small lagoon I misted us to. "But I don't know how to swim," she reminds me.

"I know. That's why I brought us here. The water is

calm and has a set of natural steps there." I point to the rock formation that's been sculpted into stairs. "It'll be about four feet deep when you reach the bottom. Then I'll be there to help you go farther into the cove, if you want to do a little swimming."

She considers that for a moment and nods. "I like this idea."

Amusement flirts with my mouth as I reply, "I do, too."

Her lips curl a little, and she rotates away from me. I study her for a moment, searching for signs of discomfort. But she appears to be mostly relaxed now, so I proceed with removing my pants and boxer shorts and walk over to the stairs.

I feel her eyes on me while I enter, aware that she's peeking over her shoulder. Though, I pretend not to notice and instead make my movements slow and purposeful until I reach the bottom.

The water covers me where it needs to, but it's rather clear, leaving me mostly on display.

Rather than turn around, I take a few more steps away from the stairs and say, "I'm ready for our adventure, Serapina." The word is purposeful, as she said she wanted to be adventurous. So I'm daring her to follow through.

The sound of rustling clothes confirms it was the right thing to say because my intended mate is disrobing.

I wonder what she'll choose to keep on for our swim. Her panties, perhaps? Maybe her tank top, too. She went without a bra earlier, so chances are—

The water ripples behind me, stilling my thoughts and causing me to hold my breath. I want to hear every movement. Sense her presence. *Feel my Omega.*

She's moving cautiously, likely because the water scares her.

"I won't let anything bad happen to you," I vow, needing to reassure her. "You're my reason for being, little dreamer. The purpose that gives me life. Just say the word, and I'll slay any demon that stands before you, even a pool of water."

A quiet moment passes between us before she asks, "How can you feel that way for someone you barely know?"

I can tell by her voice that she's only a few feet away from me, but I don't turn around yet. I'll wait until she tells me it's okay to move first.

So instead, I focus on her question and reply, "An Alpha knows his soul's mate. Which I realize is a foreign concept to you, and probably a bit intense. But it feels natural to me. My entire existence revolves around pleasing you."

She doesn't respond right away. However, I hear her moving in the water, likely taking the final two steps to the bottom.

"If Alphas know their mates, then why am I being hunted? Do they all think I'm their mate, too?"

"Some Alphas don't care about soul bonds and only value pleasure... for themselves." My jaw tightens at the notion. "There are some who believe Omegas should be enslaved and used for knotting. And, unfortunately, the disappearance of your kind worsened that need, turning a lot of my brethren into feral versions of their former selves."

I mentioned some of this to her already when reviewing the history of the Mythos Fae and the collapse of our realm.

"You're also the first Omega presence anyone has sensed in a very long time, which has many of my brethren crazed with a need that overrides reason."

"But I visited your realm, and no one seemed to hunt me there," she points out, her voice right behind me now.

"Yes, because you were very much human a mere few days ago. However, Maliki's talented tongue changed that." An explanation I haven't fully confirmed but suspect is quite true. "Further, the call you emitted told my kind you're unclaimed, which means soul bond or no, you're fair game—in their eyes."

"And in yours?" she asks softly, her nails touching my shoulder blades and tracing my spine downward.

I decide to translate that as an invitation to turn around, but do so slowly in case I misread her touch.

Though, when I find her blue eyes blazing up at me, I know I was right to move.

"In my eyes…" I trail off and look down, thrilled that she's chosen to wear nothing at all. "In my eyes, you're exquisite, Serapina." However, I don't think that's what she meant, so I meet her gaze again as I add, "You're a Goddess, little dreamer. I live to serve you and your desires. And while my soul may know you as my mate, I will forever cherish your right to choose."

She stares up at me, her palm on my chest since I shifted to face her. "Is it strange that I believe you?"

My lips curl as I reach out to tuck her hair behind her ear. "No, Serapina. Time is a human mechanism, an illusion that either affords mutual understanding or fosters distrust. But our existence is endless. We rely on our souls to guide us, and yours knows mine."

"Because you were mated to Persephone."

"Yes, though I never claimed her as mine."

She frowns, her nails digging a little into my skin. I mentioned this in passing once before, but I didn't elaborate.

134

Something that becomes apparent now as she asks, "Why not?"

"I refused to force her to choose between Hades and me, and I knew he wouldn't share her." Which is something else I commented on before, too. I think when I told her that Persephone loved him very much. And he adored her as well.

"Yet, you think he'll share me, er, her... now?" Serapina asks, her incredulous tone telling me her own opinions on that question.

But I don't let that stop me from speaking my truth. "He may choose not to share you, just as he did with Persephone, and there's nothing I can do if that's the case. But at least my soulmate will know how I feel about her—about *you*—in this life. That's what matters most to me."

Her brow creases. "Persephone never knew...?"

I shake my head. "No. I didn't want to hurt her by inserting myself into her life because I knew Hades would demand that she pick between us. So, I... I tried to protect her heart by not involving myself in her life. And I ended up losing her in the process."

It was a mistake I would not be making again.

Hence the reason I'm currently standing naked in a body of water with Serapina.

"I'm not going to lose you, Serapina. Even if you don't want me as a mate, I'll still be here as your friend. Your protector. Whoever or whatever you desire, I'm yours. I always have been and always will be."

She seems to freeze before me, her lips parting on a nonexistent breath.

Fuck. I've overwhelmed her.

She was raised human, not Mythos Fae. She doesn't know that this intensity is just who we are, what we expect, how we *exist*.

"I'm sorry, Serapina," I say with a sigh. "I don't mean to upset you. It's… it's merely my truth. And it's not one I can shy away from. Not again. Not if it means protecting you."

"I'm not upset," she whispers, her fingers sliding up my chest to my neck. "I'm… I'm in awe of everything you just said. A week ago, I would've said you were just another fae at the bar uttering a line. But I can *feel* your veracity. I can't explain how or why; I just… I do."

My lips curl as I cup her cheek. "Explanations are a human construct. And you, my heart, are a Goddess." She just hasn't embraced that part of herself yet. Not fully. However, this is a firm step forward.

Because I can see the trust in her gaze.

It warms me to know I put that there.

That I—

"You have three seconds to release my mate before I drag you to the death world, Morpheus," a deep voice says, the silky quality of it making me sigh.

Because of course Hades would choose now to return.

Just as I finally break through some of Serapina's mortal walls and reach the Omega deep within.

"Three," he begins to count. "Two…"

HADES

A Few Minutes Earlier

Onyx stands in my palace, his expression holding a note of irritation, one he's directing at me. "Thanks for the trip through the death world," he says before executing a half bow. "*My lord.*"

"Your gratitude, or lack thereof, is duly noted," I reply dryly. My hand rises when he looks ready to apologize. "Don't, Onyx. You have every right to be irritated. I'm just glad you were able to be revived. Mostly, anyway."

His once dark hair is a shock of permanent white, and his eyes are now a crimson red instead of the brown they were before. But he's otherwise alive.

With maybe a few additional talents.

Ah, he can consider those gifts from my world.

I hand him two glowing stones, which he takes with care since the other two fallen souls reside within them.

"Please work with Skull on this project." I already showed Onyx how to handle the reincarnation of the spirits.

All he has to do is gift the rock to a worthy and willing mated pair, and the life will be reborn.

Perhaps not the way it was before, but there wasn't much else I could do.

The only reason Onyx is standing before me now as he once was is because of his royal bloodline. He's an extremely powerful Corpse Fae, which allowed him to survive in my world for longer than most. If Maliki were to ever die, his soul would do the same.

He would hold on, then wait for me to find him and bring him back.

Unfortunately, not everyone possesses the same strengths in the afterlife.

And death... is complicated.

"Thank you," Onyx mutters, this time with a bit more feeling in his words.

"Just take care of those souls" is all I say before engaging my mist.

Then I realize one more task I need to give him.

Turning corporeal, I add, "And reach out to Typhos so he knows I brought you back."

Because I don't have time to waste on a call with the Hell Fae King right now.

I haven't seen Serapina in nearly two days. I need to put eyes on her, just to make sure she's all right.

Deep down, I know she's fine. I would feel it if she were hurt or in pain. But I... I simply want to see her. Maybe talk to her, too.

There's so much to say.

So much to work through.

So much to *understand*.

But the moment I materialize in my cavern, I realize all that is going to have to wait.

Because Morpheus's scent is *everywhere*.

In my room.

In the hallway.

In the kitchen.

In my guest room—which is the only space I don't completely mind.

All over the beach and the items he clearly manifested for *my* mate.

And...

And where are you now? I wonder, searching for his essence as well as that of my mate.

My teeth clench when I realize they're *together*, their mingled souls stirring a growl inside me that I barely contain as I mist myself to their location.

Air ripples around me when the sight of them unveils before my eyes.

A sight I will never unsee.

Serapina naked. Her hand on Morpheus's neck. His gaze reverent as he stares down at her.

"I'm... I'm in awe of everything you just said," my mate says, utterly oblivious to my arrival.

Fuck, not even Morpheus seems to sense me.

Or maybe he just doesn't care that I'm here.

I take a step forward, only to be held frozen as Serapina says, "A week ago, I would've said you were just another fae at the bar uttering a line. But I can *feel* your veracity. I can't explain how or why; I just... I do."

Her voice is filled with such conviction. Sweetness. *Happiness.*

I've never heard her speak like that before, I realize, my jaw tightening again.

Then I nearly bite off my own tongue as Morpheus cups Serapina's cheek.

Like he has the fucking right to *touch my mate*.

"Explanations are a human construct," he tells her. "And you, my heart, are a Goddess."

I see red.

Violent crimson.

Blood.

"You have three seconds to release my mate before I drag you to the death world, Morpheus," I warn him, my beast *raging* inside.

She is not *his* heart.

She is *my* heart. *My* Omega. *Mine*.

"Three," I spit out, fury burning hot through my veins. "*Two*." He had better let go of *my* female before I lose control.

"No," Serapina says, turning to face me and *blocking* the source of my ire. "My soul may be yours, but *I* am *mine*. *I* am Sera. *I* am my own person. And *I* don't want you to take Morpheus anywhere."

The dreamer at her back arches a brow, clearly impressed. Then his blue-green eyes meet mine, and his expression sobers. "Hades—"

"*No*," Serapina repeats. "You don't have to explain anything to him. You were teaching me how to swim, and you were going to explain a knot. There is nothing wrong with either of those activities."

"*What?*" I demand, certain I didn't hear that second half correctly. "*Explain a knot?*"

"She needs to know what to expect for her heat," Morpheus says, his tone calm. *Too* calm.

"And so, what, you were going to *demonstrate* what a knot does?"

"No, he was going to *show me* a knot," Serapina

interjects. "Not demonstrate anything." She frowns and glances back at him. "Right?"

I huff a laugh at that. "No Alpha just *shows* an Omega a knot. It has to fucking *eject*, Serapina. *Into your cunt*."

Her eyes widen and her lips part.

"Yeah," I drawl. "Now may I take him to the death world?"

"I was not going to *knot* her. I was going to show her where it is inside me," Morpheus says, a subtle growl to his tone. "I would *never* force her into accepting my knot without understanding everything you just said. And frankly, I'm irritated that you would even think that of me after all I've done for you."

Serapina blinks and begins to turn. "Morpheus, I—"

"I was talking to Hades, sweetheart," he says, his voice much softer as he addresses her.

But his eyes are hard as he stares me down.

"I never approached Persephone, despite our souls being linked. I did that for her and for you. Just as I gave you thirteen fucking months to sort this out with Serapina before I finally stepped in," he goes on.

Serapina startles again.

However, Morpheus isn't finished.

"If I wanted to seduce *our* Omega, I would have done so in her dreams. Yet I've ensured her choice. Her comfort. Her *knowledge*. Because all I desire is to please her. Not take her against her will. Not trick her into accepting my knot. That's not how I operate. And you, of all people, should know that, *Cousin*."

My jaw ticks.

"Your intentions have always been gray to me," I tell him.

"Because you refuse to accept me as an ally," he bites back. "You see me as beneath you because I play in a world of imagination, not the land of the dead. But our talents are more equal than you'll ever realize. In fact, I would argue that mine is greater than yours because I actually know how to see beyond my own ego."

"Careful, Cousin."

"No. I'm done being *careful*, Hades," he says, stepping out from behind Serapina. "Your warnings have been noted. Yet mine remain unheard. But I'm forcing you to acknowledge me now. Serapina is my mate, too. And I will be there for her in whatever manner she requires."

My hands fist at my sides.

He's painting me as the villain here.

And I don't fucking appreciate it.

Serapina doesn't know our history. She has no idea the lengths I would go to, to protect her. To love her. To *cherish* every inch of her.

Yet the way she looks at me now is through the eyes of a stranger.

Fear and hurt linger in her expression.

My mate is afraid of me.

I've gone about this all the wrong way, while Morpheus has played the role of hero perfectly.

I want to hate him for it. Destroy him. Make him choke on his own fucking knot.

But while I've been harming my Omega, he's been making her feel secure. Safe. *Heard.*

And as much as I hate that he's been her confidant, I'm thankful she has someone.

No, *two* someones.

Because Maliki means something to her, too. All because I put him in charge of her security. Among other things…

Some of the tension bleeds from my limbs, my heart beating a little faster in my chest.

I still really want to take Morpheus to the death world and drive him into an early grave. However, I can tell by the worry in Serapina's features that doing so... will destroy something inside her.

Fuck.

She's already making a choice. I don't even know if she's aware of it. But she's put her faith in Morpheus. Not in me.

His words from the other day come back to haunt me, the *warning* crystal fucking clear now.

"I don't want her to have to choose between us. But if you demand that a decision be made, I will fight for her. Hard. And dear Cousin, after all you've put our mate through... I think I'll win."

My lips tighten as I try to determine what to say and do, my heart suddenly shriveling in my chest.

Because Morpheus is right. And I fucking *loathe* the fact that he's right.

I've handled this horribly. I know that. I own that. To an extent, anyway.

No, I own it completely. I have to.

It's the only way to move on, to *fix* th—

Electricity hums down my arms, the wards notifying me of a breach.

Morpheus must sense it as well because his spine stiffens and his eyes lock with mine.

"Please don't," Serapina whispers, the plea momentarily distracting me from the approaching danger. But before I can even look at her, a harsh ringing blasts through my skull.

The alarms.

Maliki appears in the next instant, a towel wrapped around his hips and his body covered in bruises. I gape at him, shocked by his beat-up physique.

But all he does is look between me and Morpheus, lock

gazes with Serapina, and shadow to her side. "Don't let them do this," she begs him as he grabs her.

Then the pair of them vanish into smoke before he has a chance to respond.

"Find some pants," I tell Morpheus.

He's already misted out of the water, a pair of leathers seeming to materialize around his legs before he's even finished appearing at my side. He adds a matching vest, as well as some armor along his damp arms, then he glances at me.

"You were followed," he says, stating the obvious.

"I was followed," I echo the words, irritated at my own carelessness.

He shrugs. "It's fine. Someone put me in a fighting mood, so I could use a little bloodshed."

I snort.

Then mist out to the beach and introduce my fist into an approaching Alpha's jaw.

Oh, the Interrealm Fae affiliates are not going to be happy about this.

Mythos Fae in the Human Realm.

A place where mortals think they're the strongest beings in existence and ignore the reality that lurks all around them.

Well. They're about to become acquainted with some important truths.

Because those Gods from the ancient texts are very fucking real.

And we're about to go to war over a woman.

Just like we did in the old myths…

MALIKI

A Few Minutes Earlier

"WHILE I UNDERSTAND THE IMPORTANCE OF YOUR CLOAK, Fleur does not. So if you want her to stop attacking you, you're going to have to lose the robe," I tell Pip as he scurries across the bedroom with wide eyes. "Or take this game into the living area. I'm trying to get dressed."

Which is a difficult feat considering the state of my body right now. I'm healing, but *Styx*, it hurts to move.

And the shower I just finished taking didn't help a bit.

Bloody Reaper, I think as Fleur flies right in front of me, her black wings making my towel billow around my damp legs.

My familiar showed up at the end of my sparring

match with the psychotic Death Fae. Not to help me, though.

No, Fleur came to judge me.

After giving me a look that implied I was dead to her—which was entirely unfair, as I more than held my own against Reaper—she followed me back to Hades's room in the cavern.

And became instantly acquainted with Pip.

Unfortunately, the infatuation appears to be one-sided.

The nightstand crashes, causing me to sigh as Pip goes spinning across the floor.

"And you expressed disappointment in my sparring performance," I mutter, talking to Fleur as she pounces on the withering soul. "You realize he can kill you, yeah?"

She appears to be unfazed.

Probably because she'll simply regenerate.

Shaking my head—a movement I instantly regret—I start toward the bathroom again to raid Hades's closet.

It'll take some effort to find a shirt and jeans, as the attire is one Hades rarely wears. However, I know he has some casual clothes hidden in the back for the rare occasion when he wants to blend in with the mortals of this realm.

Granted, Hades looks like a God in everything he wears. So it's really a wasted effort on his—

I jump as Pip comes flying through the closet wall to halt right in front of me.

Sighing again, I say, "Look, I like you. But I'm not going to protect you from Fleur. It's better that you two figure this…" I trail off when he vibrates in front of me, going in and out of focus. "What are you doing?"

He spins, his expression full of panic.

I arch a brow. "I assure you that move will only entice Fleur more because of your cloak."

A meow sounds from behind me. Only, it's not a sound of agreement, but one of alarm.

Frowning, I glance back at my sphinx just as she flies into the room with a growl. She nudges me toward Pip, who is wildly gesturing at me now.

My brow furrows.

These two are no longer playing. They're trying to tell me something instead.

A quick mental link to my familiar tells me danger is coming.

And a glance down at Pip confirms it. "Where's Sera?" I demand, instantly on alert.

He vanishes through the wall, causing me to growl his name.

"I can shadow, but I—"

He returns, interrupting my comment, and gestures downward.

"I don't understand."

He points downward with an emphatic motion.

"Are you saying she's in the caves?"

He nods.

"Where in the caves?" *And what in the Styx caused her to go down there?*

He starts to move his arms in a strange frog-like motion, then bobs his head up—

"Oh." I don't say anything else. I just shadow to the lagoon because it's clear Pip was trying to mime *swimming* as an action. That makes some sense, I suppose. She must have gone from the beach down to a safer area to play in the water with...

My gaze widens as I materialize.

I expected to find her swimming with Alina.

But that's not what I see at all.

She's naked.

In the water.

With an equally unclothed Morpheus.

Glancing to my right, I take in Hades's fuming form and realize what set Pip off.

The Alphas are about to duel.

And Sera is about to be in the middle of their possessive madness.

Fuck.

I shadow to her in the water, and she instantly clings to me. "Don't let them do this," she begs.

But there isn't time for me to stop what's about to happen.

Morpheus and Hades need to figure this shit out. All I know is that Sera won't be here to watch them rip each other apart.

It's my job to protect her, and protect her, I fucking will.

I wrap my arms around her and shadow to the only place I can think of that'll offer us mutual protection—the Hell Fae Kingdom. It's technically close to the Netherworld Kingdom since they're all part of the Hell Fae Realm, but the heart of the Hell Fae world has a lot of power.

And my brother just so happens to be mated to the Hell Fae King.

Unfortunately, it's not my brother standing in his suite when I arrive with Sera. It's one of his other mates—a Midnight Fae named Ajax.

"I need a towel," I tell him, not at all interested in small talk or trivial greetings.

"Seems to me you're already wearing one," he replies as his wand appears in his hand. "But all right." He whispers a spell and creates a large fluffy towel that I grab from him to wrap around Sera's shocked form.

Her eyes are wandering the room, and I'm sure the fiery walls are what have her gaping at our surroundings.

This kingdom lives up to its name.

"Where's Az?" I ask, hoping my brother is nearby. "I need to talk to him."

"He's on his way," Ajax replies, glancing from me to Sera. "Can I get you anything? A coffee? A hot chocolate? Or, I don't know, a name, perhaps? Maybe even a purpose for randomly appearing in my room?"

I grunt at that. "It's Az's room."

"It's *our* room," Ajax returns.

I roll my eyes. "Fine."

"Even if it were his room, I'm sure he, too, would like a reason for your unexpected visit. I don't suppose it has anything to do with the Alphas hunting Hades's Omega?" He looks at Sera again. "Should I assume that's you?"

"Are you okay?" I ask, ignoring Ajax and giving her a means to ignore him as well.

She swallows. "They're going to fight."

"Maybe," I hedge. "Or maybe they'll talk."

Her eyes finally leave the walls and lock on me. "Where are we?"

I smile, amused by her abrupt change in topic. And also pleased that I have a way to distract her from whatever Hades and Morpheus are doing to each other right now. "The Hell Fae Kingdom."

She stares at me for a beat, then she nods like she expected that response. "Oh."

"Specifically, you're in the royal suite of the Hell Fae Palace," Ajax inserts. "A place where visitors are never welcome."

I meet his gaze, note the way the thin ring of blue resembles fire around his otherwise black irises, and say, "Clearly, we wouldn't be here if it weren't an emergency."

149

"Hmm" is all he says in reply.

I blow out a breath and drag my fingers through my still-damp hair. "Sera—"

"*Thorns*, what happened to you?" she demands, her focus suddenly on my torso.

I glance down. "Oh. That. Yeah, uh, Reaper plays rough."

Ajax snorts.

I ignore him again, which is an easy feat when Sera begins to touch me. She's gentle, her nails skimming my abs before heading up to my chest. "Are you okay?" she asks, her voice soft.

"Yeah, trouble. I'm already healing." What I don't tell her is that those fading bruises are from stab wounds.

Fucking Reaper.

I was a bloody mess before my shower.

My only point of pride was that I left Reaper equally as bloody. Perhaps even more so. Though, the lunatic was positively beaming with pleasure in response to my violence. *Such a masochist.*

"You look like you were mauled by a Minotaur," my brother says as he appears. "Who did you piss off?"

"Why do you assume I pissed off anyone?" I counter. "Maybe this is from a violent sparring match."

Which it is.

But I won't do him the honor of confirming that detail for him.

Instead, I change the subject with "Can I have a pair of pants? And can Sera borrow something from your mate?" I look at Ajax. "Or maybe you could conjure up some clothes?"

Ajax snorts again. "Not likely."

He's never cared for me. Likely because I haven't really

tried to get to know him. Or maybe he's still annoyed about the whole portal thing from last year.

Regardless, I probably deserve his irritation. It's not like I've been a great brother to Az.

Although, I haven't exactly been a bad brother either. More neutral.

Az disappears rather than answers, his shadowing skills similar to my own. Except he's also part fiery bird, our familial relation on our father's side only. His mom was a purebred Phoenix Fae, while mine is a Corpse Fae Royal.

I explain this to Sera, more so that she understands where we are and why I shadowed us here.

"So he's your half brother?" she says.

I nod. "Yep. And this unhelpful asshole is his mate Ajax."

"This unhelpful asshole magicked up a towel, which I can undo, if you prefer," he drawls.

"Please don't," Sera murmurs. "Thank you for the towel."

He smiles. "You are way too good for Maliki."

I grunt at that. He's right, so I'm not about to correct him.

However, Sera says, "He's just grumpy because Hades and Morpheus are probably trying to kill each other right now." She frowns. "They can't die, though, right?"

She's aware of the answer to that, but she clearly needs confirmation of what she already knows. So I give it to her with a nod and reply, "Yes. Mythos Fae are immortal."

Except the Omegas somehow disappeared.

So there's that mystery to solve.

But not right now.

Az materializes and hands me a pair of jeans. Given that our heights and statures are nearly identical, I'm not surprised when the pants fit perfectly. "Thank you," I tell him.

He nods. "Typhos says he'll bring something over for Sera."

Ugh. This should go well. The Hell Fae King nearly killed me last year. Of course, I fucked with his realm by opening a portal to another dimension—*for Hades*—and therefore deserved Typhos's wrath.

But that doesn't mean I fancy seeing him again.

He'll probably have a few choice words about me shadowing directly into his personal wing.

However, it was the safest place I could think of for Sera. Thus, I'll take whatever punishment he wants to deal out, so long as he lets Sera stay.

In true form, Typhos Lucifer arrives in a cloud of fiery embers, the demonstration of power not lost on me.

Yet Sera appears unfazed, as though she sees these sorts of parlor tricks every day.

She stares at him and says, "I assume you're Typhos?"

His eyebrow arches as he meets her gaze. "I am."

She nods. "Okay."

"Okay?" he echoes.

"I'm a little overwhelmed right now and just trying to make sure I know everyone's names."

"I take that to mean you have no idea who I am, then," he says slowly.

She frowns. "You just confirmed you're Typhos."

"Yes. Typhos Lucifer."

Her brow furrows. "As in the Hell Fae King, right?"

"Oh, so you do know who I am," he drawls.

She exhales loudly. "Yes, I do. But to be completely honest, I already have enough arrogant Gods in my life. So if you don't mind, I'm going to just talk to you like an ordinary fae."

"But I'm not an ordinary fae," he points out.

"And I respect that, Your Majesty. I'm also sorry for teleporting…" She glances at me. "What's the right term?"

"Shadowing," I tell her.

She nods. "Thank you." Her focus returns to Typhos. "I'm sorry for *shadowing* in unannounced, but Morpheus and Hades are trying to kill each other. So I assume Maliki brought me here to keep me safe. In which case, I think that says a lot about what he thinks of you, so… I think highly of you, too."

Typhos stares down at her. "You remind me of my mate," he says, then holds out a pair of jeans and a tank top.

Sera grimaces at the sight but accepts the items.

"You can change in there," Az says.

He didn't offer me the same place to put on my pants, but I just slipped them up under my towel. Sera might have a harder time with that.

She thanks him and mutters the same words to Typhos, then leaves to get dressed.

"What's her name?" he asks.

"Serapina," Hades answers as he materializes beside me. "And no, you can't have her."

Typhos huffs a laugh. "I don't think Camillia would be open to the notion of a fifth member in our circle. And aside from that, I'm not interested."

"I wasn't referring to you wanting her as a mate, but as some other lucrative means, Typhos." Hades gives him a meaningful look. "She's *mine*."

"*Ours*," Morpheus corrects as he appears on my opposite side.

I sigh. "Haven't you two worked this out yet?"

"No," they both reply in unison.

"Great," I mutter.

"A trio of Alphas followed me back from your realm to the human world," Hades says, changing the subject and focusing on Typhos. "I don't know how that happened, but I ensured it won't happen again."

"*We* ensured," Morpheus corrects him.

"Wait, is that why Pip told me to grab Sera?" I interject. "Because of the other Alphas?"

Hades glances at me. "What other reason could there have been?"

"Because you two were apparently trying to kill each other," Ajax drawls, just as Sera steps out in the clothing Typhos provided.

She takes one look at Hades and scowls. "*You.*" But when she sees Morpheus on my other side, her eyes widen and she repeats, "You," in a very different tone. One filled with relief. "You're okay," she adds, starting toward him.

"We have to go," Hades says, stepping between them and blocking Sera's path. When she tries to skirt around him, he mists to her and pulls her into his arms.

"Go where?" Morpheus demands at the same time I say, "Now, hold on a second…"

"You know there's only one place I can keep her safe," Hades replies, his gaze on Morpheus.

"I don't—"

"It wasn't a suggestion," Hades interjects, cutting off Morpheus's protest before he can finish speaking.

Then Hades and Sera disappear.

I growl. "*Where* did he take her?"

Morpheus heaves a loud exhale and shakes his head. "His underworld," he mutters, his eyes meeting mine.

"You mean the Netherworld?" I ask. Because there's no way Hades took her to the death world. And I have no idea what else the "underworld" could mean.

"Not quite." Morpheus's uneasy expression tells me

I'm really not going to like whatever he's about to add. "His underworld is the maze he made for Persephone's heat. And it's so heavily warded that neither you nor I can enter. Because the only power that can combat his hold over that creation comes from Persephone herself."

Styx...

Yeah, I definitely don't like that.

Not one fucking bit.

SERA

Hades's scent is all around me, drowning my senses with the false promise of a beautiful winter morning.

I'm so eager to escape it—and *him*—that I shove away from him the moment my feet hit the ground.

And instantly stumble into something hard and cold.

A shiver bolts up my spine, the temperature a startling difference from the Hell Fae Kingdom. Glancing around, I see stone walls and intricate designs that look like vines, except they're made of rock, not leaves.

The ground beneath me is hard as well, matching the walls, reminding me of a concrete prison. However, this one has texture. *Like the garden at the palace*, I realize, examining the intricate engravings more closely.

There are flowers etched into the corridor, giving it the illusion of being amongst wildlife.

Only it's all cold and dead.

How fascinating, I marvel.

Then remember that I'm not here to enjoy the view or the company.

Because *he* brought me here. To wherever *here* is.

"Where are we?" I demand as I spin toward Hades.

He regards me carefully. "In a safe place," he answers vaguely.

"Like the cavern in the Human Realm?" I ask, unable to mask my annoyance. "Which you made *unsafe* by trying to kill Morpheus?"

He frowns. "I didn't try to *kill* Morpheus. Why would you think that?"

"Because I was forced to leave when you found us in that lagoon together?" I suggest.

"That's not why you had to leave," he replies. "I was careless in my pursuit of returning to you and failed to check my surroundings, thus putting you in danger. And for that, I apologize."

I blink. "Wait, what? You weren't fighting Morpheus?"

"I may have been about to at one point, but no. I didn't fight Morpheus. He helped me handle the Alpha issue after Maliki took you to the Hell Fae Kingdom. However, unfortunately, it means the cavern is compromised. So I brought you here… where I know I can keep you safe."

My lips curl down at the hesitation in his voice. "How do you know I'll be safe here?" My question comes out almost as slowly as the latter part of his statement. I may not know Hades well yet, but it's obvious there's something he isn't telling me.

He stares at me for a long moment before saying, "Because I built this place for Persephone's heat. Only our souls can exist here." His jaw ticks after uttering the words, suggesting that he's still holding something back.

"And?" I prompt, my hands on my hips.

Hades looks ready to growl, but his voice is interestingly steady as he replies, "And I never meant to bring you here."

My brow furrows. "What? You just said this place is for Persephone's heat, right?"

"Yes. *Persephone*. Not *you*."

My lips part a bit at the way he says that, the anger underlining the words, the frustration crossing his features, the narrowing of his dark eyes.

I swallow. "Oh." He built this as some sort of gift for his mate. I... I'm just... the human who has his mate's soul trapped inside her. "I see." That makes more sense.

This place means something to him, and he's not pleased about having to bring me—*Sera*—here.

"That's why you took me to the Human Realm first, then, I assume?" I phrase it as a question. A distraction. A way to keep the conversation going while I consider what he's admitted. What it *means*.

"Yes. You don't deserve this place, Serapina. I'm sorry for bringing you here. But I have no other option."

I wince, his words hurting me in a way I could never have anticipated.

This male—this infuriating, arrogant, *God*—has been cruel to me from the beginning. First, when he thought I was actually Persephone and playing some sort of game with him. Then, by *testing* my truth by making Maliki please me.

And now... *now* he tells me I don't *deserve* to be in the place he made for Persephone.

Because I'm not her.

And he's sorry I'm here.

Yet he had no other option.

"That's not true," I whisper. "You could have left me with Morpheus and Maliki and let them take care of me."

He scowls at that. "You are *mine*, Serapina. That means protecting you at all costs, even ones that may be unfair of me to pay."

"Right. Because your mate's soul exists inside me," I reply, swallowing. "So you feel obligated to protect me."

"Obligated?" he repeats, his brow creasing.

The echoed word reverberates around my mind, beating at a nerve that has my hands fisting at my sides.

Because I didn't ask to be this Alpha's *obligation*.

It's not my fault that I have his mate's soul inside of me.

Just as it's not my fault that I'm not truly her. That I'm not worthy of this little "safe place" that he built for her.

I don't deserve to be talked to this way or treated like this.

Maybe Persephone does—if she hurt all those Omegas —and maybe he thinks that's why it's okay to manhandle me and talk down to me.

But none of that means I have to stand here and take it.

"I don't—"

"If I'm such a burden to you," I say, interrupting him. "Then why not give me back to Morpheus and Maliki? Surely that would be better than keeping me in your precious safe space for Persephone, right?"

Now he just looks confused. "Precious?"

I roll my eyes. "Sacred love nest?" I offer instead. Then I wave my hand through the air, like I'm trying to erase the words. "I don't even care what you call it. What matters is that I'm not Persephone, right?"

He stares down at me for a long beat before replying, "Yes, I've already said I believe you don't possess her memories."

"But I am not her, correct?" I reiterate. "That's why I don't deserve to be here, yes?"

"I'm starting to think you've misunderstood me," he says slowly.

"Am I Persephone?" I ask again.

He still appears to be confused but answers with "No. You're Serapina."

"Right. So I'm not worthy of your love nest, or whatever this place is, yet you still feel a possessive need to keep me from Morpheus—despite not actually being your Persephone. All because of my soul?" I phrase that last part as a question while he gapes at me.

"Now I'm certain we're having a miscommunication."

"That isn't an answer to my question," I state flatly, exhausted by this whole interaction. "So tell me this—do you want to share me?"

"I've already demonstrated how I feel about that by letting Maliki touch you," he hedges.

"That was to test whether or not I'm Persephone," I point out. "Yet you wouldn't share her at all, would you?"

"No, of course not."

"However, you let Maliki touch me, so maybe you already knew I wasn't Persephone." I shake my head, suddenly feeling like I'm talking in circles. There's just so much to unpack between us. So much anger. So much insanity. *So much history*.

Thorns, it feels like we have a decade of issues to work out.

Which is impossible given our short tenure together.

"Hades—"

"No," he interrupts. "Somewhere in this conversation, we took a strange turn, and I think it's because I didn't appropriately explain what I meant about *why* I never intended to bring you here."

"I don't need you to—"

"Please, Serapina. Let me explain," he stresses, his tone stern yet soft. "This maze is the product of two thousand years of anguish. I built it with the sole purpose of punishing Persephone for her betrayal. That's why I took you to the cavern first; I wanted somewhere nicer for your heat. Not…" He gestures to the walls. "Not *this*."

My lashes flutter as I try to process everything he just said. "What…? What did you plan to do to her here?"

His jaw ticks again, but he doesn't answer.

"You said it was for her heat," I add, my stomach twisting. "*What* was the plan, Hades?" I need to know what kind of monster I'm facing. To understand how dark he's willing to go to *punish* his mate.

Because this male thinks he owns me, too.

What will he do to me if I say no? If I say I want Morpheus or Maliki instead?

Hades's expression shifts into something I don't recognize. Not fury. Not condemnation. Not sorrow, either.

If I didn't know any better, I would think he's *hurt*.

"Fuck, the way you're looking at me right now…" Hades shakes his head and takes a step backward. "Omegas like to be hunted during their heat. It's how an Alpha shows his worth. So I built this maze to hunt Persephone."

I shiver. "And force her…?"

His gaze widens. "Fuck, Serapina, *no*. You don't understand me at all."

He moves even farther away, like he's afraid of me. Or maybe trying to give me room. I don't know the purpose, but I suddenly feel even colder than before.

"I would never *force* her to do anything. Nor would I *force* you…" He trails off again and closes his eyes. "You could say I was going to force you to marry me, but I thought you were Persephone. I thought you were already my *wife*. That…"

He drags his fingers through his hair and blows out a breath like he's trying to harness his self-control.

"The purpose of this maze was to indulge Persephone in her hunt, to see her through her heat, and take care of her like an Alpha should. All while surrounding her with the reality of what she did to us. These lifeless walls represent who I've become without her. They demonstrate the harsh reality of who she made us become."

He finally looks at me again, his tormented expression undoing something inside me.

He looks ravaged.

Pained.

And above all else… *contrite*.

"I never meant for your first heat to be in this maze, Serapina. That's why I said you don't deserve this place. But I know I can properly protect you here, and your safety matters most right now. I… I'll do whatever I can to help you find comfort here. But I will not *force* you to do anything you don't want to do. Despite what you might think of me, that is not who I am."

He stands there, looking utterly defeated. And I'm pretty sure my heart breaks for him.

Which is ridiculous to an extent. He's not been kind to me. He hasn't earned my wavering emotions.

But this is no ordinary situation for either of us.

"So what happens now?" I ask him, glancing around. "Am I supposed to run? Because I don't particularly feel like being chased or hunted right now."

He huffs a laugh, but it lacks humor. "No, I imagine not." He clears his throat. "I can show you the home I created. There's a bed. A kitchen. Magic similar to the one in the cavern. And I... I can attempt to manifest other things, if you like."

"Can you manifest Maliki or Morpheus?" I wonder aloud, and immediately regret it when Hades winces. "They can't come in here, can they?" I guess, my stomach twisting.

"Not in its current state, no," he replies, looking visibly uncomfortable again.

"Can they enter in a revised state?"

He studies me and then nods. "Yes. I can revise the wards to allow them entry, if that's your desire."

The words feel loaded, like he's testing me somehow. "If I say yes, are you going to hold it against me?"

"That you're even asking me such a question shows how badly I've fucked things up between us," he replies, sighing.

I don't say anything since my inquiry is a valid one. I don't know how he'll react if I say I want Maliki and Morpheus here.

Maybe he'll allow Maliki entry, but probably not Morpheus.

And I... I want them both here.

Maliki offers me comfort.

Morpheus gives me answers.

I've only ever trusted my sister—

"Oh!" My eyes widen. "Is Alina okay?" I thought Hades and Morpheus were going to fight and that's why Maliki shadowed me to his brother's place in the Hell Fae Kingdom.

But Hades mentioned that an Alpha issue was the reason the cavern was no longer safe for me. I was so distracted by why *this* is a safer location that I didn't seek clarity on what he meant.

"They're all fine. Orcus took her to an undisclosed

location until… until your heat has passed." He swallows and looks away. "We agreed to separate if found again. Alina might be claimed, but the feral Alphas won't care."

"Oh." That… that makes sense. Not the feral part, but separating. "They need to protect Thea, too."

"Her designation won't be as obvious until she's thirteen or so," he tells me. "Though, yes, it is likely she's an Omega, just like her mother."

I nod. "That's what Alina told me, too."

"Has she shared any other details?" he asks. "Like information about what to expect for your heat? Or your need to nest?"

"She's given me some basics about what a nest is, but essentially said I should talk to Maliki or Morpheus about my, er, heat." Warmth spreads up my neck. "Sorry. I…" Yeah, I don't know how to finish that, or why I just apologized, so I simply stop talking.

Hades says nothing for a moment. "All right. Let's… let's go this way to the cabin. Then we'll… we'll talk more."

My lips twist as he turns and walks away.

I'm not sure what more there is to say between us. Probably a lot. But I'm not feeling all that talkative anymore. Just tired.

Like I could sleep for a year.

Which is crazy after how much I slept last night.

However, I follow him since I don't have any other choice. It's that or go the opposite direction. And given that this is a maze, I don't think that's a good idea.

Though the walls really are beautiful. So intricately designed, the flowers forever etched into stone.

I trace my fingers along one of them, noting the pretty lily petals. *Fire lilies, maybe*, I think.

When the image seems to flutter, I jump back and find

myself up against a wall of masculine male. Hades grabs my hip, then reaches around me to pluck the flower off the wall.

My lips part as it begins to sizzle and burn, the orange and yellow petals coming to life right before my eyes. When the stem glistens in a dark green, he holds it out in front of me. "I know it's not much, but hopefully… hopefully it's a start," he says.

"A start for what?" I ask, confused.

"A new beginning," he replies, his palm leaving my hip as he steps to my side, the flower still hovering between us in his opposite hand. "A way to seek amends. An introduction to who I truly am." He shrugs. "Or consider it a token of my destruction. Whatever you prefer."

I hold his gaze and reach out to take the token from him. "It's a fire lily, right?"

"Yes."

"What…? What does it do? Just constantly burn?"

He smiles. "No. It simply blooms. Eternally." He turns again, and I frown at his back.

"But all the ones Pip brought me were black," I tell him. "If they bloom eternally, why were they charcoal when he gave them to me?"

"Because he's a creature of death, like me," Hades says without looking at me. "And most things we touch die."

"Yet this flower just blossomed," I point out. "So that can't always be true." At least where Hades is concerned.

He pauses at a bend in the maze and glances at me over his shoulder. "I suppose fate isn't always black and white," he murmurs.

I blink at him, curious as to what he means.

But he disappears around the corner without another word.

I rush to follow him, just to freeze at the sight before me.

He called this a *cabin*.

This... this isn't a cabin.

It's a skull, just like Death's Den.

Only there are no blue fires lingering in the eyelike windows here.

Just *ice*.

HADES

Welcome to our little nest of lies, I think as I pass through the threshold of the cabin. *Fuck, how many times have I thought about voicing those exact words aloud?*

It was the greeting I intended for Persephone.

But a different version of her joins me now.

A stronger version.

One still holding the fire lily I manifested for her.

The embers flicker and glow, illuminating her fair skin and providing her with a healthy blush.

It's beautiful.

Fuck, *she* is beautiful.

This Omega masquerading as a human. Though, I suppose *masquerading* isn't the right term, as it implies nefarious intentions. Yet nothing about Serapina Everheart appears to be conniving in nature.

Of course, the same could have been said about Persephone, too.

Only Persephone exuded a childlike innocence, one I used to adore. However, I can't help but be intrigued by Serapina's boldness. She's still innocent in a way, but there's nothing childlike about her.

She's determined.

Strives for independence.

And isn't afraid to speak her mind. It's… refreshing.

It also kind of reminds me of Maliki. He's always been fearless where I'm concerned, a trait I find exceptionally rare.

Serapina isn't exactly fearless so much as assertive. She doesn't shy away from voicing her wants and needs.

Unless she thinks I'm going to "hold it against her."

My jaw clenches at the reminder of her question. It wasn't voiced in a sarcastic tone but in an honest one. Because she actually thinks I'm capable of cruelty.

Which makes sense, given everything she's seen from me.

And now she's here—in the heart of the underworld that I built for Persephone.

It exists beneath the Netherworld Kingdom. A secret labyrinth of passages meant to entertain and punish my mate.

Now it feels like a prison.

Because I'm trapped here with the darkness of my decisions. Forced to face my sins in the most unanticipated of ways.

"It's freezing in here," Serapina says as she enters.

"Yes. It's as cold as death," I reply. "This is what happens when life ceases to exist." I glance at her. "As I said, everything I built here is layered with pain and bitterness." Perhaps I didn't explain it quite like that, but the point was clear.

Something flickers in Serapina's blue eyes, and for a moment, a twisted part of me hopes Persephone can hear me.

But I regret that desire in the next second.

Because I... I don't know how I would feel about her replacing Serapina.

It's a jarring realization.

For two thousand years, I've searched for my mate. Not to save her, necessarily, but to simply find her. And I was willing to do whatever it took to locate her.

I love her. I do. But the desire to hunt her is intrinsic. It's part of who I am as an Alpha.

Yet there's something about Serapina that I... I don't want to see disappear.

She's—

"There's beauty in stillness," she says, distracting me from my thoughts. "Like this..." She walks up to the wall and traces a design etched into the icelike glass. "This crystallized snowflake is forever frozen in perfect lines."

Serapina sounds awed as she admires the unnoteworthy pattern while clutching the fire lily with her opposite hand.

She's not like Persephone at all. Persephone hated the cold. Despised snow. "Everything is dead," she would whisper sadly. It would break my heart and make me wish I could control the seasons.

Alas, I couldn't.

So we would venture to warmer climates instead.

Oftentimes to visit her mother, Demeter.

"And this," Serapina whispers, her attention going to a nearby vase holding a frozen bouquet of petalless stems. "It's like you crystallized life right before death."

She looks at me, a puzzled expression on her face.

"Is that meant to be a dark concept?" she asks. "Torturing a flower in its final moments? Or maybe it signifies rebirth?"

I stare at her, fascinated by how her mind has crafted such intriguing spins on what was meant to be a simple display of lifeless flowers.

"Everything here is frigid… like death," I reply. "That's the purpose."

She frowns. "But even ice is alive." She looks down at her lily. "Flowers and plants are not the only symbols of vitality. Sometimes it's in an artistic depiction. Or simply in an activity you enjoy." She shrugs. "However, I will say I hope the bedroom has a warm comforter, or I'm going to freeze in this igloo."

A startled laugh escapes me. "I'll manifest you a chest of the finest blankets. Whatever you want."

Which effectively kills the moment for me.

Because there's only one *want* she's voiced. Well, *two* wants. *Maliki* and *Morpheus*.

Fuck.

I can't fault her desire. I'm the monster in her tale.

But I can turn this around. I have to.

She's still my mate. Just… just reincarnated.

It makes me wonder if all the other Omegas are in different forms now, too. If Demeter somehow stole their souls and put them in new forms.

Human and otherwise.

It's a mystery I long to solve. No, I don't *long* to solve it; I *need* to solve it. Because I have no idea what's going to happen when Serapina goes into heat. Will her Omega soul truly take over? Will Persephone wake up?

Or is this Persephone's permanent existence?

A true rebirth.

The notion stirs a myriad of emotions inside me, ones I

don't want to identify. Because some of them feel like a betrayal to my mate.

However, a hypothetical question whispers through my mind. I try to push it away, not wanting to hear it, but it's too loud to ignore. *Is it cheating to fall for a new version of my mate, especially when she's nothing like the Omega I've loved for so long?*

It's... it's a conundrum.

Except it's becoming my reality.

Because I can't help but observe as Serapina wanders through the cabin, admiring my creation with an expression of interest.

"You realize that manifesting all of this is another version of creating life, right?" she asks when she reaches the kitchen. "You keep calling it dead, but it's alive with energy. *Your* energy. And while you may be the God of Death, you're not exactly dead."

"Why do you sound disappointed by that?" I ask, somewhat teasing.

She stills. "I... I didn't mean to... I... I'm just trying to make conversation since you're being all broody."

"Broody?" I repeat, amusement flirting with my lips despite everything. "I think you mean *thoughtful*."

"Maybe," she replies, clearly missing my attempt at lightening the air between us.

I sigh, aware that I have a lot to answer for here. "How about a tour?" I offer. "It's not much, but I can... show you around."

"The igloo or the maze?"

"The cabin," I say, correcting her term. Though, I suppose it is reminiscent of an igloo with the icelike walls. "I can't show you much of the maze. It'll ruin your fun later."

She looks at me. "You mean... during my heat."

I nod. "You'll want the space to play, and if I show you around the labyrinth, it'll defeat the purpose. You need to learn the area yourself and decide how you want to play."

"I don't... I don't think I'll want to play in the maze you made to punish Persephone."

"The punishment is about the cold surroundings, which don't seem to bother you," I tell her. "The maze itself is harmless." I would never hurt Persephone in that way. "You're very safe here."

"Yeah, until I go into heat... and you make me run through your maze."

All hints of my previous amusement die in a breath. "I'm not going to make you do anything, Serapina. Your inner Omega will be the one in control, as it should be."

She stares at me. "And you think my Omega is going to want to play in the labyrinth?"

"Yes. Your inner Omega will want to use it as a way to test your potential mates. It's how Alphas and Omegas bond. And given that this will be your first heat, the setting is quite important."

The way she's looking at me right now tells me this is all news to her.

Another failure for my list, I think.

I run my fingers through my hair and debate how to handle this. "When was the last time you ate?" I blurt out.

She gives me a startled look, likely because I just abruptly changed the topic. But I did it with a purpose in mind. "Breakfast," she says slowly. "I don't know when that was. Hours ago, though."

I dip my chin. "All right. How about I make some food, and then we'll... talk?"

"Talk," she echoes. "Like we're doing now?"

I smile. "No, like *really* talk. I'll tell you more about

Omega heats, how the mating hunt works, and we'll go from there."

Her nose crinkles. "I..." She trails off as her stomach grumbles, maybe in outward disagreement with the refusal she may have been about to voice.

Or perhaps she was going to accept and the hunger pang distracted her.

Either way, her belly just agreed to my plan.

My lips twitch. "Go get comfortable on the couch. And I'll conjure up something for us to eat."

"Couch," she repeats. "What—"

The appearance of a leather sofa in the middle of the otherwise stark room causes her mouth to snap shut. I add a fireplace in the wall next, then manifest a table in the middle of the wraparound sofa, and create a vase for her flower—since she's still holding it.

And lastly, I fashion a remote that will allow her to turn on a screen, if she wants to try to watch something. Though, I suspect she doesn't typically enjoy television.

Unless Maliki has introduced her to some of his dreadful mortal movies.

I nearly groan at the thought but distract myself by adding another creation—a warm, fuzzy blanket, the color of which matches Serapina's eyes—and head toward the kitchen.

Except when I get there, I realize I have no idea what kind of food she might like to eat.

If Maliki were here, I would ask him.

And he would probably tell me to go to Styx instead.

Rightfully so.

Fuck. Talking to him later is going to be... a chore. But I deserve his wrath. And probably a few good stabs.

I'll deal with him after I settle Serapina's nerves. She

has to come first. If he's the fae I think he is, he'll understand.

Because he, too, will put her first.

As the Omega in the center of my... I frown, the thought rephrasing in my head. *As the Omega in the center of* our *circle*.

He's my best friend for a reason. The one I let taste Serapina first. The fae I've trusted for eons.

Maliki pushes my limits daily, which is exactly what I need in a partner. Because he'll force me to be a better Alpha.

Fuck, he's been trying to demand that of me for thirteen months. I've only just recently realized why. Because he saw what I refused to see—Serapina's truth. Her worth. Her sincerity. Her greatness.

I should have listened to him.

I should have listened to Morpheus, too.

Damn it.

They've both been trying to force me to open my eyes, and unfortunately, my stubbornness prevented me from listening.

And I may have lost my soulmate in the process.

No. I refuse to think that way. I can fix this. I *will* fix this.

Alas, time isn't on my side.

Serapina's heat will begin soon. Maybe in a few days. Definitely within the next week or two.

It'll be intense.

Overwhelming.

Maybe even terrifying.

Which is why I'm going to prepare her. That includes a lesson on consent.

Because if she refuses me, I won't touch her. Even when she's out of her mind with lust and begging, I'll uphold the choice she made while coherent.

That's what a good Alpha does, and while I've not been a prime example of greatness lately, I will not let her down now or ever again.

I'm going to be the mate she should have known from the moment I first sensed her.

No more anger or grudges.

Just an Alpha who misses his Omega.

And loves her... in all her forms.

MALIKI

A Few Minutes Earlier

THE UNDERWORLD HADES BUILT IS BENEATH THE Netherworld Kingdom.

Which is utter Styx. Because not once did he mention the existence of a damn labyrinth. Hades has always been mysterious in that superior God sort of way, but I never realized how much he kept me in the dark until these last few days.

First with the escape plan.

Now with taking Sera to some sort of twisted maze created to *punish* his Persephone.

Normally, I stay out of his affairs. But this… this is too fucking far. "There has to be a way to break through the wards," I say to Morpheus, interrupting whatever he and Typhos Lucifer were just discussing.

Because I don't give a Styx about politics.

I care about Sera. And I am *not* leaving her with Hades in what is likely a complex network of horrors.

"Who can we talk to?" I press, aware that everyone in the room is now staring at me. "Give me a name. Any name. I'll go wherever we need to go if it means saving Sera."

"Interesting that you think the Omega needs to be saved," Typhos drawls. "Isn't Hades her Alpha?"

"He's mated to her soul," I tell him. Not that he needs or deserves an explanation. But if he has an idea that could help, it may be worth taking a few seconds to elaborate. "But Sera—the *person*, not the *Omega*—is unclaimed. That's why her impending heat sent off that signal. Right?"

I look at Morpheus for confirmation. I don't actually require it, but solidarity in this situation is important. I know Typhos. He values and rewards demonstrations of loyalty. And perhaps he'll be more amenable if he sees us as a united front.

Or maybe he'll just try to cut a deal.

That's fine. I think he'll find that I'm willing to do whatever it takes to get to Sera.

She's mine to protect. My charge. My responsibility. And that includes protecting her from the one who assigned her to me in the first place. *Hades.*

Because at some point, I decided she was my priority. Not him.

I'm guarding her because I want to, not because I have to.

And Hades has made me question everything.

"Well, this is fascinating," my brother says, his violet eyes looking me over with interest. "I had no idea you finally found a mate. I just assumed you and Hades were, well, you know."

I glare at him. "What the fuck are you talking about?"

"Oh." He glances at Ajax. "He hasn't figured it out yet."

Ajax snorts. "Shocking."

"I believe his relationship with Hades is similar to yours with Typhos. Claimed, but not in a sexual way," Morpheus murmurs.

"I am not *claimed*," I tell him. "I also haven't found a mate. Sera is my *charge*. And you all are wasting my time with your idle gossip." I focus on Morpheus. "Do you have any suggestions or not?"

"Actually, Hades's claim on you might be useful," he says, his expression pensive.

"He hasn't claimed me."

"He has," Morpheus murmurs thoughtfully. "I assume through a token of some kind. A coin, perhaps?"

"I don't..." I trail off, recalling the gold coin he gave me the other day.

The one he told me to put on my wrist. Only it dissolved into my skin the second I took it from him.

I told him at the time that it felt like a trap to accept his "gift." He responded that I felt that way because I knew him well.

So he never denied it.

Nor did he ever *explain* it.

"He told me it would keep you from bothering me," I say slowly.

Morpheus snorts. "I suppose he's not wrong; his claim protects you from my abilities. But it does a lot more than that. It identifies you as part of his mate-circle, something I believe he properly initiated when he let you play with Sera."

My jaw clenches. "I fucking hate all your Alpha games."

"I'm not the one playing right now," Morpheus murmurs. "However, I am thinking, and Hades's claim may be your ticket into the maze."

All right. If that's the case, then... "I'm listening."

"First..." He turns to Typhos. "The Alphas shouldn't be a problem for your realm any longer. While the maze Hades built is technically beneath the Netherworld Kingdom, it's not a tangible location. More like a paradigm, I suppose, only far more intense in terms of creation magic. That's why you can't sense it or access it."

Typhos narrows his gaze. "When I permitted you access to my realm, it was with the purpose of expecting you to watch over and protect my fae, not—"

"Which we've been doing," Morpheus inserts. "The Netherworld Kingdom and the Morpheus Kingdom are both safe."

"Tell that to my Strigoi," Typhos deadpans.

"Well, that whole situation with the throne wasn't my responsibility," Morpheus returns. "And you know how I feel about interfering in games of fate, Typhos. I observe. I bless them with dreams. I do not *fix* nightmares."

Typhos grunts.

"Or are you saying you needed my assistance?" Morpheus presses. "Because it seems to me that *fate* worked in your favor, yes?"

The Hell Fae King folds his arms across his broad chest, his dark blue eyes on Morpheus. "I don't *need* anything from you. I would just appreciate improved communication, given that I allow you to reside in my realm."

Morpheus grins. "Consider me duly chastised, Your Majesty. Now, as far as communication goes, it seems to me that your Strigoi require an heir. Unfortunately, I hear he's quite, shall we say, stealthy. Perhaps removing his 'shadow' would help, hmm?"

I have no idea what he's talking about. Nor do I know how any of this is relevant to the situation with Sera. "Can we go back to discussing how Hades's supposed claim can help us break through the maze wards now?"

Typhos looks at me and then at Morpheus. "Just get out of my palace."

Morpheus's smile grows. "Happily." He grabs my arm before I can comment and mists us to my room in Death's Palace.

My gaze narrows. This area of the palace is riddled with Hades's magic. Morpheus bringing us here with such ease shouldn't have been possible. "I assume the maze wards are different from the ones in this palace?" I guess, prompting him for an explanation.

He shrugs and releases me. "When Hades tasked me with cleanup duty, I made some changes."

I snort, not at all surprised by his response. And any other day, I might even be amused by it.

Alas, I'm not in a humorous mood today.

"Well, if you know how to undo or alter Hades's wards, then surely we can figure something out with the maze," I tell him. "So start talking."

"Your demanding nature is rather attractive, Ghost," he drawls, then collapses into my favorite chair—just like Hades always does.

Fleur chooses that moment to fly in, my familiar clearly having followed me back from the Human Realm. She takes one look at me and then Morpheus before choosing the God's lap to land in.

"Your loyalty is noted," I mutter as she curls up.

She responds by closing her eyes.

And begins to purr.

Brat, I think at her.

Morpheus combs his fingers through her black fur. "You're a pretty little one," he coos at my sphinx. "A fine familiar, too."

"Stop complimenting my cat and focus on the maze."

"Maybe if you spent more time complimenting your precious beast, she would choose you over a stranger," he muses, his purr igniting to life and startling Fleur.

But rather than run away, the little traitor curls up even more, her contentment clear.

I roll my eyes. "She just likes Alphas."

"Most females do," he murmurs with a smile. "Wait until you see Serapina react to our knots. It'll be a beautiful display indeed."

"If we can even get to her," I say through my teeth. "Why are you not more concerned right now?"

"Because I know Hades won't hurt her, and he was right when he said his maze was a safe space."

"Except you also said it was built to punish Persephone."

"It was," he replies, frowning a little. "But Serapina isn't Persephone."

"Clearly," I state dryly. "So she doesn't deserve any of this."

"No, what I mean is that Serapina might not see any of it as a punishment."

"Something I would believe if she weren't trapped there with Hades right now," I ground out.

Morpheus shrugs. "Maybe it's what they both need— some solitude so they can finally talk."

I stare at him. "You think this is good for them?"

"I think it's good for *Hades*," he corrects. "And I'm trusting Serapina to be able to handle herself."

"So you're not worried at all," I press, my ire mounting. "You think she's just fine in that labyrinth of horrors."

"Depends on her point of view." He scratches Fleur behind the ears. "But let's talk about his claim on you and how that may be of use to us."

Oh, now he wants to get to the point.

Rather than comment, I just continue to stare at him.

"In theory, you're already a member of the mate-circle. Which means his wards should grant you entry. But that requires us to find a proper door. I assume it's somewhere in this palace. And it won't be in an obvious place."

"That's helpful," I mutter.

He shrugs. "This is Hades we're discussing, is it not? Nothing is ever what it seems where the God of Death is concerned." He cants his head. "So where do you propose we begin?"

I blink at him. "You're asking me where to start?"

"Well, yes. You know him best."

"Do I?" I ask, serious. "Hades didn't tell me about the escape plan, and he's certainly never mentioned the underworld to me before. So do I actually know him best? Because you knew where to go *and* you knew about the maze."

"I only knew where he took Serapina because of my link to her soul," he informs me. "As for the underworld... it's been a point of contention between us for nearly two thousand years. I sensed when he started to build it, and, well, I didn't approve of the intention behind it."

"Because you don't want to punish Persephone."

"No, I do not," he says softly. "I don't believe she intentionally hurt anyone. But Hades has been blinded by her perceived betrayal and refuses to see beyond it. Until now, anyway. Serapina, I believe, is going to change everything."

I study him for a moment, then take the chair across from him. "That's why you want them to talk."

"Among other reasons, yes," he admits, his gaze taking on a faraway look. "She's the key to undoing millennia of wrongness. And potentially the one who will help us save the Mythos Fae Realm."

My eyebrow inches upward. "That sounds like a prophecy."

His lashes flutter, his blue-green eyes capturing mine. "Maybe it is." He looks down at Fleur. "Sorry, pretty girl, but I need to check on something." He glances back at me. "See if you can find that door. I'll be back."

He disappears before I can comment, leaving me growling an expletive in his wake.

"*Bloody Alphas.*" I don't even know what *door* to search for.

But as Fleur meows, I suddenly have an idea.

Maybe Howl and Mort can help me...

Pushing off the chair, I go to look for Hades's beast. Maybe the three-headed creature followed Fleur back here.

If not, I'll go trash Hades's suite in search of the elusive door.

And raid his liquor cabinet.

Because that arse owes me a stiff drink. As well as a Styx-ton of answers...

SERA

"AM I ALLOWED TO HAVE PIP HERE?" I ASK WHEN HADES appears with two trays in his hands.

The question is one that's been rolling around in my mind since I set the fire lily in the vase, which I assume Hades created for this purpose. However, seeing it there, all glowy and orange, made me think about Pip's dead version.

And I... I miss him.

But I'm not sure if he can get through whatever wards Hades put up around his labyrinth.

"Pip is your familiar," Hades replies as he sets the trays down on the table he manifested a bit ago. "He can go wherever you desire. Just call for him and he'll appear."

I frown. "Call for him?"

He settles onto the sofa beside me, his focus on the trays as he shifts them around on the table. "Yes. Via your mental bond."

"My mental bond...?" I echo, phrasing it as a question.

He looks at me. "Do you not sense Pip?"

I blink. "No? I don't think so, anyway. I…" My lips twist as I try to figure out what to say here. "Sorry, I don't know what you mean."

He leans back, seemingly surprised. "You essentially conjured him, so I'm surprised you can't feel him. Maybe you'll feel more connected after your estrus?"

"Maybe? I mean, I have no idea what to expect during my heat or after it. So why not add this to the list of uncertainties?" I don't mean to sound so flippant about it, but I'm feeling just a tad overwhelmed. And exhausted.

And hungry, I realize as the scent of melted cheese touches my nose.

I look down, half expecting to find pizza. But instead, it's… it's… "What is this?" I ask, not recognizing the meal he's prepared. It's various bowls of what looks like melted cheese on one side and a large array of fruits, vegetables, and breads on the other.

"Fondue," he says, shifting forward to pick up a metal prong. "You stick this into one of the items on this tray and dip it into one of these three pots." He points to the bowl farthest from me as he says, "That's sharp cheddar. This one is a more traditional swiss-and-gruyère blend. And that one is my own creation."

I eye the three options. "Okay." I take the prong as he holds it out for me, stab a piece of white bread, and opt to try his "creation" first.

Flavor instantly bursts on my tongue, causing my eyes to widen at the smoky tendrils twined with sweet notes. "Oh," I moan, not caring at all that my mouth is full. Because wow. *Wow.* "This is really good."

His lips twitch, probably because my words come out muffled from the food I'm still chewing. At least I blocked the view with my hand.

"Try the cheddar with the green apple," he suggests.

"Is that one of Persephone's favorites?" I guess after I swallow.

He frowns. "No, actually. It's my favorite."

"Oh." Rather than say anything else, I try what he suggests and nod my approval. "It's good."

He doesn't reply, just watches me as I pick up a third item—a piece of broccoli—and dip it into the cheddar. After it's in my mouth, he says, "I realize things between us are tense, Serapina. However, I'm going to try to explain a few things. I don't know if it'll help, but hopefully it'll be a start."

I finish my vegetable, then reply, "Okay," since it seems like he wanted my agreement before continuing.

His responding nod confirms it.

I pick up another apple piece instead of broccoli and try it in his cheesy creation while he observes.

The cheddar is better with it, I decide. But I don't voice that opinion out loud because he starts speaking.

"I'm going to begin with an apology," he tells me. "I should have come to you the moment I knew you existed, and explained all of this to you then. As I'm your Alpha, it was my responsibility to prepare you, and I failed you. I'm sorry."

I'm in the middle of eating another piece of bread, so I can't respond to that.

But he doesn't seem to expect me to, as he continues by saying that most Omegas learn their distinctions around thirteen years of age—something I already knew because of Alina's comments about Thea.

And then he says most Omegas go into their first heat between eighteen and twenty years old.

Which clearly wasn't the case for me.

"I suspect Demeter did something to you after saving you from Monsters Night," he goes on.

Saving seems like an incorrect term, but I don't comment. Primarily as I don't know a better word for what she did. She set it up to ensure my name was picked from that chalice, then kidnapped me and put me in a garden. Or a dream. Or whatever she did to me.

Regardless, his assessment that Demeter may have altered my heat seems to be founded on truth.

"I think Maliki pleasuring you fractured whatever Demeter did," he continues. "I just wish I understood more, but nothing about this is precedented."

"That's what I keep hearing," I mutter as I stab a celery stalk with a little too much force. Then I dunk it in the cheese before popping it into my mouth.

All while Hades observes me with an expression I can't quite read.

He clears his throat. Then starts explaining what a "normal" estrus looks like.

"The Omega may feel some stomach pains. Exhaustion. A need to nest. Or become increasingly interested in sensual play. But eventually, an instinct takes over that inspires the Omega to run. Because she wants to be chased. So I created this maze to satisfy that desire."

I swallow, my throat suddenly dry. I knew this part already, obviously. But somehow him reiterating it makes the experience more real.

"It's about testing an Alpha's strength before the fog of lust sets in," he explains.

"Fog of lust," I repeat, my voice softer than intended.

"Omegas tend to lose their sense of reality during estrus, as they're consumed by passion and pleasure. That's why they run shortly before the heat sets in—while they're still coherent enough to evaluate an Alpha's worth."

My lips form an O without sound. I... I knew the heat would be intense. But he makes it sound like I'll be out of my mind. *Lost in a fog of lust...*

"See, Omegas in estrus want to breed, and they need to ensure their Alpha's seed is worthy of procreation. That's the point of the chase. And an Alpha's instincts are driven by the need to hunt and claim."

And now my throat just feels tight. Like I can't breathe. Or maybe that's my lungs.

Yet somehow I manage to whisper, "So... so you're going to hunt me and breed me... in this labyrinth."

"Yes." No hint of hesitation, and just the word alone makes my stomach drop. Only, in the next breath, he adds, "Unless you refuse me."

I'm not sure how to respond to that. "You just said I'm going to be out of my mind with lust and that you're going to pursue me through this maze and knot me... Now you're saying I can refuse? How?"

"Because I won't even attempt to hunt you without knowing it's your wish for me to do so," he says.

I stare at him. He's called me his mate and his wife countless times. Yet now he's saying he won't pursue me unless I give him permission? That feels... off base... given everything we've been through.

"Serapina, I understand if my intentions feel unclear to you," he tells me, obviously having read the incredulity in my features. "But I do value consent. That's why I never impregnated Persephone. She didn't want to risk bringing another Omega into our world. And I respected those wishes. Just as I'll respect whatever requests you make of me."

I... I want to believe him.

But I refuse to be that naïve.

And he must see that opinion because he sighs and

says, "We'll return to this discussion in a moment. I want to talk about your actual heat. You're going to crave a knot, which I gather Morpheus has discussed with you." His jaw seems to tighten as he utters the words, something dangerous flashing in his gaze.

I don't want to worsen whatever dark emotion that is, so I say nothing and let him make assumptions.

"Has he explained that knotting will hurt at first?" he asks.

"N-no," I reply, swallowing. "But Alina kind of mentioned it would be overwhelming... and then okay." Or that's what I gathered from what little she told me.

He nods. "Once the initial pain of your first time dissipates, you'll enjoy it. But the knot is what ties the Alpha to an Omega for procreation."

"So you didn't do that with Persephone?" I ask, my brow furrowing. "Since she didn't want a child?"

"I, um, no. I still knotted her. But Alphas can control our seed. It's linked to our ability to manifest, just in a unique way." He pauses before adding, "Basically, we ensure life doesn't blossom."

My eyebrow arches. "You chose that flower reference for me, didn't you?"

"I did." His discomfort is clear. "But you understand?"

"Yes. I think so."

He nods. "Then it was worth the reference." He clears his throat again. "Anyway, as I said, you'll crave a knot during your heat. And if you choose to reject an Alpha, your estrus could become excruciating. But I'll do my best to help you mitigate that pain, if you go that route. However, there will only be so much I can do."

I stare at him. "Are you telling me this so I accept your knot?"

His eyes widen. "No, I'm trying to... Fuck, you're

right; that's how it comes across, but that's not what I meant. My point is, Omegas always have a choice, and many have chosen to go through their first few cycles without Alphas, as they were searching for an appropriate mate. It's not unheard of, but it can be painful."

"So my body will punish me if I reject you," I translate.

He closes his eyes now and blows out a breath. "That's not what I'm trying to say either. I just want you to understand the process." He pinches his nose for a long moment before dropping his hand and looking right at me. "I'm not good at this, am I?"

The question is so earnest that I can't help but smile a little at his self-deprecation. "It's not exactly an easy conversation to have, is it?"

He doesn't seem to find humor at all in the situation because he scowls. "I swear I wasn't always this inept."

"I don't think you're inept, Hades. I think we're both overwhelmed." I lean forward to stab an apple piece, then coat it in the cheddar cheese—which must be magically enhanced since it's not solidifying—and hold it up to his mouth. "Eat."

He arches a brow but leans forward to take the morsel I've offered him.

I create one for myself as well, then we both chew in silence for a long moment.

"By my estimation, you have a few days before your heat comes," he says after I'm done swallowing. "Once that happens, you'll have to give us your decision, so we can properly care for you. If—"

"Us?" I echo. "*We?*"

His eyebrow wings upward again. "You asked if I could alter the wards for Maliki or Morpheus." The latter part of that comes out with a slight hiss to it, one that vanishes as he adds, "As that's your desire, I'm going to work on it. At least for Maliki. For Morpheus... I need to talk to him first."

"Oh," I whisper.

"And, as I was saying, *if* you choose to accept us—any of us—during your heat, you'll also need to voice your desire to be claimed. Which, from an Alpha, requires a bite, not just a knot." His gaze slides to my neck before returning to my eyes. "You'll also need to provide guidance on your preferences for procreation."

My lips part. "I..."

"You don't need to decide now, Serapina. It's a lot. Unfortunately, time is not on our side, and I accept blame for that. Just know that... whatever you choose, I will respect it. And I'm fully aware that being bound to your soul does not give me exclusive rights to you or your body."

He studies me for a long moment, then looks away.

"This is the only way I know how to support you, Serapina. By bringing in Maliki, I mean. He doesn't have a knot, but he has other skills... I know he can make you comfortable. And when your heat starts, I'll leave you with him while I lock myself away."

I frown. "You'll lock yourself away?"

He nods. "Yes. So I don't attempt to kill him for fucking my mate."

My eyes widen. "Hades—"

"I know you think I'm a monster, Serapina. And I am to an extent. All Alphas are. But I am *your* monster, mate or not. With that comes a possessive need to *claim*." He looks at me, and I can almost see his beast peering out at me through his intensely dark eyes. "You have no idea how difficult it will be for me to stay away from you during your estrus, but I will. If that's your choice."

He pushes up and off the couch.

"Hades," I start again.

"I'm sorry, Serapina," he whispers before I can say anything else. "But I'm going to fix this. And to do that, I need to have a long-overdue discussion with Maliki."

He looks at me, and the agony in his eyes renders me speechless.

"I'm going to ensure that the bedroom is properly prepared for your comfort. When I return, I'll answer whatever questions you have… then I'll go find Maliki."

I frown after him, confused by his abrupt departure.

So I get up and follow him.

And find myself in a massive bedroom adorned with crystalized skulls.

Not real remains, but intricately carved stones and icy decor.

"Wow," I breathe, causing Hades to still by the bed. "This is… unique." I mean that as a compliment. It's cold and beautiful. Yet eerie, too.

He stares at me like he can't quite believe his eyes. Maybe he didn't hear me follow him.

Or perhaps he's surprised by my reaction to the macabre adornments. But I like the chilling scene. It's oddly inviting, despite the undertones of death.

Hades visibly shakes himself and waves his hand over the bed—where a pile of fuzzy blankets forms. "Let me know if you need more," he says.

I study the luxurious mound, then look around for the other amenities. A sudden craving hits me, one I can't quite explain. But after the day I've had, I decide to indulge in the instinct.

Because what do I have to lose? Absolutely nothing.

I also *deserve* a little comfort.

"Is there a bathtub?" I ask.

"Yes, and a shower."

"With hot water?" I press, staring him down.

His lips twitch. "Also yes."

"Good." I stretch my arms over my head. "I think I'm going to take a bath... and consider everything you've said while doing so." Because I... I don't know what questions to ask right now.

And honestly, stepping in here has me just wanting to relax.

Maybe that's an insane reaction to my situation. But I don't really care. My life is essentially insanity personified.

"I'll go get one started for you. Any preferences on scents?" he asks, playing along with my moment of lunacy.

"Something wintry, maybe with a hint of leather, too. Oh, and cotton." The description leaves me without much thought, causing my brows to furrow. Because it certainly sounded specific.

And his expression tells me he picked up on that as well.

But all he says is "I know what you need" and disappears into the bathroom.

Minutes later, I know he understood me perfectly because the mixture of aromas meets my nose and makes me sigh.

This is crazy.

However, I don't care.

I'm going to relax. Maybe think a little. And... and probably take a nap.

Yes to sleep.

After a bath.

I feel like I'm in a daze as I enter the bathroom, the chilly stone barely registering as I move.

Hades studies me, his brow furrowing a little. "Are you feeling all right?"

"Maybe," I murmur. "Maybe not."

He hums and leans against the wall beside the filling bathtub. "You're overwhelmed."

"Likely," I agree.

He nods. "Then take your bath. I'll be in the other room if you need me."

"I thought you were going to find Maliki?" I ask as I bend to check the water temperature. It's warm and perfect.

"I will. After you're tucked into the nest."

I frown, not sure what he means by that. But I choose to let it go and instead start to disrobe.

Hades doesn't turn away, just watches as I drop the borrowed tank top and jeans to the floor. "I'm going to need new clothes," I tell him conversationally as I pull my hair loose. "Preferably something less clingy, and no denim."

His lips twitch, like I'm amusing him.

But I'm not trying to be funny. "I mean it, Hades. *No denim.*"

"I hear you, darling," he murmurs, the endearment one I think he's only used once before. Or maybe not at all. I'm not sure. But I... I kind of like it. And I *really* like it when he says, "No more jeans."

I nod. "Thank you."

He holds out a hand, and I accept it without thinking.

Then sigh as he helps me into the giant bathtub. "This is far too big for me."

"It's meant for a party of two or more," he replies.

I glance at him. "I'm not inviting you into my bath."

He smiles. "I know." He waves a hand, causing a few candles to appear, their colors reminding me of the fire lily. "If you need me, just say my name. Otherwise, I'll be in the other room waiting for you to finish."

"Okay," I say, leaning back against the marble and

closing my eyes. "Thank you." The two words slip from my mouth, and I'm not quite sure what I'm expressing gratitude for. Maybe the bath. Or perhaps… perhaps other things.

Right now, I feel a little too dazed to focus on meanings.

I just want to exist in the warmth, surround myself with these scents… *and rest.*

HADES

I ONLY TAKE TWO STEPS BEFORE SERAPINA STARTS TO SLIP beneath the water.

Her exhaustion came on fast, leaving her a bit delirious in the end.

That's not surprising. She's an Omega who is about to go into heat, and while not all Omegas experience this level of extreme tiredness, I'm not at all shocked that it's impacting her in this way.

She's an extraordinary case.

And with that come extraordinary reactions.

I bend to lift Serapina from the bath, her petite form instantly curling into me as I begin to purr. She's soaking through my suit, but I don't care. She can't sleep in the bath, or she'll drown. So I carry her to the bed, where I manifest a warm towel to lay her on.

I create a second one to run over her damp limbs to

thoroughly dry her, then conjure up a sleep gown for her to wear. It's golden silk, reminding me of her hair.

She doesn't stir as I pull the sleepwear on, though her nipples harden beneath the fabric as I tug it down to her hips. I try to ignore the view, but it's difficult. She's just so fucking beautiful.

And so different from Persephone, I think, an uneasy feeling stirring in my gut.

I've spent two thousand years being devoted to one Omega. The only time I deviated was when I watched Maliki fuck. But I never touched or indulged in the experience. Just watched.

It fed a foreign part of my soul, one I chose not to acknowledge until recently. *When I asked Maliki to kiss my wife...*

I swallow, my gaze running over Serapina once more.

She looks so soft. So beautiful. So deceptively fragile.

Oh, she's absolutely breakable in her human form. But she possesses a warrior's spirit. Which is utterly bizarre because Persephone wasn't a fighter.

Which again has me wondering if my mate was truly reincarnated.

Thus, her soul is mine.

But this version of her is not.

I tuck her hair behind her ear. The ends are damp from her ten-second bath. They'll dry. However, I help speed that along by patting them with the towel. Then I lift her again and set her more firmly in the center of the bed and grab one of the blankets to drape over her.

After firmly tucking her in, I pick up the towels and discard them in the bathroom.

With a low whistle, I call for Ossa and her brothers. They appear in a heartbeat, our connection resolute. "Guard my Omega," I tell the trio. "Alert me immediately if there are any issues." There shouldn't be any, as this maze is the best-protected creation of my existence.

But Serapina may wake up scared or confused, and I'll need to mist back to reassure her.

Though, I hope she sleeps. She's going to need it for the heat to come.

I give in to the need to admire her again, my gaze observing as her chest lifts and falls as she succumbs to a deeper sleep. My purr is likely a source of contentment for her, which I use as an excuse to linger a little longer.

However, after several minutes, it's clear that she's lost to her dreams now.

So I leave her to go clean up the living area.

Once done, I stop in one final time, just to see if she's moved.

She hasn't.

Though, my beast has settled onto the foot of the bed, their three heads resting on the mattress as they guard my sleeping mate.

Fortunately, they're facing away from her, their focus seeming to be on me in the doorway.

"Try not to scare her when she wakes up," I say softly. "She doesn't know you like I do yet."

Ossa snorts, almost as if to say, "And whose fault is that, hmm?"

I ignore her and look pointedly at Mort and Howl. "If you want to play fetch, use balls, not skulls."

They look at each other in a way that suggests they're confused by my request, but I feel them agree via our connection.

Meanwhile, Ossa basically rolls her eyes.

"I mean it," I say. "Be gentle."

She huffs, and I'm pretty sure she's saying, "We've got it. Now fuck off."

Sighing, I do just that and mist back to the palace where I sense Maliki's presence. He has no idea that I marked him. It wasn't exactly intentional. I really just wanted Morpheus to leave my best friend alone. But I suspect Maliki isn't going to see it that way.

And honestly, I probably should acknowledge that my *mark* went a lot deeper than a simple charm.

I essentially claimed him as part of my mate-circle.

Which… I didn't fully realize or accept at the time. But I understand it now. And I'm prepared to—

A fist flies at my nose as Maliki materializes in front of me, his fury a whiplash that has me misting backward just before contact.

Only, the asshole anticipated my movement, as evidenced by the knife now lodged in my fucking back. "*Maliki.*"

"Hurts, doesn't it?" he says. Then saunters off down the corridor like he didn't just fucking stab me.

I'm about to go after him when a series of electric currents hums through my veins, telling me he laced the blade with some sort of venom.

Fuck.

"What the fuck?" I demand, my knees giving out.

"You stabbed me in the back, so I returned the favor," he informs me from what sounds like far away as my vision begins to black out.

It's only a momentary blindness, but it's enough to infuriate me.

"Have you lost your fucking mind?" I snap. Or try to, anyway. My voice is a bit hoarse. And what is he going on about, saying I did this to him? "I never stabbed you."

"It's an idiom," he drawls, his voice stronger now as he crouches in front of me.

That's when I realize his hit has sent me to the damn floor.

And I'm flat on my stomach.

"Also a metaphor, I guess," he adds, his head cocking to the side. "It means you betrayed me. So I physically returned the favor. As I said ten minutes ago—hurts, doesn't it?"

Ten minutes ago?

Fuck.

I must have blacked out longer than I realized.

Hence my placement on the floor.

But the knife appears to be gone.

"Now get up and take me to Serapina," Maliki commands.

I huff a laugh. "Not going to do that." *Not after you fucking stabbed me, asshole.*

Yet I'm oddly aroused by his violence. It isn't because I want to fuck him, but because it confirms my decision to claim him for Serapina.

He truly is the ideal mate for my circle.

He'll protect Serapina from every threat imaginable—including me.

Which will be important if she doesn't want me to see her through her heat. I meant what I said about locking myself away. But on the chance I find a way out of the box, he'll need to be able to take me down.

I'll have to provide him with the tools to do so. However, he just proved he won't even hesitate to follow through.

Because Serapina has his loyalty now.

Just as she should as *our* mate.

"That wasn't the right answer, Hades," Maliki says in a silky tone.

I mist to my room before he can stab me again, then

mist a second time to *his* room, just in case he's trying to anticipate me again.

And finally return to the hallway on my feet rather than on the floor, and grab his wrist before he can stick another knife in me.

Except the clever fae was apparently ready for that, as evidenced by the stinging sensation climbing up my arm.

I release his wrist with a curse, belatedly realizing he put on some sort of silver-studded bracelet—laced with *more* venom. "*Maliki.*"

"You pissed me off," he says conversationally. "So I found some extra slug venom." He smiles as my knees give out. "But because I need you to be coherent, I didn't use too much. Now take me to Sera."

"I can't," I grit out. "Not yet."

He cants his head. "Meaning what, exactly?"

"Meaning we have to talk first."

"Talk," he repeats, like the word is foreign to him. "Fancy that. You could have *talked* to me about an escape plan, but didn't. Could have fucking mentioned a maze built to torture your mate, too. But no. You kept me in the dark."

I wince, and it has nothing to do with the venom humming through my veins. "I didn't intentionally keep you in the dark, Maliki," I growl. "Fuck, you're my best friend. I just... I didn't..." I wince again, this time from the pain echoing up my arm from my fingertips. "I didn't think... it would be needed."

Darkness overwhelms me again, the venom winning as I crash into the floor once more.

But this time when I come to, I'm on my back and Maliki is standing over me. "Best friend?" he says, arching a brow. "I'm your *best friend*?"

"Well, you were until you fucking stabbed me," I

mutter, my tongue feeling so damn heavy that it's hard to speak, let alone talk.

"You're going to have to repeat that, as I didn't understand it," he says, folding his arms.

It's then that I realize he's dressed in assassin leathers—black pants, a tactical vest, and boots.

"Fuck, you look ready for war," I grumble, my hand coming up to touch my pounding head. "I'd kill anyone else in this position. You know that, right?"

"Still can't understand you."

I glare. "Liar." My tongue is already back to its normal size, which means my words are more than coherent.

And the grin he gives me confirms it.

"Asshole," I add.

He shrugs. "You pissed me off."

"You said that already."

"It was worth repeating." He holds out a hand.

I eye it warily. "I'm not falling for another one of your tricks."

He grunts. "I'm done torturing you for now." He wiggles his fingers. "*Best friend.*"

Fuck, I'm never living that down. "Don't let it go to your head."

"Oh, that ship has sailed."

"Your mortal idioms are tiresome," I inform him. Because that one I've heard.

"Your lackluster communication is tiresome," he returns.

I sigh. "Fair."

"Not nearly," he replies, bending down to grab me by the shirt to yank me upright. "I want you to take me to Sera."

"I told you I would—after we talk."

"So *talk*," he demands.

Ignoring him, I mist to my room for a much-needed drink.

He shadows after me.

"Stab me again and I will consider taking you to the death world," I warn him from the bar area.

Maliki snorts at that. "Sounds like a date, *best friend*."

I roll my eyes and grab a bottle of bloodpagne. I don't ask if he wants a glass, just pour us both one and hand it to him when I turn around.

He takes it despite not really caring for the liquid. "Are we celebrating our friendship?" he asks, a tinge of sarcasm in his voice.

My teeth clench. "I think we're celebrating our mate-circle."

HADES

I force my jaw to loosen enough to take a long swig of my drink. My eyes close with the process, only for Maliki to clear his throat.

"Mate-circle?" he prompts when I look at him. "We're celebrating *our* mate-circle?"

I sigh. "You're going to make me work for this, aren't you?"

"I'm going to make you fucking explain it, yeah," he returns. "Starting with the *claiming mark* you supposedly gave me with that damn coin."

I arch a brow. "Morpheus told you?"

"He has nothing to do with this."

He has a lot to do with this, actually, I think. But that's a conversation for later. Right now, I need to address my claim. "It wasn't my original intention. I only meant to provide you with the protection you needed when facing another Alpha. But I've since realized there may have been more to it than that."

"May have been?" he repeats, sounding incredulous.

I take another drink, notice that my glass is already half empty, and refill it before heading over to my couch.

That's when I suddenly see that my surroundings are… uninhabitable.

Arching my brow, I glance around my suite. It's like Mort and Howl tussled through the lounge and shredded everything with their claws.

But this wasn't done by my beast.

Nor is this the result of the Alpha attack from the other day.

No. This has Maliki's signature all over it.

"Was this really necessary?" I ask him, exasperated.

He shrugs. "Necessary? No. Fun? Abso-fucking-lutely."

I face him again. "You know I would kill most fae for this, right?"

Another shrug. "You say that like I fear death."

I shake my head. "You're almost as psychotic as Reaper."

His lips curl, but the smile lacks true amusement. "Thank you," he says, his tone telling me he doesn't mean that at all. "Now talk to me about this mate-circle. Tell me what it means to you. That I pleasure Sera for your benefit…? That everything I do with her is for you? Because if that's the case, then I'll pass."

"You can't *pass*," I inform him flatly. "And no. It's for Serapina, not me. However, I will absolutely get pleasure out of it." Because watching him play with Serapina will be… *enjoyable*. "And probably some pain, too, since you'll likely be the first to put me in my place when needed."

As evidenced by these last few days.

"You're the only one willing to challenge me, which I

need. You'll ensure that I'm the best Alpha I can be—for Serapina."

"So now I'm babysitting you?" Maliki asks, releasing a humorless laugh. "No, thank you."

I glare at him. "You're being purposely obtuse."

"Pot, meet kettle."

"Another human phrase that makes no sense."

"Actually, it does make sense. It means—"

"I don't fucking care what it means, Maliki," I say, setting my glass down on the bar—since that's the only piece of furniture he didn't ruin.

Whatever. I don't even care about the mess, either.

"What matters is Serapina," I growl. "She's alone right now because I'm up here trying to convince you to come help me worship her. And you're making me jump through hoops to gain your acquiescence. If that's how you're going to treat our mate, then forget everything I've said. She matters more than your bruised ego."

"Bruised ego," he echoes. "Hades, my *ego* is fine. What isn't fine is the way you've used me where Sera is concerned. I care about her, more than I'm probably allowed to care. That's not about ego. That's about pain. She means something to me, and she's not mine the way I want her to be. Because she's yours. And you've made it quite clear that you'll only share her if it benefits you. So I'm saying no. I won't pleasure her to please you. I'll only pleasure her to please her."

"As you should," I reply, frowning. "Our mate-circle revolves around her, not me."

"Fancy words," he mutters. "Do you understand them? Because I'm not quite sure you do. Everything I've done has been under your advisement or commandment. What if I want to do more without your permission?"

My frown deepens. "You don't need my permission to touch or claim our mate, Maliki."

He stares at me, his golden irises seeming to burn like twin flames. "You consider her to be mine, too." It's not a question but a statement.

"Isn't she?" I ask. "She seems quite content with you."

"I've never wanted a mate."

"I've never wanted to share my mate," I point out. "Fate creates changes we could never have foreseen, yes?"

He continues to study me. "Is it fate when you're claimed without your consent?" he asks.

"You mean my mark?" I guess.

"Yeah. That."

My eyebrow wings upward again. "Do you want me to remove it?"

"Can you remove it?" he asks, arching a brow. "Is that even possible?"

"It is, yes. Now ask if I want to remove it."

"I can already guess that you don't want to," he says flatly.

"Of course I don't." Why would I want to break our mate-circle? We're stronger together. And as I already told him, this is about Serapina and what's best for her. Not us.

"Then why offer?" he asks.

"Because you're right—I shouldn't have claimed you without consent," I admit.

"That's not exactly what I said."

"It was implied, Maliki."

"True," he agrees.

"But I don't regret claiming you. Serapina needs you as much as I do. Actually, probably more." Because he'll be the one to hold me accountable. And fate knows I need that.

He sets his glass down by mine and folds his arms. "All

right. Let's say I consider this. You understand that I can't protect her properly if I don't know what the fuck you're doing, yeah?"

I release a breath, my chest feeling a bit tight. "I realize I fucked up by not sharing all of my plans with you. I didn't think it would be needed. Because, as I said, I had no intention of ever sharing my mate."

"Well, as you pointed out, fate changes Styx."

"That's not quite what I said," I hedge.

"So if this is about Sera," he goes on, ignoring me, "then we need to talk about Morpheus, too. Because you've alienated an ally, which is unacceptable, especially when Sera needs more protection, not less protection."

"We can protect Serapina just fine," I mutter.

"Just fine isn't enough," he counters. "*Sera* wants Morpheus. Therefore, we *need* Morpheus."

This, right here, is why Maliki is part of my mate-circle. He's the only one brave enough to say blasphemous things to my face.

Blasphemous things like suggesting I include Morpheus in our circle.

"I know you feel possessive over her, Hades, but I don't think you have a choice here," he adds, a little more solemnly now.

"Did Morpheus put you up to this?" I wonder aloud.

"No. The asshole disappeared after spouting some cryptic Styx about Sera being the key to undoing millennia of wrongness and saving the Mythos Fae Realm." He shrugs. "I've been waiting for him to return."

"While destroying my property?" I ask.

He smiles. "I was pissed and bored. What can I say?"

"Hmm," I hum. I would suggest an apology, but I know he won't give me one. Just like I haven't really provided one either.

We're beyond that.

We're united for Serapina.

And now… now I need to think about what he said. *As well as what Serapina wants.*

"So you agree… to be in the mate-circle?"

"I think you're asking if I agree to *remain* in the mate-circle," Maliki rephrases. "Since I've already been claimed by Your Royal Highness."

My eyes roll upward. "As I said, I can undo it."

"You won't, though," Maliki replies. "Because you want me to fuck Sera."

"I want you to care for her," I say through my teeth.

"By fucking her," he presses.

"Are you trying to make me punch you in the face?"

"No, just trying to make you acknowledge what's going to happen if I accept our mate-circle. She's going to be mine, too. To touch. Kiss. *Claim.*" He stares me down. "And I may not let you watch. Some things will be private between us."

"I suspect some things already are," I tell him.

"You suspect right."

Part of me wants to ask what he means by that. But the more intelligent part of me doesn't press.

Because he's right.

Sharing doesn't mean being part of every moment together. It means trusting one another to love and cherish our mate. And I need to let Maliki do it his way, not my way.

So I nod. "I understand, Maliki. And I respect… your choices."

He continues to look at me. "If I end up in your death world after I fuck her, I am not going to be pleased."

"Meaning you'll just destroy my rooms again?" I ask.

"Worse," he promises. But doesn't elaborate.

"Now I'm intrigued."

"And you call me psychotic," he drawls.

I lift a shoulder. "Two peas in a pod, right?"

His eyes widen. "Did you just use a humanism?"

I grunt. "Don't get used to it."

"Ohhh, I'm going to get used to it. In fact, I'm going to *encourage* it." His smile grows. "I'm going to introduce Sera to all of my favorite phrases, make her whisper them to you while you sleep."

I turn away from him, duly annoyed. "You're wasting my time now."

"I'm improving your vernacular," he counters. "Making you more cultured. Introducing you to a whole new realm of—"

"I'm going to go work on the labyrinth wards now," I tell him, interrupting his inane chatter. "And I'll consider talking to Morpheus."

I don't give him a chance to respond. Just mist.

All while thinking about the infamous God of Dreams. My cousin. The one who has also challenged me for millennia.

I really don't want to have a conversation with him. But it seems I'm going to have to. *The things I'm willing to do for my mates...*

MORPHEUS

THERE YOU ARE, PRETTY OMEGA, I THINK, FINALLY FINDING my intended in the dream world. She's naked and floating in a deep blue sea, her eyes closed, her arms outstretched.

My lips curl at the sight as I disrobe and step into the warm water, eager to join my little dreamer. "You told me you didn't know how to swim," I murmur. "Yet you seem to be doing just fine out here."

She startles, her blue eyes opening toward the sky before searching for me. "What?" she asks, blinking a few times. "I don't— Oh!" She tries to sit up and ends up spinning her arms in an awkward circular motion that leaves her floundering in the water.

I dive toward her, my arms coming around her and

righting her in the shallow lagoon, the water maybe three feet deep at most.

She stands and clings to me, her lashes fluttering as she takes a big gulp of air.

"You're okay," I murmur. "I have you. And more importantly, you can stand here." *This is also a dream*, I nearly add, but she's shivering, her adrenaline rush evident.

So I simply hold her instead.

"Just breathe," I whisper, my lips against her ear. "Inhale... exhale... that's it, Serapina. Now be a good girl and inhale again. Mmm, that's right, sweetheart. Exhale." I repeat the mantra a few more times, helping her to regulate her breathing, and eventually the shaking subsides.

"How did I end up h-here?" she asks, only a slight quaver in her tone.

"You're dreaming," I tell her. "And apparently your mind wanted to return you to the lagoon." I glance around. "Only this is a pretty different backdrop. All dark skies with glittering stars and two very distinctive moons."

It reminds me of the Netherworld.

Except there are no blue seas like this in that kingdom. Just the Blood River and a recently resurrected Creek of the Dead.

So this is a glorious combination of her experiences from Hades's world and Mykonos. "I approve of the scenery," I tell her, meaning it. "Especially your choice of wardrobe." I look down at her breasts pillowed against my chest. "You're beautiful, Serapina."

She frowns, then follows my gaze down and gasps. "Oh!" Her palms go to my pecs like she's going to push me away, but her nails bite into my skin instead as electricity hums between us.

I arch a brow.

And she slowly looks back up at me. "This… isn't real?"

"It's as real as you want it to be," I tell her.

"But it's a dream?"

"Yes." I draw my fingers up her spine to the back of her neck. "You're in my world now, Serapina."

"So you're… actually here?"

"In a way," I hedge, smiling. "You're still in Hades's labyrinth, but obviously asleep."

Her nose scrunches. "Oh. So you could just be a figment of my imagination."

I nod. "That's true. But I'm the God of Dreams, sweetheart. So I could truly be here, too."

"Hmm, maybe. However, I also know that, which means this could still be in my head," she replies before looking around. "It would make sense that I wanted to continue what was happening in the cave."

My eyebrow glides upward. "And what was happening in the cave?" I ask, my voice dropping to a lower volume, one meant for the bedroom.

The way her nipples stiffen against my chest tells me she's not immune to my charm. Or maybe it's because she's thinking about what led us to disrobing and walking into that lagoon. "You were going to teach me about your knot," she whispers.

"I was," I reply, my lips curling a little. "I still can, if that's your desire." Because I would do anything to please her. To know her. To *earn* her.

She's incredible. So resilient. Intelligent. Strong. Independent.

Her life hasn't been easy, and she's currently trapped in Hades's maze, yet she looks up at me with such sincerity and interest in her alluring blue eyes.

"Hades told me I'll crave a knot during my heat," she informs me.

"Oh?" My intrigue is piqued. "Did he say anything else?"

She swallows and nods. "He said I'll want to be hunted... because I'll want to test my potential mates."

I dip my chin. "He's right. Omegas love primal play, as do Alphas. And although Maliki isn't an Alpha, I'm sure he'll enjoy chasing you, too."

Serapina shivers. "Because I'll want to... breed?"

"That's the purpose of a heat, yes," I murmur. "But all of us will understand if that's not what you truly desire, little dreamer." Though, admittedly, it will be a bit disappointing, as the notion of a pregnant Serapina is arousing as fuck.

I won't care whose seed takes inside her womb; I'll still love her and the life inside her equally. Because creation is magic. And the concept of being part of that creation is divine in nature. A miracle.

I just want to be a witness to that moment and help nurture the gift of life.

"Your expression... you look wistful?" she says, one of her hands traveling up my chest to my neck to trace the line of my jaw with a single fingertip. "You desire a child?"

It's such an observant question, one that confirms how well Serapina pays attention to those around her. Always studying and reading into situations. That skill is no doubt a product of her harsh upbringing, the ability to evaluate everyone and everything around her a means for survival.

But she uses it now as a way to ascertain my wants and wishes, even though I was primarily focused on her.

"Alphas exist to gift our seed to Omegas and aid in the creation of life," I tell her honestly. "So yes, it has long been my desire to have a child. But I've waited millennia,

Serapina. A few more decades or centuries won't bother me."

Her eyes widen. "Centuries?"

"Or decades," I add. "I did say 'decades,' too."

"You would wait *centuries* for me to be ready?" she asks, ignoring my "decades" commentary altogether.

I cup her cheek as I tighten my hold around her lower back with my opposite arm. "Serapina, I would wait for eternity if you asked me to. I'm your Alpha. Always and forever. In whatever capacity you desire."

She stares up at me, her gaze searching. "You're not doing a good job of convincing me that this is real," she whispers.

I smile. "Dreams are very real for me, my heart. But this can be as fantastical or as true as you wish. Because I'm your God of Dreams, and your fantasies are my literal commands."

Her lashes flutter a little, her pupils seeming to dilate. "So you'll give me anything I want… in this dream?"

"Sweetheart, I'll give you anything you want." I pause to ensure she knows I mean now and in general.

So long as it's within my power to do so, I will always provide whatever she requests.

Dream or no dream.

"But if you would like to begin with the parameters of this fantasy," I go on, "I can work with that."

"Then I want to continue our conversation from the lagoon," she tells me softly. "I… I want to know what would have happened next."

My gaze slides down to her mouth and then back up again. "I'm fairly certain I would have kissed you, Serapina." I graze my thumb along her bottom lip. "And then I would have guided your hand to my knot, to let you explore."

She shudders. "Okay." Her expression takes on a lustful quality. "Show me, Morpheus. I want to experience what should have been."

My breath leaves me, her words sounding more like my own fantasies—me wanting to show my Omega what life should have been like between us. How our souls should have bonded all those millennia ago.

But this is Serapina.

My perfect intended.

My Goddess.

And that makes my fantasy so much more intense. My desires burn hotter. My love shines even brighter.

"Dreams, Serapina," I whisper, my forehead falling to hers. "I'm starting to wonder if our roles have reversed, and perhaps you're truly here to make my fantasies come true."

Because I want nothing more than to indulge her.

To embrace her.

To worship her.

I brush my lips against hers in the softest of kisses, aware that when she wakes tomorrow, this will be nothing but a memory inside her mind.

But for me, this is so fucking real. I'm here. I'm in the dream world with her. Embracing her. *Tasting her…*

I kiss her again, applying a tad more pressure, and draw my hand back into her hair to properly hold her.

Everything melts away around us, the sea morphing into a different kind of pool. A secluded bath. One with walls all around us to give us privacy.

Not that anyone can disturb us here.

The only way to end this is with Serapina telling me to stop… or someone rousing her back in the real world.

However, I want to provide her with a semblance of

privacy, while also introducing her to the magic of my domain.

I create four pillars around the bath, all of them stone and adorned with gold leaves.

Then I add a bench layer to the massive basin, giving us a place to lounge… or do other things.

Whatever she wants. However she wants. *I'm hers.*

Serapina doesn't seem to notice any of this, her body simply melting into mine with each stroke of my lips against hers.

But the moment I slip my tongue into her mouth, our embrace changes.

Her nails scrape along my skin as she moves her hands up to my shoulders, then wraps her arms around my neck.

I groan, the feel of her pressed up against me the most intensely amazing sensation I've ever experienced. She's so warm. So soft. *So mine.*

I deepen our kiss, my arm a steel band around her lower back.

Because I need more. I need *her.*

Gods, I've been starved for so fucking long. No Omega. No true mate. And now… now my ultimate fantasy is playing out in my dream world.

Serapina moans, her tits practically vibrating with the sound.

I shouldn't continue. I should stop. But my hand drifts of its own accord, needing to feel her. To *know* her.

I cup her breast, eliciting another delicious sound from my mate as she arches into me. This wasn't part of the plan. But I can't stop now. I want to feel every inch of her. Memorize this moment… in case there's not another one.

She gasps when I give her a little squeeze, then practically purrs when I thumb her nipple.

My mouth leaves hers to kiss a path down her neck, but

her fingers suddenly thread through my hair as she yanks my head back up for more.

I smile just before our lips touch, then indulge in her demand.

Only this is more than an indulgence.

It's a claiming.

Not just from me, but from her, too.

Because our kiss turns from explorative to feral in an instant, her tongue dueling mine as I thumb her nipple and press my lower half against her belly.

There's no question as to where my knot is or how hard I am for her.

My cock is like a fucking brand against her soft skin, my body throbbing for her in ways I can show more than describe. "Fuck, Serapina," I breathe.

She clings to me. "More, Morpheus. Please."

My hands go to her hips, and I pull her flush against me, then lift her. "Wrap your legs around me," I tell her.

She does.

Because of course she fucking does. She's my good girl. My *dream*.

I walk us backward to sit on the bench, where she straddles me with ease, but I don't let her sit. I force her to stay on her knees and place her exactly where I want her—with her tits closer to my face.

Leaning forward, I take a nipple between my teeth and bite.

She gasps in surprise, then startles when I lave the sharp sting away with my tongue.

"Ohh," she moans, her back arching as she tries to encourage me to do it again.

I don't.

Instead, I suck, which draws even more beautiful mewls from my Omega.

Her fingers find their way back into my hair while her other hand goes to my shoulder. "That feels… feels so good…"

"Mmm," I hum, agreeing with her.

Only, I would change *feels* to *tastes*, because fuck, my mate is *sweet*.

I want more.

To lick every inch of her.

To sink my teeth into her flesh and mark her.

To drag her beneath me and *fuck her*.

But I can't rush this.

I need to savor every second of her admiration and approval. Revel in her attention. *Enjoy her choice.*

Switching to her other breast, I lavish it with the attention it deserves, cherish her with my mouth, and pleasure her with my tongue.

By the time I pull away, a pretty flush has spread all over her chest, the color matching her cheeks as she pants in my lap. "More?" I ask her.

She nods. "Yes, please."

I twine my fingers in her hair and pull her down for a kiss. But just before our mouths meet, I tell her, "My heart, with me, you never have to beg. All you have to do is ask."

I demonstrate my vow with my tongue, embracing her with millennia of passion building inside me, all for the Omega of my dreams. My mate. *My intended.*

She quivers, her body lowering onto mine as I gather her closer, placing us intimately together and allowing her to feel my knot right up against her slick cunt.

Serapina reacts by pressing herself even more firmly against me, her lower half giving an exploratory shift as she seeks friction against my shaft.

I indulge her in her needs. Because fuck, how could I stop her now? Why would I even try?

"Dreams, you feel amazing," I whisper.

This might be a product of her own mind, but it's still the most incredible experience of my existence.

And it makes me crave her that much more.

I'm going to have to find a way into Hades's maze, which was originally why I sought out Serapina in her dreams. She has the power somewhere inside her to alter the wards. I wanted to teach her.

Instead, I ended up in this bath with a very turned-on Omega in my lap.

She's so close to her heat. I can *feel* it. This need inside her is only going to build.

Until she loses her mind with lust.

And begs Hades to knot her.

I want to growl at the unfairness of it all, the very real threat of losing my mate all over again to his possessive touch.

She's mine, too…

But I can't claim her in a dream. And I also won't bite her until she asks me to.

"I want to touch you," Serapina says on a pant, her mouth against mine, her pussy so fucking hot against my aching cock.

"Touch me," I tell her. "Touch me wherever you want, little—"

The world vibrates around us, causing me to growl.

Her eyes go wide. "What is…?" She trails off, her voice dissipating as her visage begins to fade.

And suddenly, she's gone.

My head falls back, my body strung tight as agony simmers through my veins. For a brief moment, Serapina introduced me to a true fantasy.

Now, I have to face the nightmare of reality.

A nightmare where I once again realize that she's not yet mine.

"Fuck," I growl, my fists clenching as the illusion melts away around me. "*Fuck.*"

I'm so fucking tired of battling Hades for my right as an Alpha. But I'll fight him for eternity if it means one day winning a kiss from my intended.

She chose me in her dreams.

Hopefully, she'll choose me outside of them, too.

But the only way I'll ever know is if Hades lets me see her.

Or if I teach her how to let me into the maze.

Next time you dream, Serapina, I'll focus on finding you, I decide. *Until then, I'll be waiting for you in the dream world, my love…*

SERA

Morpheus, I think, searching for him as the world fades away.

And suddenly I'm staring at a ceiling adorned with crystallized flowers.

I blink, trying to determine what caused me to wake up. Or… or how I even fell asleep to begin with.

My brow furrows. The last thing I remember is following Hades in here and going to take a bath. Then… then nothing.

Glancing downward, I find myself in a gold silk gown, one that's clearly meant for sleeping and not a dinner party. It's not what I usually sleep in at all, which suggests that Hades dressed me.

But when did I fall asleep?

Swallowing, I try to push myself up, and come face-to-face with a three-headed beast.

"Oh!" I scramble back into the headboard, the pillows

cushioning my abrupt scurry, all while the animal watches me curiously.

Two of them have their heads cocked, while the third —*Ossa*—gives me a goofy, pant-like grin.

I stare at them. "Erm." I... I don't know what to say or do. Are they going to eat me? Attack me if I move? Bark? "Hi?" I say uneasily.

Ossa's jaws close, then open again to release a tiny little yip, one I'm pretty sure belongs to a puppy, not a wolfish beast.

Howl and Mort follow, releasing two varying sounds, but equally as, well, *cute*.

I blink at them.

And they blink back.

Then loll their tongues to the side in matching grins while Ossa pants happily.

I scoot a little closer to them on the bed—which I now realize is massive since the beast is only taking up the foot of it, and there's still room to maneuver around them.

Stars, this mattress would easily fit a party of five or six...

Or at least me, Morpheus, and Malaki... and maybe Hades.

I shiver at the thought, my thighs clenching at the idea of being with all three males at once.

Oh, that would be... something.

I swallow, my heart suddenly racing. "Something" is an understatement.

Ossa lays her head down with a little whine, her silver eyes big and round as she stares at me with an adorable begging expression.

When Mort and Howl follow suit, my heart begins to crack. Because, oh my thorns, they are *adorable*.

And their tail is wagging.

I lift my hand toward Ossa and cautiously go for one of

her floppy black ears. When I give her a scratch, her eyes begin to close, and I swear she starts to purr.

I reach for Mort next, his ears equally as soft and floppy. His eyes are a golden color that reminds me a bit of Maliki.

Then Howl gives me the saddest look with his blue irises, and I feel compelled to move both hands to his head and give him a thorough scratch.

When I'm done, they're all panting happily again, and I can't help but smile.

"You're very cu—"

Ossa's snarl cuts me off and has me yanking my hand back in alarm.

"I'm sorry," I rush to say as Howl and Mort both look at her and yip. *Loudly*.

I scurry backward again, convinced I'm about to become dinner for this beast, when the creature launches itself off the bed and sprints out the bedroom door.

Goose bumps pebble along my arms as I hear Ossa vocalizing her anger.

Something is happening…

I… I don't know if I should stay here, or…

My lips twist.

Then my brow furrows.

Hades said this maze was safe. So whatever has his beast reacting this way must be related to the labyrinth.

With narrowed eyes, I slide off the bed and wander toward the door, determined to face whatever has Ossa growling like that. Because I refuse to be a damsel.

Hades created this place to punish Persephone. But he loves her. That much I know. And I really don't think he would ever truly harm her—or me.

So whatever this is, I can hand—

My eyes widen as I see Mort and Howl leap up to give

224

Maliki twin kisses with their long tongues, all while Ossa grumbles and growls.

He chuckles and gives the two heads pats, then reaches for Ossa and snorts when she tries to bite his fingers off. "So touchy," he says to her.

She snarls again.

Which just has him shaking his head. "One of these days, you'll give me a chance."

She grunts, then looks away from him while Howl and Mort continue to show their affection.

My eyebrow arches at her clear annoyance. She's very obviously miffed that her brothers are loving on Maliki, which is endearingly amusing to observe.

Only, after a few seconds of enjoying the scene, a realization hits me square in the chest—a realization that instantly dismantles my amusement. "You're here," I say, my eyes widening. "You're here!"

Maliki looks at me and smirks. "Yeah, trouble, I'm here." He disentangles himself from the massive paws and comes toward me in a pair of dark jeans and a black button-down shirt.

I throw myself into his arms and inhale his leathery scent, the smoky tendrils seeming to curl around me in a subtle claim. He kisses my neck and then my cheek before pressing his lips to my ear. "Did you miss me, little mystery?"

"Yes," I whisper.

Except another thought occurs to me right after, causing me to pull backward and look up at him.

"This is real, right?"

He frowns. "What?"

"This isn't a dream?" I press.

He stares at me for a beat, then cocks his head. "Well, I suppose that depends on what you want to do. Would you like to make this a fantasy, trouble? Because that could be kind of fun."

"I'm serious, Maliki. Am I still dreaming?"

"Still dreaming?" he echoes. He arches a brow for half a beat before adding, "Oh, I see. That's where Morpheus misted off to. He's been playing with you in the dream world, yeah?"

His use of the word *playing* has my stomach twisting as fresh heat warms my veins.

Playing is certainly an accurate term.

In fact, I want to go back to *playing* in the water. Straddling him again. *Feeling his warmth against mine...*

"Mmm, playing indeed," Maliki murmurs, his hands going to my hips as he lifts me effortlessly into the air. "I'm going to assume the bedroom is this way, then." I grab his shoulders as he starts carrying me back the way I came. "Maybe we can make our own dreams come true."

"Maliki..." His name comes out a little breathy.

I'm still not convinced this is real.

But I'm not sure I care anymore.

Maliki is here. He's warm. *And he's taking me to the bed.*

"This gold gown looks beautiful on you, by the way," he says, his mouth at my ear again. "I assume Hades manifested it?"

"I... I don't know," I whisper. "I think so, though. I don't remember falling asleep."

"Yes, he mentioned that you nearly drowned."

My eyes widen. "I did?"

He sets me on the floor by the bed and looks down at me. "Hades said you passed out in the bath."

"Oh." My nose crinkles. "I don't remember that." But I do vaguely recall asking for a bath. Which... which isn't like me to do.

But I'm not exactly sure what's normal for me anymore.

Everything feels... strange. New. And oddly exciting.

Er, well, that latter emotion is purely a result of the way Maliki is admiring my gown right now.

That, coupled with what Morpheus did to me in my dream, anyway.

I tremble, my thighs clenching. And Maliki seems to notice because he slowly returns his gaze to mine and arches a brow.

"You all right, trouble?" His hand travels up my side to cup my cheek. "Or did Morpheus not properly care for you in your dream?"

"I woke up before..." I trail off, not able to finish that sentence. As I'm not really sure what would have happened if I'd stayed asleep.

But I know what I would have liked to have happened.

And it involved learning more about Morpheus's knot.

"Hmm, I suppose that's my fault, then. The moment Hades showed me how to find you, I shadowed straight in." He draws his fingers back into my hair. "Would you like me to make it up to you, Sera?"

I... I don't know how to respond to that. "Isn't it wrong?" I ask, thinking out loud. "To... to go from Morpheus to...?" My eyes widen as I continue processing my thoughts. "I mean, wait. Are you even here because you want to be?"

It's a jarring subject change.

But he said Hades showed him how to find me... because Maliki wanted to find me? Or is he here because I asked Hades to grant Maliki access to the maze?

"Am I still an assignment?" I wonder aloud. "Or did Hades—"

Maliki's mouth silences me, his tongue slipping past my

lips to indulge me in a kiss that leaves me dizzy and confused against him.

Dizzy because *wow*.

Confused because… because I have no idea what I was just thinking or saying. I simply want *more*.

His fingers slide into my hair to hold me against him as he devours me. "If this is still an assignment, Sera, then this is the best fucking assignment of my life." He picks me up again and tosses me onto the bed.

I blink up at him, my head swimming with his words and mingling with the passionate desires echoing through my heated thoughts.

"I'm here because I want to be here." He starts unbuttoning his shirt, his golden eyes holding mine. "I can't define what this is between us, little mystery. And frankly, I don't want to. I just want to be with you. That's all that matters to me."

There's a reverence to his tone that leaves me breathless, but it's his expression that captivates me.

Hunger radiates from his gaze.

And his mouth, so sinful and full, continues to move as he says, "As for going from Morpheus to me being wrong?" He smiles. "From what I understand, Omegas craving multiple mates is expected. And, fortunately for you, I like the concept of sharing."

His shirt parts, and he places a knee on the bed.

"In fact, I *love* to share," he adds as he crawls over my prone form. "So if you want to invite Morpheus into your nest, I'll very much enjoy pleasuring you with him."

Okay. Now I'm sure I'm dreaming. Because that sounds like a fantasy come true, one I didn't even realize I desired until recently.

Or perhaps I've known for a while now. Ever since

Alina introduced me to her mates. *Plural.* And left me wondering what it would be like to have a circle.

I quickly dismissed it at the time, as I didn't think that could ever be my future.

But now... now I'm wondering if it might be possible.

With Maliki. Morpheus. And maybe even Hades.

He let Maliki into the maze, like I requested. That has to mean something, right?

Unless I'm dreaming.

But reality or no, I want this. I want Maliki.

So when he settles on top of me, I spread my legs around his hips and lean up to kiss him.

His palm wraps around my throat as he indulges me with his tongue, his mouth hot and intent against mine. I moan, needing something I can't define. Something intense. Something Morpheus awoke inside me that I need Maliki to fulfill.

Is that wrong of me? I wonder, repeating the concern but only to myself. However, Maliki's comment from moments ago echoes through my mind.

"I like the concept of sharing."

I shiver as his thumb traces the column of my neck. It feels threatening, yet reverent, and the combination leaves me squirming beneath him.

Which causes me to arch up into his hips, searching for friction. He presses me right back down and gives my throat a little squeeze. "Don't rush me, trouble," he murmurs. "I'm not done tasting you."

His tongue slides back into my mouth before I can reply, his kiss subduing me and heating me up at the same time.

I want more. So much more.

But he's holding me down and mesmerizing me with his mouth.

Thorns, he's a good kisser. Not that I have anyone to compare him to. Except Hades and Morpheus... in my dreams.

Does that count?

Do I care?

No.

I just... I just want to fall into this kiss and be utterly consumed by Maliki.

His grip loosens on my throat while his opposite hand skims up my side. A moan escapes me as he palms my breast, his thumb stroking my already stiff nipple.

It reminds me of Morpheus.

Yet it's different, too.

This is Maliki. His touch is electric. Morpheus's is more fantastical, like a dream. And Hades... Hades is intensity personified.

"I really do like this silky gown," Maliki murmurs, his finger circling my areola. "But I want to touch your skin, Sera."

A rip follows his comment, the strap popping right off from him tugging at my dress and yanking it down to my waist. I barely even felt him move, but he's settling on top of me once more in the next second and kissing me again.

The sensation of his bare chest meeting mine lights my blood on fire. He's muscular and hot, and his tattoos... his tattoos are *moving*.

I feel them against my skin, writhing in a rhythmic pattern that teases my breasts and causes my nipples to tighten even more.

He smiles. "You like that, Sera?"

I nod and moan in confirmation as I try to somehow touch even more of him.

"That's my version of a purr," he tells me. "But it'll do so much more than soothe you, trouble. It's going to drive you over the cliff into an ecstasy unlike anything you've ever experienced before. I promise."

I don't even question his words. Because I know everything he just said is true.

And I trust him.

I want him.

I want *this*. Whatever *this* is. I don't want to think anymore, just indulge.

So I do.

Kissing him.

Grabbing his shoulders.

Pushing his shirt off so I can explore his muscular back.

All while wrapping my legs around his hips and pressing up into him. When he spins us, I yelp and suddenly find myself straddling him. Which is when he takes the gold silk gathered around my waist and pulls it up over my head.

"Fucking stunning," he says, his gaze roaming over my naked form. "Now free my cock, Sera. I want to show you what my tattoos can do."

MALIKI

THIS WAS NOT MY INTENTION WHEN I ENTERED THE MAZE. I wanted to check on Sera, ensure she was safe, and ask her if she needed anything.

But the damn lingerie-like gown Hades had put on her changed my mind the moment I laid eyes on her.

The fact that she was obviously already turned on— *Thank you, Morpheus*—only heated me up more. And the next thing I knew, I was carrying her to the bedroom.

Having her naked and astride my lap right now does not have me regretting my choices.

Hades might kill me, as we haven't exactly defined any rules here.

Oh well. It'll be a worthy death.

A decision that becomes evident as Sera reaches for my belt.

Her lust-filled gaze meets mine, and I know she's letting her instincts guide her. I'm prepared to help her along where needed, but we'll go at her pace.

This is just an introduction, a way to make her comfortable before I defile her innocence and teach her all the ways she can experience pleasure.

She's not ready for that yet.

However, I think she will be soon. Especially with the eagerness she's portraying now as she unfastens the button of my pants. She's only barely undone my belt, too. My girl isn't taking her time. She's eager.

Which makes me wonder what Morpheus showed her in her dreams.

If he taught her this, then, once again... *Thank you, Morpheus.*

The zipper is next, the sound a reverberation that sends my tattoos writhing along my arms and down my torso.

Sera pauses, obviously noticing the movement, and watches as some of my smokelike bands disappear beneath her fingertips.

Her eyes slowly lift to mine, causing my lips to curl. "Curious, trouble?" I ask her as I tuck my hands behind my head.

"Yes," she admits.

"Then finish your job," I tell her. "Free my cock."

Because I'm not doing this for her.

This is all about learning one another, our preferences, our tastes, *our needs*.

She's going to explore me just like I've explored her.

Her pupils dilate, and her tongue comes out to sweep across her lower lip.

Then she shifts back onto my thighs and tugs on the zipper.

I'm about to tell her to slip her hand inside my boxers, but she moves off of me entirely to drag my pants down my legs.

I watch her, loving the way she's disrobing me.

There's a boldness to her movements, one I know is fostered by her spirit and not experience.

Did Morpheus show her how to do this, too? I wonder. *Or is this all Sera?*

Neither reason actually matters.

All I care about is her hands on my bare legs, skimming upward to my boxer briefs.

She doesn't ask or comment, just hooks her thumbs inside the black fabric and yanks them down—similar to what I did to her gown. Except the boxers don't rip; they just glide down my legs.

Being the thorough woman that she is, she removes my socks with the boxers, leaving me as naked as her on the bed.

And from the expression on her face, I can tell she's impressed.

"Like what you see, sweet mystery?" I ask, wondering if her mouth will compliment me in a manner similar to her eyes.

"Yes," she whispers, admiring my muscular thighs before studying my cock. Her nostrils flare, her tongue sneaking out to dampen her lips again.

"Are you thinking about tasting me?" I murmur, curious as to what she's thinking.

She glances up to meet my gaze. "Can I touch you?"

"You can do whatever you want to me, Sera." I mean it. She could drag a knife along my skin, make me bleed, and I would allow it.

I'm hers in a way I've never belonged to anyone.

I can't define it. Can't say how or when it happened.

But at some point, my babysitting assignment turned into something so much more. So much deeper. So much more intense.

Now, Sera owns my loyalty. My compassion. *My everything.*

Is it fast? For her, maybe. But I've had eternity to find a connection like this. I know what I feel. I trust it. And I'm not going to shy away from it.

Perhaps, it'll be temporary.

Perhaps, it'll be for eternity.

But as her palms skim my thighs, I hope for the latter. Because *fuck*, that feels good. *So. Fucking. Good.*

My tattoos warm in response, swirling along my skin and creating a pleasant hum. Her eyes widen a little, telling me she feels it, too. When she notices the way the smoky lines whirl and move along my shaft, her fingertips pause.

"I told you I would show you what my tattoos can do," I tell her, amused by the way she's studying my arousal. "Stroke me, trouble. *Feel* me."

Because I want to demonstrate my power against her palm, make her realize just what I'll be able to do once I'm inside her.

She visibly shivers, then drifts her touch upward to tentatively trace one of the tattooed lines. When it moves, she yanks her hand back. But then narrows her eyes and touches me again. Bolder now. *Hotter.* Her lips part when my tattoos react to her exploration. "Oh," she breathes, her cheeks reddening. "*Oh.*"

I smile. "You asked about my gifts, Sera. I told you I can make others feel whatever I desire. Pain… pleasure…" I increase the frequency and add, "*Ecstasy.*"

Her eyes practically roll into the back of her head, her nipples beading tightly, her body so flushed with arousal that I sit up and grab her hips before she can fall off of me. "*Maliki*," she says, her chest suddenly heaving.

A chuckle leaves me as I pull her up my legs and onto my lap. She releases my shaft in the process and grabs my shoulders, her overexcited state leaving her beautifully submissive beneath my touch.

"Wrap your legs around my waist," I tell her softly.

She obeys, lost to the vibrations my body is releasing to hers.

It's not a purr. It's something better.

Or, at least, *I* think it's better.

And the way she's pushing into me now suggests she agrees.

"Reach down and part your pussy lips for me," I tell her. "I want you to feel my tattoos against your clit."

Her lashes flutter, the only indication that my command is registering through the haze of lust likely overtaking her mind.

She hasn't orgasmed yet.

But my tattoos certainly put her on the edge.

Now I'm going to drive her over that cliff and thrust her into oblivion.

Sera grabs my shoulder with one hand, then slips her opposite palm downward, just like I told her to do, and spreads herself for me.

"Good girl," I praise, my palms still on her hips. "Now prepare yourself, Sera. This is going to be intense."

Her eyes widen just a little, but I don't give her time to reconsider. This is still an introduction. And it's not like I'm going to fuck her in this state.

She needs to be warmed up. Stretched. *Prepared*.

This is just about pleasure. *Her* pleasure.

And… mine, too.

I jerk her up against me, causing her to gasp as my

cock perfectly aligns with her cunt. It's an intimate kiss that allows her to feel how large I am, because her clit is against my shaft, not the head. Her eyes widen, then her lashes flutter again as my tattoos do their job.

A scream leaves her, the orgasm almost instantaneous.

It makes me wonder if she's ever used a vibrator before. I'm guessing not. But now she has her own personal toy—one I'll let her use whenever and however she desires.

"Maliki," she pants, her thighs tightening around my waist as the sensations increase.

"Embrace it," I tell her, upping the pressure and holding her as she comes undone again.

She grabs hold of me with both hands now, her nails digging into my skin as she falls apart in my lap. I groan in kind, her slick coating my cock in a rapturous invitation.

It takes restraint not to flip her onto the bed and drive into her needy cunt.

But she's not ready for me yet.

However, I absolutely indulge myself by guiding her hips against mine and sliding through her damp folds. Vibrating her clit some more. Soaking my shaft. Feeling the reward of my actions through the warmth of her pussy.

"Shadows," I whisper, my lips hovering near hers. "You feel fucking phenomenal. I'm going to need you to keep coming for me, Sera." I apply even more pressure, my tattoos increasing their reverberations to intensify her pleasure.

She tries to pull away from me, her panting turning violent.

But I don't release her hips. I hold her in place. "Endure it, Sera. Take every second of this climax and understand how much more I intend to give you. Because this is only the beginning for us. I'm going to keep you in a state of arousal for hours."

And I mean it.

She's going to keep coming until she passes out.

Because *fuck*, this feels so good.

I'm not even inside her, and I'm content to simply exist with her pussy gushing against my cock.

"*Maliki*," she says, my name sounding like a curse on her tongue.

"That's right, trouble," I murmur against her mouth. "That's my cock making you come just by *touching* you."

Her nails bite into my skin so intently that I begin to bleed.

But I don't fucking care.

She feels too good on my lap for me to stop.

And I tell her that with my tongue as I kiss her deeply, forcing her to accept this, to accept us, to accept *me*.

By the time I'm done introducing her to my talents, she's quivering as violently as my tattoos, and I lay her out on the bed.

Then I lick a path down her sweet form, pausing at her tits before continuing to the prize below.

"Oh, pretty mystery, your clit is fucking swollen," I tell her before tenderly stroking the source of her pleasure.

She bows off the bed, but I hold her down with my hand against her stomach.

"Shh," I hush her. "I'm going to kiss it better."

"*Thorns*," she hisses when I seal my mouth around her.

She grabs my hair, yanking at my head, but I'm not stopping until I'm satisfied. She tastes too good and feels too amazing for me to consider pausing now.

I lick her deep.

Kiss her.

Lick her again.

Suckle her.

And smile when she starts to pant just like before.

Hades once told me about an Omega's penchant for coming on repeat, how they're practically insatiable while in heat, and I'm seeing how true those claims were now.

Because Sera is no longer trying to pull me away. She's practically pushing me against her pussy and demanding *more*.

I slide two fingers into her to apply some pressure and drive her toward oblivion with my tongue against her clit.

By the time she's falling apart again, she's barely coherent.

So I climb back up her body and kiss her for a while, allowing her to recover from the intensity, and simply indulge my need to be close to her. To hold her. To *worship* her.

It's such a bizarre need. So unique to her. Yet I've never felt more important than I do right now as she clings to me. It's like I'm her source of life. Her anchor in this reality. Her one true path.

And I fucking love being that for her.

Protecting her goes beyond the desire to guard her. It's about ensuring her happiness, too. Pleasuring her. *Making her smile up at me like she is right now...*

"You look lust-drunk," I murmur, amused as she presses against me like a content little kitten.

"I want to make you lust-drunk, too," she says, sounding sleepy and a tad delirious. "Can I lick your cock, Maliki? Taste you?"

My eyebrow wings upward. "You never have to ask permission to lick me, trouble. I'm yours to touch and fondle and play with as you wish."

She smiles, her eyes closing. "Mmm, 'kay."

I chuckle. "Something tells me you're not going to stay awake long enough to properly play with me."

She nods. "Mm-hmm. Soon. Maybe. Yes."

My lips twitch. "Okay, sweet mystery."

She yawns. "I'm going to…" She trails off, nuzzling into me. "Make you… come… too."

"Whatever you want," I tell her.

"'Kay," she replies groggily, yawning again. "Soon."

My tattoos shift into something more soothing, the need to comfort her overriding every other instinct.

Which naturally has my dick aching in protest.

But we'll make time to play after she wakes up.

And if she still wants to lick me then, I'll indulge her.

However, until then, I'll hold her while she sleeps.

I close my eyes with her, reveling in the moment.

Only to stir a second later as a familiar presence enters the room.

I don't look at him, though. I keep my eyes closed as I ask, "Did you enjoy watching me play with your wife?" Because I have no doubt Hades was lurking nearby throughout the entire exchange. Though, I didn't think about him once.

Bloody voyeur.

"Yes," he says. "And also no."

My lips twitch. "Sounds right. Are you going to punish me now?"

"Was a potential punishment what held you back from fucking her?" he asks.

I finally peek at him, not at all surprised to find him standing right beside the bed with his hands in the pockets of his dress slacks. "I didn't fuck her because we're still getting to know each other," I tell him. "It had nothing to do with you."

He considers me for a moment. "It's not like you to move slowly with a lover."

"Sera is more than just a lover," I counter.

The comment has his lips curling. "I know. She's our mate." He cocks his head. "So, no, Maliki. I'm not going to castigate you for treating her right. But I fully accept your punishment for the way I've treated her thus far."

I frown at him. "You want me to punish you?"

"You already are," he tells me. "Watching you play together brings me great pleasure, and significant pain." He winces a bit. "Which is why I need to talk to Morpheus."

I arch a brow at him, curious as to what he means by that.

But before I can ask, he says, "Keep her happy, Maliki. I'm going to try to do the same." With that cryptic comment, he vanishes.

I sigh. "The mandate was unnecessary," I tell him, aware that he's long gone and can't hear me. "Sera's pleasure is my main priority now. Which makes her my boss, not you."

Not that Hades was ever actually my boss.

But the words needed to be said regardless.

Even if he didn't actually hear them.

Though, I swear I hear a snort from the shadows. Perhaps from Hades. Maybe from his beast.

Regardless, I've said what I wanted to say.

Now all that matters is keeping Sera warm and safe while she rests.

And being ready for her when she wakes...

HADES

A Few Minutes Earlier

MY BLOOD SIMMERS, THE SOUNDS OF SERAPINA'S ECSTASY making me so fucking hard that I nearly reveal my presence.

But I can't join them.

Not this time.

It'll ruin the moment. And I don't want to intrude.

Fuck, I shouldn't even be here.

Except, no. That's not true. This is *my* maze. And that's *my* bed. The one I created for Persephone to nest in.

Only, this isn't Persephone.

Watching Serapina come undone against Maliki's cock, and again with his mouth, just further drives that point home.

However, the Goddess on the bed holds me captive. This reincarnation of my mate is… *stunning.*

I always loved watching Persephone fall apart, but Serapina is a whole new experience. She's innocent, yet bold. Curious, yet confident. And the way she submitted to Maliki was nothing short of extraordinary.

Because she didn't just succumb to his desires. She *joined* him. She allowed him to lead, all while playing an equal part.

This woman is a fucking queen.

And I want to bury my knot so far inside her that she tastes my claim for *years*.

It's a visceral need that has me struggling to remain in the in-between.

I can *feel* her pleasure, the beacon of it riding my soul and causing my inner beast to growl in response. It's a feral reaction, one driven by the desire to mate.

She's mine.

My soul's other half.

My Omega.

Yet, she hasn't chosen me. Her spirit may be linked to mine, but the physical entity—*Serapina*—isn't truly mine.

And that knowledge undoes something inside me. Something painful. Something that nearly brings me to my fucking knees.

I've never felt this sort of agony before, this notion of *separation*. My heart is practically torn in two. And my soul feels *lost*.

My mate is right in front of me, but she's not mine to claim.

Because I haven't earned her desire.

Which is my own fucking fault.

Serapina screams again, her euphoria washing over me in a blissful caress that ends in a blistering burn.

A burn that heightens when I watch her seeking comfort from Maliki.

Not me. Not an Alpha. *Not her mate.*

And I realize I can sense all of it. The pleasure she's experiencing, the satisfaction, and the renewing need deep inside her.

She's my Omega. We're linked, even if only on a soul level, and my inner beast is aware of every second.

Her heat is going to kill me, I think.

If she doesn't choose me, or accept me, I'll have to lock myself away, or I'll end up in a rut.

Because all I want to do is go to her now, worship her between her thighs, and give her the knot she craves.

And that intrinsic need will only worsen when she's in a full-blown estrus.

Fuck, how did Morpheus stand this? I wonder, my hands curling into fists at my sides. He had to have felt this every time I was with Persephone.

Yet he never interfered, despite their obvious link—a link I've only just begun to acknowledge. But he's proved it existed then, just as it does now.

Which means he went through unthinkable agony every time he couldn't answer Persephone's mating needs.

Serapina nuzzles into Maliki, the tenderness tugging at my heart.

It should be *my* chest she's nuzzling into right now, her inner Omega seeking *my* purr.

However, it's Maliki she's talking to now.

Maliki that she's falling asleep on.

Maliki with the taste of my mate's cunt on his tongue.

I want to know her this way, too. Lick her deep. Feel her clit throb against my lips. Make her clench around my knot. *Kiss her while I fuck her.*

Everything about this craving feels new.

Mostly because I want to do those things… while Maliki helps please her.

Have him inside her ass while I take her pussy.

Or maybe watch her suck his cock while I take her from behind.

This notion of group play is foreign, yet it provokes a yearning deep inside me, one I refuse to ignore.

I've never wanted to *share.*

But Maliki has changed everything.

Serapina, too.

And maybe even Morpheus.

I clear my throat, aware that Serapina is sleeping now.

Maliki has his eyes closed as well, but I know he's awake. He won't leave our mate undefended. Not that this labyrinth can be penetrated.

We're all safe here.

Which Serapina just proved with her multiple orgasms. No Alphas came running. No one intruded.

Only me.

As I watched from the shadows.

Shadows I step out of now as I materialize in the room.

"Did you enjoy watching me play with your wife?" Maliki asks, obviously sensing my presence. Though, he doesn't look at me, his body still utterly relaxed despite the sensuality of his question.

Did I enjoy watching him play with my wife? I think. "Yes. And also no." Because it hurt. *A lot.*

I don't get a chance to elaborate on that since Maliki's next question is about punishment. It confuses me. I invited him to join my mate-circle. Why would I punish him?

It makes me wonder if perhaps that's why he didn't try to fuck Serapina—something I half expected him to do, given their aroused states. Though, I'm somewhat relieved he didn't. I don't think I could have stayed at that point; I would have needed to see more. To be part of the moment.

Maliki, however, surprises me by saying he held back because he's still getting to know Serapina. It's not like him to go slow, something I point out.

And he states the obvious back to me: "Sera is more than just a lover."

I smile. "I know. She's our mate." The wording is intentional, a way to remind him that she is *ours* because we're a mate-circle now. But in case he needs more elaboration, I also clarify that I have no intention of punishing him for pleasing Serapina.

Keeping her happy is our priority.

And I've failed that priority.

Which is why I'm the one who has earned damnation. I accept that.

"You want me to punish you?" Maliki asks, after I infer as much aloud.

"You already are," I tell him. "Watching you play together brings me great pleasure, and significant pain." I wince as my words remind me of something I need to do. "Which is why I need to talk to Morpheus." Because if anyone will understand this agony, it's him.

And knowing I caused him some of this torment has left me feeling a bit… uneasy.

"Keep her happy, Maliki," I say. "I'm going to try to do the same." *By talking to Morpheus*, I think. Though, I don't add that out loud, just return to the in-between.

"The mandate was unnecessary," I hear Maliki say, even though he knows I've disappeared. "Sera's pleasure is my main priority now. Which makes her my boss, not you."

I snort in response, amused by his commentary.

I've never been your boss, Maliki, I think at him.

Then truly vanish and go in search of my cousin for a long-overdue conversation.

SERA

I'M DREAMING AGAIN.

Or maybe I never woke up and everything with Maliki was a dream, too. I'm not quite sure. What he did to me with his tattoos certainly felt like a fantasy.

And this… this is surreal.

Clouds. Flowers. The scent of a morning mist.

It's everywhere.

Yet nothing is familiar.

I feel lost. Alone. *Desolate.*

Like I'm trapped in a maze…

The thought makes me frown. *Am I in Hades's labyrinth?*

I spin around, noting the fog and lifeless walls. There are skulls everywhere, the faces etched into the cement-like corridors.

I shiver.

This place isn't as beautiful as I thought. It's… it's *death.*

"Hades?" I whisper, searching for him. "Are you… hunting me?"

The question sends a jolt down my spine. If this is real, then perhaps my heat is about to begin. Maybe I'm supposed to run.

But I... I don't feel like being chased. He said an Omega likes to test her potential mates. Shouldn't I want to—

Movement from the corner of my eye grabs my attention as a blue cloak scurries past me. "Pip!" I cry out in relief.

Only... only, he doesn't stop or face me. He just scampers off and around a corner.

"Hey!" I chase after him, confused and a little miffed that he didn't acknowledge me. That isn't like him at all.

When I turn the bend, I see him floating off in a hurry, like he's running from something.

Is he trying to guide me out of this maze? I wonder. *Has something happened?*

The urgent sway of his cloak makes me pursue him, my steps growing faster as he picks up speed. "Pip!" I try again. "Wait!"

He's practically sprinting now, winding us through the hazy labyrinth and dragging me deeper into the murky darkness.

Only to halt at a solid black wall decorated with intricate symbols. I stare at it, mesmerized by the magic pouring off the barricade.

"What is this, Pip?" I ask as he studies the barrier.

He doesn't respond. Not that he usually talks, but he often tries to communicate with gestures.

Instead, all he does is touch the engravings with a gloved hand.

I take a tentative pace forward, my own hand lifting as I try to understand what he's doing. "Pip," I start, then notice a strange flickering in his robe.

It's… it's not the right blue color. It's tarnished and a bit black.

My brow furrows, and my hand starts to drop to my side. Something isn't right. This isn't—

The creature grabs my wrist and yanks me forward, forcing me to touch the enchanted barrier just as a pair of big red eyes meets mine from beneath the hood.

A scream bursts from my throat, the sound echoing all around me as the world fades into a dark oblivion.

And then there's nothing.

No maze. No black wall. No engravings. *No Pip.*

It's just a dark abyss, one that lacks sensation and makes me feel even more lost than before.

My lips part as I try to scream again. But noise doesn't exist here. Not even air appears to be present. It's simply a vapid cavern.

A chill skitters up my spine. This feels very real. Too real.

Am I awake? Do I even exist?

The latter thought stirs an ache inside me, one that has me shivering.

Except that I no longer have skin. Or bone. Or *anything.*

It's like I'm a soul.

Wait… My eyebrows lift. *Is this… is this how Persephone feels?*

Did we switch places?

Is she corporeal now?

And I… I'm here?

Is that even possible?

I spin around. Or I think I do, anyway. But I feel nothing. Sense nothing. *Am nothing.*

I have no mouth to open. No vocal cords to use for a scream. No arms to wave. No legs to run with.

I… I don't exist here.

How does one escape from a void?

All I have is my thoughts. My mind. My yearnings. My *wants*.

It's like the worst form of a prison. Terrifying. Cold. *Lonely*.

Frigid sensations overwhelm me, freezing me from deep within.

It's debilitating. Paralyzing. *Horrifying*.

I experienced fear on the Day of the Choosing, the moment my name was called.

However, this… this is true terror.

If this is a nightmare, then surely Morpheus will free me from it.

But this doesn't feel like a dream anymore.

This feels very real.

And I'm pretty sure waking up isn't an option.

"It's chilling, isn't it?" a feminine voice murmurs against my ear. "A prison unlike any other. One where the souls are trapped for eternity and guarded by the God of Wrath."

I try to turn around, to *see* the source of those words.

Because I know that cultured tone. It's similar to the accents spoken by Morpheus and Hades, only haughtier somehow.

It's the same voice that used to call me "Daughter."

"Alina subjected me to this fate. After all I've done for Omega kind, it's truly a disheartening experience. And then there's you, my own daughter, betraying me with *him*."

Her tone takes a frigid turn, the coldness inside me seeming to spread through every inch of my being.

"How *dare* you return to him," she says. "After all I've shown you, all I've done for you." She tsks, the sound reminding me of metal scraping against stone. "And you let him touch you?"

Wind whirls around me, the sensation both welcome and unnerving. Welcome because I can finally feel something other than an icy sense of nothingness. And unnerving because it's unworldly in nature. Angry, too.

"You deserve this fate, Persephone," Demeter goes on. "It's a lesson you need to learn. Alphas are monsters. They'll take you against your will. Do unfathomable things to you. I tried to save you, sweetheart. I did. But you chose this. You chose *him*."

The wind heightens, a rush of power washing over me. It's hot and unfamiliar. A kiss of lively electricity, one that sets my veins on fire.

A scream echoes in my mind, the agony razor-sharp as the heat threatens to burn me alive.

Only for a kiss of cold magic to calm the flames.

Demeter growls, the reverberation deep and intimidating. "What is this?" she demands.

But I can't answer.

I have no mouth. No corporeal form. No identity.

I am simply a mixture of fiery intensity and ice.

Cold bands wrap around me, yanking me out of the void and into the maze.

Demeter's roar follows close behind as flames erupt all around me in a blinding flash of brilliant light.

I lift my hands to shield my eyes, only vaguely aware that I'm me again. Human. *Corporeal.*

And then everything stills, the silence reminding me of the abyss.

A sob escapes me, the notion of being nothing again chilling me to my very core.

"Sera," Maliki breathes, his voice and presence the most welcome experience of my existence.

I lower my hands to find him hovering over me, his dark brows angled downward in concern.

I don't think; I react, and throw my arms around his neck, needing to feel him, to ensure he's really here. That I'm safe. Not lost. Not alone. *Not forgotten.*

"Is this real?" I ask, desperate to be told I'm awake. I still exist. *I'm here.*

"Yeah, trouble, this is real," he replies, his fingers threading through my hair as he hugs me against his bare chest.

He's naked.

I'm naked.

Everything is warm.

Everything is tangible.

Everything is okay.

I press my face into his neck and breathe him in, indulging in his leather scent tinged with smoke. Though, the latter smells stronger now, like he's wrapped me up in his smokelike tattoos.

"What happened, Sera?" he asks. "Why did you get so hot?"

My shoulders stiffen. "I felt hot to you?"

"Like you were burning up with a fever," he replies, his fingers combing through my hair. "I had to cool you down with my shadows."

My eyes widen. "The bands…" It was Maliki's cool power that I felt wrap around me.

But that… that means it was all real.

How is that possible?

"Bands?" Maliki prompts.

"In my nightmare. Dream. Whatever that was…" I trail off and swallow. "I dreamt that I was nothing, just a soul. And Demeter was there."

I proceed to tell him everything I can remember, from the Pip look-alike to the words Demeter said to me.

"You probably think I sound crazy," I say at the end.

But he shakes his head. "No. I don't think you were dreaming at all. And I don't think it's a coincidence that this happened after you experienced pleasure again. There's something linking you to Demeter." He cups my cheek. "When Hades returns, we need to tell him about this."

I swallow and nod. "Okay." Then I frown. "Where is he?"

Maliki's lips curl a little. "Oh, he's talking to Morpheus."

My eyebrows fly upward. "What?"

His smile grows. "I think your mate may have learned how to share…"

MORPHEUS

A Few Minutes Earlier

I slam my fist into the nearest figment, the dreamlike creature one I manifested specifically for this purpose.

The problem is, since I created it, the being hits back.

Because I like a challenge.

And today, I need that challenge more than usual.

Which is also why my figment resembles Hades. Because fuck my cousin. And fuck his possessiveness.

Serapina is just as much mine as she is his.

Waking her up right when I'm about to make her come.

Fucking low blow.

I punch my version of his face, then swing around to hit him again as he appears behind me.

Only, the very harsh impact of my fist meeting bone

sends pain up my arm. "*Fuck*," I mutter. My mind has gotten too good at this.

"Okay. I deserved that. But hit me again and I will hit back," Hades says, his cool tone far too real to be a creation of my mind.

I straighten, then strike him again for good measure.

He growls.

I growl.

And the world rumbles beneath us as our powers manifest, our inner beasts ready to battle for dominance.

"It wasn't enough that you had to finish what I started? Help her get off after waking her so abruptly from her dream?" Because yeah, I felt that orgasm.

And the several that followed.

"You've come here to gloat?" I guess, not giving him the chance to answer before shoving a bolt of energy directly into his mind.

For just a second, I want him to experience my pain. My agony. The very real torment of once again feeling my mate's need and not being allowed to answer her call.

"*Morpheus*," Hades hisses.

I ignore him and yank him even deeper into the pit of despair I've crafted from my personal experience, forcing him to face the truth. The hurt. The *torture*.

His face contorts, the sight one I've yearned to see for so long that I give myself more than the promised second and instead allow it to go on for a handful of beats.

Then I release him with a sigh and turn to walk away. "Go gloat somewhere else, Hades."

Because I'm not fucking interested.

His responding growl echoes in my wake as I mist back to my palace.

Not the one in the Morpheus Kingdom, but my true home in the Mythos Fae Realm.

Athena appears with me on the balcony, her starry eyes scanning for any threats. I acknowledge her with a nod and start toward my bedroom doors when she squawks out a loud warning.

I spin just as Hades appears in a wave of shadows and darkness. I gape at him, shocked that he dared to enter my domain.

A domain he rarely ever visited even millennia ago.

"Wow, I had no idea gloating meant this much to you," I say, folding my arms. "By all means, then, Hades, brag to your heart's content."

I don't bother holding back on my sarcasm. He has a lot of fucking nerve showing up in *my* palace to taunt me with words about *my* mate.

Maybe he craves death, I think. *After all, he is the God of Death.*

"Maliki pleasured her, not me," he informs me. "And for the first time in my existence, I somewhat understand your plight."

Athena walks over and pecks Hades on the head, earning her a warning snarl from the Alpha.

I ignore her antics, aware that she's merely doing her job as my familiar and expressing my frustration. It's not like she attacked him. Not really.

"Fuck off," he says to my majestic owl.

She snaps her orange beak in response, her silver and gray feathers flaring as she flaps her massive wings.

"Morpheus." Hades sounds exasperated. "Tell your bird to back off."

"She's an owl," I reply. "And no."

Athena can do whatever the fuck she wants. This is *our* home, not his.

"I came here to apologize," he says through his teeth. "And to have a real conversation."

"So just because you're finally ready to discuss our mate, I have to be amenable and receptive?" I ask, purposely being difficult. Mostly because I'm shocked that he's here. But also because he deserves my ire.

Maybe Maliki pleased our mate this time.

But he wasn't around with Persephone. Hades was. And those years were hell for me to endure.

Yet I did. *For her.*

But our Omega wants me now. I'm sure of it. So I won't be enduring this pain any longer.

"She's mine, Hades," I tell him. "End of discussion." I step through the curtains framing my balcony and enter my rooms.

And Hades mists inside.

Athena releases a loud squawk, clearly disapproving of his antics. "She's *ours*," he tells me flatly.

I huff a laugh. "How many times have I said that?"

"Too many," he returns. "And I'm still struggling to accept it. But I'm here, Morpheus. I'm trying to make this right."

"For you or for Serapina?" I wonder aloud.

"Do you think I want to share her with you?"

"I know you don't," I reply.

"Then clearly this is for her," he says, his hands slipping into the pockets of his slacks. "She... she worried that it was wrong to play with Maliki after dreaming of you. And that sadness, that misunderstanding of her needs..." He looks away. "I'm aware that I've failed as her Alpha, Morpheus. I'm here to correct a wrong."

My eyebrow arches upward. But I don't speak. I've said more than enough over the millennia. It's his turn now.

Hades's jaw clenches. "You're not going to make this easy on me, are you?"

"Likely about as easy as you've made this for me," I admit.

He studies me for a long moment. "What about Serapina?"

It's a quiet question, one I understand instantly. He's asking if I'll forgive him for our Omega.

Or perhaps *forgive* is too strong a word.

He's asking if I'll reconsider my stance… for Serapina.

"I would suffer another eternity of loneliness if it pleased her," I say, miffed that he even had to ask. "Forgiving you—or whatever you want to call this—would be a simple concession. If that's *her* desire."

"I think her desire is for me to let you into the labyrinth." His response is soft, like he's having a hard time accepting her wishes but is willing to set aside his discomfort if it means pleasing her.

Which is how an Alpha should respond.

And exactly how I'll react, if that's what my mate needs. "Did she ask for me?"

"She asked if I could manifest you and Maliki in the maze," Hades tells me with a wince. "Then she asked if I would hold that request against her."

"Are you truly surprised?" I wonder aloud. "You've made your possessive claim crystal clear, Hades."

His jaw ticks. "I would never begrudge her for anything."

"But she doesn't know that."

"Clearly," he deadpans. "She's completely misunderstood me."

"Can—"

He holds up his hand, cutting me off. "Her misunderstanding me is my fault. As I said, I've failed her as an Alpha. But you haven't. She seems to trust you. And while it pains me to say this, she's going to need you during her heat."

I stare at him. "If she asks me to knot her, I will."

He stares right back at me. "I know."

"I'll claim her, too."

"I know," he repeats.

"And you expect me to believe that you'll be okay with that?" I demand.

His expression tells me he won't be okay at all. Yet, aloud, all he says is "Serapina's needs are my priority. She wants you in the labyrinth. So I'll grant you entry."

I study him, noting the stiff lines of his shoulders and the not-so-subtle tic in his jaw.

He doesn't want to accept me into his circle, let alone into the maze. But he's putting Serapina's comfort before his own.

As a good Alpha should.

"Will you come with me?" Hades asks, a note of exhaustion in his tone. "She needs to be properly cared for. And I trust you to succeed where I've failed."

That's not an apology. But for Hades, it's pretty much the same thing.

"Where will you be while I 'care' for her?" I use his term, though we both know there's another meaning behind the word.

"I'll... I'll either control my urges or lock myself up."

A snort escapes me. "Control is impossible when your mate is in heat and releasing her mating call." I take a step toward him, curious about whether he's even thought this through. "Do you know what I had to do every time Persephone fell into an estrous cycle?"

The way he looks at me tells me he doesn't know at all, that he probably hasn't even considered that aspect of my plight.

"I felt the pain today watching her with Maliki," he grits out. "I can handle it."

I laugh humorlessly. "Oh, Cousin, that's only a fraction of the agony you'll experience. And you were able to watch, which would have taken out some of the sting as well."

Fuck, I would have loved to observe Hades and Persephone during even just one of her cycles. It would have hurt, yes. But simply knowing my mate was taken care of properly would have soothed some of the burn.

"You'll be a slave to her call when the time comes, Hades. Knowing someone else is there to care for her won't be enough. Our beasts live to serve our mates. To not be allowed or accepted to do so is the most agonizing form of punishment you could ever imagine."

He doesn't respond right away, his gaze assessing. "If that's true, then how did you keep yourself from misting to Persephone's side?"

I smile, but it's not a kind grin. It's one born of exquisite pain. "Ares helped me."

Hades's nostrils flare.

It doesn't take much thought to understand what I'm telling him.

Still, he utters the translation aloud by saying, "You spent time in Pandora's Box."

"Yes." I don't elaborate beyond adding, "It was the only place that could throttle my abilities."

He has the grace to glance away, his throat working to swallow.

Whether that's a response to his pending fate or a sign of guilt, I'm not sure. Something tells me it's the former more than the latter.

Hades will never apologize for claiming Persephone. She was his.

But perhaps he'll have more compassion in regard to Serapina. Or at least understand why I refuse to go through that agony again.

He clears his throat. "I suppose it's my due."

"Is it?" I wonder aloud. "Because of how you've treated Serapina?"

Rather than acknowledge my question, he says, "I need to rewrite the maze barrier, then you'll be able to enter. It won't take me long." He starts to mist, but I grab his arm.

"I'm coming with you," I tell him.

The look he gives me expresses extreme discomfort with that idea.

"Being a mate-circle means collaborating," I tell him. "And collaboration requires forgiveness. If you want to please our mate, you'll need to learn how to work as a team."

He narrows his gaze, and I have no doubt he's about to tell me that he doesn't need a lecture on how to please "his" mate.

But he surprises me by shaking off my hold and grabbing my wrist. "Fine" is all he says, his misting ability wrapping around me as he takes me with him to the Netherworld Kingdom.

I glance around the Soul Yards, my eyebrow inching upward. Hades escorted us to the dead center, right next to one of the geyser-like holes.

He releases me to glance over the edge, then jerks back just as a swarm of deadly energy blasts into the sky. "I hate entering this way," he mutters, shuddering as a chill swirls through the air in the wake of the explosion.

Then his black wings burst from his back and flare wide, his beast instantly present as he transitions into Alpha mode. He looks at me with equally dark eyes.

"You wanted to *collaborate*." With those ominous words,

he shrugs and jumps into the hole that the souls just shot up out of.

"*Fuck.*" I call upon my inner Alpha, my wings appearing in an instant with a flourish of wind. "This had better not be a trick, Hades."

He doesn't reply.

So I sigh.

And follow my cousin into the hole.

MALIKI

Sera sits across from me at the table, her expression thoughtful as she tries the cinnamon roll I just conjured up in Hades's enchanted kitchen.

Or I guess it's *our* enchanted kitchen now.

I'm not quite sure how all this mate-circle Styx is supposed to work, but we'll figure it out.

"Thank you," Sera says after taking a sip of the hot chocolate I magicked up for her. It has a hint of cinnamon in it because that's the way I prefer to make it at home. As I created a sample for myself, I know the enchantment crafted the drink correctly, and I'm pleased Sera likes it.

"You're welcome, trouble," I tell her.

She's wearing a tank top and black pants, the clothes ones she found when we went to explore the closet. The outfit simply appeared for her, just like everything else in this place.

Meanwhile, I stole a pair of Hades's pants.

Or perhaps those, too, were *manifested*.

"This place is like living in a dream," I muse aloud. "Even the decorations are appropriate." I glance at the skulls and bones etched into the walls. "At least, it suits my tastes." Not so sure about Sera's, though.

Her lips curl a little. "I know Hades built this maze to punish Persephone, but I actually find it kind of beautiful."

My eyebrow lifts. "Did you tell him that?"

"Yes."

I grin. "And how did he take it?"

"He seemed surprised." Her nose crinkles. "Maybe a little confused, too."

"Good. He deserves a little confusion after existing in a constant state of arrogance for eons. Maybe he'll learn something useful." In truth, I believe he already has, but I don't add that out loud. Time will show us what Hades has truly learned.

Regardless, I hope he returns soon, as I want to discuss Sera's vision because I don't believe for a second that what happened to her was a dream. Morpheus would never allow his intended Omega to experience a nightmare, especially not one where she felt like she didn't exist.

My teeth grind together at the notion of Sera being lost in a spiritual state. I know she's wondering if that's what has happened to Persephone, but I refuse to believe that. They're the same person, or being, or whatever. Sera is a reincarnation of Persephone's spirit.

I don't know what all that entails. However, I do know it won't end in us losing Sera. Because I will chase her to the depths of the obsidian void to bring her back.

"Do you—"

A crash from outside cuts Sera off, the interruption followed by a fierce growl from Ossa.

Up until now, the beast was slumbering in the living area. Not anymore. With a blink, the three-headed creature disappears, and a snarl erupts just outside the door.

Followed by a screeching meow.

My eyebrow lifts as I push away from the table. "Hmm." That meow was from Fleur. I didn't even realize she was here, but it makes sense that she followed me into the maze.

The scurrying of paws greets my ears when I reach the front door.

I jump back upon opening it, sighing when a ball of fluff comes rolling inside.

Ossa releases a furious noise while Mort thrashes his head.

"Drop it," I demand, recognizing the feathery limbs and furry legs sticking out from his large jaw.

Mort's ears perk up, his big gold eyes glittering as he meets my gaze. I stare him down, asserting my dominance, which causes Ossa to grumble her discontent.

"Now," I tell Mort.

The giant creature sighs, then spits out my familiar in an obsidian ball of slobber, feathers, and fur. Fleur screeches and tries to fly but can't since she's covered in wolfish drool.

"*Thorns*," Sera breathes, rushing forward to scoop my cat up in her arms. "Oh!" She looks horrified. "How do we help it?"

Fleur releases a mewl that echoes through the room, her agony overexaggerated and meant to attract all the pity in the world.

I snort. "Drama queen."

Sera's eyes widen. "*What?*"

"I'm talking to Fleur, trouble, not you." I move forward to give Mort a good scratch behind the ear, ensuring he knows I'm not upset with him for turning my familiar into a chew toy, then step in front of Sera.

Who is now cradling my whimpering sphinx.

"Wow," I say, drawing out the word for Fleur's benefit. "Keep crying like that and Ossa is going to declare herself as the superior beast."

The female in question growls, clearly already considering herself to be the *superior* one of the two.

Meanwhile, Fleur starts to rub against Sera, all while making more of those pathetic sounds.

I fold my arms. "Mort didn't even bite you. There's no blood. Just slobber and a few broken feathers. You're fine."

"Her wings are bent at odd angles, Maliki," Sera interjects. "And she's shaking like she's traumatized."

I huff a laugh. "She's being a drama queen so you'll baby her. She's fine."

Sera narrows her gaze at me. "She doesn't *feel* fine, Maliki."

Fleur peeks up at me and gives me a look that's all triumph, causing me to roll my eyes. But another crash from outside keeps me from answering.

I shadow out there this time, on instant alert.

Only to shake my head when I see Pip trying to smooth out his torn robe. It looks like it's been shredded by claws. If he possessed eyebrows, I think they would be furrowed over the narrowed glow of his blue eyes.

I hum again, this time shadowing to the closet inside to magic up a new cloak, then return to Pip and hold it out. I may not be the cause of the damage, but my familiar is technically an extension of me. So, I owe him a new cloak.

He studies my offering, then points to the ground.

I set it there and go back inside, guessing that the little soul wants some privacy to change. Or whatever.

It's not like I would see much if he disrobed in front of me, just a blurry soul with skeletal features.

When I reenter, I find Sera on the couch with Fleur, petting her while cooing.

The victorious look Fleur gives me has me rolling my eyes again. She's milking the attention for all it's worth. "Enjoy it for now," I tell my familiar. "Once Sera sees how you treat Pip, she won't be so attentive."

Sera's brow crinkles as she looks up at me. "What?"

"Fleur is obsessed with Pip's cloak. I assume she was attacking him outside, which resulted in the first crash that caused Ossa, Mort, and Howl to react." A glance at Ossa confirms my assessment. The female's head is up, and the beast's chest is puffed out in pride. "They were protecting Pip from Fleur."

My sphinxlike cat gives me a look of utter betrayal.

"What?" I ask her. "Suddenly concerned you'll lose your new best friend?"

"You wouldn't attack Pip, would you?" Sera coos, running her fingernails through my cat's sleek black fur.

Fleur purrs and sets down her head, neither agreeing nor disagreeing with Sera's words.

But the moment Pip floats in through the still-open door, it's pretty clear where he stands on the topic of Fleur. He takes one look at the sphinx curled up in Sera's lap, widens his eyes, and goes right back outside.

Sera frowns. "Pip?"

He doesn't come back.

I lean against the wall, arms folded, and arch a brow. "Still falling for Fleur's act?" I wonder out loud. "Or are you going to go check on your familiar?"

Sera looks at me, then down at my purring cat. Fleur

appears to be exceptionally content, like she's found her utopia.

"She's not hurt," I promise Sera. "And even if she were, she would regenerate. But all Mort did was shake her around a little bit. He was playing. It's Ossa you need to worry about."

Ossa grunts in response. I can't tell if she's agreeing with me or mocking me. Regardless, I'm not wrong. I've been on the receiving end of her teeth more times than I would like to admit.

"Did you hurt Pip?" Sera asks quietly, the words for my cat. "Because if you did, that's not very nice. Pip is my friend."

Fleur stretches her front paws in an innocent gesture, but I note the way she flexes her talons. "She shredded his cloak. I just gave him a new one."

Sera's eyebrows lift as Fleur cuts me a glance that suggests she's plotting my murder.

"If I die, you die," I remind the little ball of obsidian. "And I don't think Sera would like it if you attacked me."

Fleur stares me down for a moment, then stands on her paws with a grace only she's capable of and casually leaps from Sera's lap to fly off toward the bedroom.

Sera gapes after her.

"I told you she was fine," I say, amused by Sera's surprise. "Fleur has nine million lives, give or take a few eons." I shrug. "She's as immortal as I am."

"Little trickster," Sera whispers.

"She's just an attention seeker." I push off the wall and whistle for Pip. "She's gone to take a nap, little soul!"

He doesn't immediately return but eventually sticks his head inside to look around. When he sees a cat-less Sera, he cautiously enters.

Mort gives the soul a lopsided smile, as does Howl. But Ossa simply lowers her head and closes her eyes.

The lack of a growl tells me the more dominant of the trio actually likes Pip. Otherwise, she would have released a sound of discontent.

Interesting.

"Are you mad at me?" Sera asks when Pip turns away from her.

He doesn't acknowledge her commentary at all, just floats off into the kitchen.

She scrambles after him. "I thought the cat was hurt!"

Pip huffs, the only evidence of the sound found in his fluttering robe and the way it billows around him.

I follow the pair with a chuckle, amused again.

"I didn't know she shredded your cloak, Pip," Sera says. "I'm sorry."

Pip glances back at her, his head cocked. Then he spins around and does a little dance, showing off his new robe. Or I assume that's what he's doing.

Sera giggles, the sound one that has my chest feeling a bit warmer than it should. But I don't overthink the reaction, simply embrace it, and walk over to the table to clean up our snack.

She says a few things to Pip while I work, the pair of them seeming to rekindle their bond in a matter of seconds, then she follows him outside, as he apparently wants to show her something.

Frowning, I trail after them, a bit concerned by this behavior, given her dream.

But all he does is lead her to a garden of flower statues and point to the one that looks like a fire lily.

Sera nods, saying she recognizes it as the one he's tried to bring for her before.

Then Pip holds up his hand, like he's telling her to wait

for a moment, and disappears. When he returns, he has his gloves on and the pot of soil from her Netherworld Village hut. We brought that to Hades's palace, but I haven't seen it since then.

However, Sera is thrilled to have it again. She carefully takes it from Pip and brings it inside to set on the dining table. Then she frowns and says, "I don't have any sunlight."

"Maybe we can try to manifest some?" I suggest.

She looks at me. "You think we can?"

I shrug. "Only one way to find out."

We're safe here for now. Might as well do something productive.

Because there isn't a chance in Styx that I'll be letting Sera sleep again anytime soon. Not until I've had a chance to talk to Hades about her supposed "nightmare."

Better hurry up, Hades, I think, aware that he can't actually hear me, but mentally talking to him anyway. *And if you can, bring the God of Dreams back here with you. I suspect that we're going to need him...*

HADES

SOMETHING'S WRONG.

I sense it the moment my feet touch the ground, the air all around me disturbed by an undesired presence.

Morpheus worsens that feeling when he lands beside me, his white wings a stark contrast to the obsidian rock around us. He resembles an angel descending from above, his silver hair a halo of glittering brightness, thanks to the candlelight flickering around us.

His wings beat once, the gold tips glistening like his hair, then the feathers disappear at his back. "You built a back entrance in the death pits?"

I grunt. "Not quite."

The magic is born of my powers, which are associated with death. Thus, this is where I come to access my creations.

But I don't explain any of that out loud.

He has his dream world to manage, and I own death. That's simply who we are.

To showcase that, I press my palm to the black wall and watch as a dozen runes light up, just like the candles did upon my descent to the lower levels of the Netherworld Kingdom.

This layer is only ever accessed by me and the dead souls being temporarily released for an exterior jaunt around the realms.

They all return eventually.

Either by choice or by force.

The death world calls to them naturally, drawing their essences back home in waves.

Unless, of course, one is resurrected.

But that's not why we're here. I just need access to my power, the energy flourishing in these walls enough to give me a boost.

Except that sensation of wrongness only grows.

"Do you feel that?" I ask Morpheus.

"The icy chill of death?" he asks. "Yes, Hades. I do. I believe it's coming from you."

I narrow my gaze. "So much for collaborating." Because clearly this was a waste of time.

"Collaboration typically involves communication, Cousin," Morpheus drawls as he folds his arms across his chest. "Tell me what you're sensing, and I can better comment."

The muscle in my jaw ticks. It would be so much easier to ignore him. However, I would be a fool to do so right now, especially as it involves Serapina's safety.

I may not like or want him to be involved in her life, but I can't deny his usefulness. He'll protect Serapina until his dying breath. Then regenerate and continue guarding her. Over and over again.

I know this because I feel the same way.

Which makes him a competitor… and, grudgingly, an ally.

"Hades?"

"Life," I tell him before he can say anything other than my name. "I sense *life*." Which shouldn't exist down here. This is my world. My creation. *My power*. So why does it feel *alive*?

Serapina possesses Persephone's soul, which suggests her link to a lively power. But she's still human.

So this isn't from her.

"Someone has been tampering with my energy," I go on before Morpheus can comment. "And there's only one Goddess powerful enough to do so."

"But she's locked up in Pandora's Box," Morpheus says, the words ones I was about to utter.

So I repeat them with a nod before adding, "Now tell me what you sense. Because I need to know if this is something only I'm noticing or if you feel it, too."

He considers me for half a beat before pressing his palm to the obsidian rock. His wince is the only indication that he feels uncomfortable, but I know that touching the chill of death has to hurt him more than most. He lives in a world of fantasies, his dreamland full of aspirations and desires.

My world is where those aspirations and desires come to die.

His cheekbones protrude as he clenches his teeth, showing a bit more of a disturbance now. However, as he pulls away to look at me, I know it's not death that upset him, but something else entirely…

"Demeter," he says, fury in his tone. "She's been here."

"How is that possible?"

He shakes his head. "I would have to ask Ares.

Though, I suspect he won't be of much use. This has something to do with Serapina and whatever Demeter did to her in the Monsters Night world."

I nod again, agreeing with him. "The timing isn't a coincidence, either. I just checked the walls before granting Maliki entry into the maze, and I didn't sense Demeter then. However, she somehow reached out…"

"After Serapina experienced pleasure," Morpheus says, finishing the statement for me. "I agree. The timing isn't coincidental."

At any other moment, I wouldn't appreciate how like-minded my cousin seems to be to me. But right now, I can't deny the usefulness.

"Be quick," Morpheus tells me, clearly aware of what I was about to say.

Thus, I don't even bother voicing my intention to go alter the maze. We need to check on Serapina immediately, which means we don't have another second to spare.

I have half a mind to go to her first, just to ensure she's okay, but I focus on my task. If there was an issue, my familiar would have alerted me. I also trust in Maliki's ability to protect our mate. He wouldn't even attempt to handle Demeter on his own; he would simply take Serapina and shadow.

He's not an arrogant fool. He's resourceful and intelligent. And I know he'll put our mate's safety first above all else.

He's been doing it for over a year.

Hence his challenging me at every turn.

It just took me too long to realize the intent and purpose of what he was doing, and what we had become over the centuries.

A mate-circle.

Well, I see it now.

And I'm... trying to embrace it.

Disappearing into my network of power, I visit the death world and search for the strands of energy protecting my intended's labyrinth.

A few of them are no longer black, but tinged with strands of white. *Life.*

They're not exactly visible or tangible, the roots ones I see inside my mind's eye more than in reality. Yet I touch them anyway, my power weaving through the damaged threads to dismantle the intrusion.

The foreign energy hisses at my dominance but slowly dies, a reaction I find exceptionally appropriate.

Then I weave in a new presence—one I never expected to invite into the sacred place I made for Persephone.

But I don't hesitate.

Mostly because I can't. Serapina requested Morpheus's presence, even went as far as to suggest it might be wrong to play with more than one mate. And I can't help but feel responsible for leading her to that assumption.

I never wanted to share Persephone, and she never expressed a desire to be shared.

However, Serapina is different. Perhaps because I ensured she met Maliki first. Or maybe because her soul was always meant to be protected by a circle of mates, not a single Alpha.

Which suggests I fucked up two thousand years ago.

My stomach churns at the notion that Morpheus has been right all along.

Persephone never wanted anyone else, I think as I add his presence to my magical web. *But I also never asked. Does that make me a bad Alpha? Selfish? Wrong?*

I swallow, not liking this trail of ponderment.

It's not useful.

There's nothing I can do to change the past, only the future.

And I'm... My hand hovers over the final enchantment, my eyes closing as I push Morpheus's presence into the wards. *I'm trying to make amends.*

Swallowing, I straighten my spine and turn to find my cousin standing right behind me.

His blue-green irises swirl with knowledge and understanding. "Apology accepted," he says softly. Then disappears before I can comment.

My jaw clenches. "I didn't apologize."

But there isn't time to argue the semantics. That's something Maliki enjoys more than I do. I prefer straightforward commentary and action.

Though, I won't shy away from the occasional riddle.

Shaking my head, I mist after Morpheus and find him standing in the middle of the maze, staring at the cabin I created for Persephone.

I anticipate his criticism, ready to accept his ridicule regarding the punishing labyrinth I designed. But rather than speak, he stares. And in a beat, I realize why.

He's not looking at the cabin at all, but at Serapina as she wanders the garden beside the home. Pip is floating along with her, and Maliki is leaning up against one of the pillars. His golden eyes meet mine in a flash, his expression informing me that he has something to tell me.

"What is it?" I ask him, not bothering to waste time on formalities. "Demeter?"

Serapina's head comes up, her blue eyes widening. Then her lips part upon seeing Morpheus standing beside me, and she drops whatever she was just holding—a stone flower, maybe?—and runs toward the God of Dreams.

My stomach twists when he holds out his arms and

catches her in a hug, the pair of them suddenly whirling just a few feet from where I stand.

It's alarming.

Frustrating.

Overwhelming.

Because I want to be the Alpha she runs to. The male she seeks shelter and peace from. The mate she *trusts*.

However, she looked at me with concern, then looked upon Morpheus with relief.

"How did you know?" Maliki asks, drawing my attention back to him as he walks toward us. He's wearing a pair of my pants—something I know because they're dressier than his usual preferences—and nothing else.

"We could sense her in the death pits," Morpheus says, answering for me.

"She touched my magic," I add, a subtle growl underlining my words. "We have no idea how. She's in Pandora's Box. Did you see her?"

Maliki shakes his head. "No. Sera, for lack of a better term, *dreamt* of her."

Morpheus freezes. "Not possible. I would never allow Demeter into my realm, nor would I permit her to reach out to Serapina."

Our mate is already shaking her head. "It felt like a dream at first, but then it turned… into a void."

I frown at her. "A void?" I share a glance with Morpheus, and he takes a step backward as I approach her. "Can you describe it?"

She reaches for Morpheus, like she wants him to save her from me.

It's a reaction that fucking burns.

But I don't have time to correct it now.

"This is really important," I tell Serapina, doing my best to gentle my tone. "Tell me what you mean by 'void'... please." The final word reluctantly leaves my mouth, the term not one I typically voice. However, it felt necessary.

And the subtle loosening of Serapina's shoulders confirms that my instinct was correct. "My dream started with Pip," she whispers.

Then proceeds to tell me how she chased him through the maze, only to realize it wasn't him.

"You touched the wall?" I ask, seeking clarification before she continues.

"Y-yes. Pip—or the thing pretending to be him— grabbed my wrist and forced me to."

I nod. "Okay, and then what happened?"

She swallows and goes on, saying how she fell into an abyss of darkness where she was nothing but soul. The sad way she speaks about the experience causes my purr to ignite, the need to soothe her overriding reason.

Serapina stills, her eyes drooping a little.

Morpheus moves to stand behind her, his hands on her hips as she leans back into him. He meets my gaze as he begins to purr, too, his cadence more rhythmic than mine. But my reverberation is all baritone and bass.

Our mate seems to sway between us, her comfort apparent in the way she relaxes.

Normally, I would hate that he's helping me in this way.

But right now, our Omega needs us. So I don't comment on Morpheus's involvement and instead say, "What you're describing sounds like Pandora's Box."

"It is," Morpheus murmurs. "That sense of nothingness is exactly how it feels to exist there."

His words and tone hold meaning, one I wouldn't have picked up on before. However, our conversation from less than an hour ago is still very fresh in my mind.

"She told me I deserved my fate," she says, her brow furrowing. "No, she told Persephone that she deserved her fate there. I... I..." Her eyes widen. "What if Persephone is trapped there? Is that why she hasn't taken over my body? Become, er, me?"

I stare at her, then look at Morpheus. He appears to be equally confused. "Serapina, you are Persephone," I say slowly. "A reincarnation of her, anyway. Her soul isn't trapped anywhere."

If it were, I would feel it.

Instead, all I sense is that the woman before me is my mate. My Persephone. *My Omega.* She's just been reborn. *As Serapina.*

"But what if she's trapped there?" she asks. "What if I was reliving a memory? Like I have with you?"

My brow furrows. "What memories have you seen of me?" Because this is the first I'm hearing about it. She's mentioned dreams, but not memories.

"I... I'm referring to..." Her cheeks redden as she glances at Maliki and then back at Morpheus. When her eyes meet mine again, I can tell this isn't something she wants to discuss in front of them.

Which suggests *intimate* memories.

"Would you be comfortable speaking with me privately about these memories, Serapina?" I ask her, oddly nervous about how she might respond.

I want her to feel safe with me. But I wouldn't blame her if she refused me.

"It's... I don't know how to describe..." She trails off.

"Serapina, if you're talking about your dreams of Hades, I don't think those were memories," Morpheus inserts quietly.

She gives him a startled look over her shoulder. "You've seen...?"

"Only the beginnings of them," he tells her. "Whenever you enter my realm, I'm aware and drawn to you. But I always try to give you privacy. With one exception."

Her cheeks darken even more, and I know he's talking about the dream she recently woke up from—the one that led Maliki to satisfying her.

"Have you witnessed anything that leads you to think it was more than a dream?" I ask Morpheus, my words drawing us back to the topic at hand.

He shakes his head. "No. If they were memories, you would have been dressed differently."

I arch a brow.

"You didn't wear suits two thousand years ago, Hades," he adds, staring at me. "In fact, our wardrobe was quite different. Yet every dream I've seen in her mind has begun with you in a modern suit."

"And you don't think it could have been manipulated in some way?" I press. Not because I don't believe him, but because I want to ensure we've evaluated every point of potential relevance.

"No. I think it was simply her soul's way of trying to help Serapina find you," he says, his attention shifting to her. "Unless you've dreamt of Hades in obsidian armor?"

The way her forehead crinkles tells me she hasn't before she even replies with, "Er, no." Because if she had, she would know what he meant by that. Instead, she's glancing at the rock walls of the maze now like she's trying to envision me wearing that sort of texture as armor.

Any other time, I might have smirked at the idea and teased my mate.

But we're not in a place for that right now.

So instead, I return to her commentary on Persephone's soul. "I don't think you had a vision of a memory," I tell Serapina. "I think Demeter reached out to you somehow and tried to manipulate you into altering the protective barrier surrounding this labyrinth."

I go on to say that only Serapina and I have the ability to change the security parameters surrounding this maze, which Demeter must have figured out.

"That makes sense," Morpheus says when I'm done. "I knew that as well."

"I assume that's why you initially went to her in her dreams?" I guess.

He smiles. "Initially, yes."

I don't remark on the taunt lingering in those two words and instead focus on Serapina once more. "I've already removed Demeter's influence, but she will absolutely try again. I'm going to have a word with Ares to see if he's noticed anything strange happening in Pandora's Box. However, I suspect this is linked to whatever Demeter has done to you… and perhaps all of Omega kind."

Serapina's throat works as she tries to swallow. It's clear this has all unnerved her.

"You're going to talk to Ares?" Morpheus asks, sounding surprised. "You don't want me to talk to my best friend?"

I look at him. "Normally, yes. But Serapina needs you right now. So I'll be talking to Ares instead."

I'm about to leave when Morpheus halts me by saying my name.

Sighing, I meet his gaze again and say, "Yes?"

"You're a good Alpha, Hades, and while Serapina may not know it yet, she needs you, too. So hurry back." Those last three words seem to be layered in warning.

We're running out of time.

Because Serapina's heat is imminent.

He can smell it, and I can smell it, too.

It'll be maybe a handful of days now.

Likely less.

So I nod.

And disappear.

All while hearing my cousin's words play through my head. *"You're a good Alpha, Hades."*

I'm not.

But I'm trying to be better.

For Serapina Everheart.

SERA

Two Days Later

No more dreams.

Or visions.

Or chance meetings with Demeter.

Just solid sleep and a lot of food.

"I feel like every time I wake up, you stuff food in my mouth," I complain when I open my eyes to find Maliki holding a tray of what looks like pancakes. "I'm not hungry."

"Rest and sustenance are vital staples for an Omega when leading into a heat," Morpheus says from behind me.

His bare chest is pressed against my back, his arm wrapped around my waist.

This is the most touching we've done since he arrived, which confuses me greatly because we were about to do a lot more in my dream the other day.

Yet he's been handling me with exquisite care, which I've both appreciated and disliked at the same time.

Appreciated because I'm nervous about all of this.

Disliked because I want him to do more. To kiss me. To introduce me to his knot. To *something*.

Maliki hasn't been any better.

He's kissed me, yes. Touched me, too. But not like the other night.

Both males have said it's not a coincidence that Demeter reached out to me after I played with Maliki. So apparently we're just not going to do any of that again until Hades returns with answers from Ares.

While time is elusive here, I'm pretty sure that was many days ago. And I... I'm worried about him.

Why hasn't he returned yet? I wonder. Morpheus told him to hurry back. At the time, I wasn't sure I agreed. But the longer we've been apart, the more uneasy I've felt.

He let Morpheus and Maliki into the maze.

That... that means something to me. He's made his stance about sharing clear. Just as he's apologized in his own way for some of the misgivings between us.

However, now he's gone.

And I can't help but wonder if he's left me here to be taken care of by Maliki and Morpheus... without him.

I'm not his version of Persephone, something that's become obvious between us. *Maybe he's decided he doesn't want me as a result?*

My stomach clenches at the thought.

Everything with Hades is so complicated. One minute, I belong to him. And the next, he just... disappears.

"Sera?" Maliki says softly, drawing me from my thoughts. "Are you all right?"

I blink at him. "I mean, sure. I'm being plied with food and sleep. What more could a girl want?"

His lips twitch. "Your sarcasm is noted and heard." He sets the tray aside and pulls off his shirt before sliding into the bed with me and Morpheus. "So let's talk more about what you want, yeah?"

Morpheus chuckles behind me.

And I narrow my eyes. "Are you teasing me?"

"No, mystery, I'm not. But I can, if that's what you want," he offers, his eyebrows waggling.

"One thing to learn about a mate-circle is that we value communication," Morpheus says, his lips near my ear. "And we both know something is bothering you. So either you talk about it, or we coax it out of you."

Maliki presses his finger to my lips as he adds, "Don't try spouting nonsense about being overfed, Sera. We'll see through it. Now tell us what's really on your mind, or I'll kiss you."

I stare at him. With an offer like that, why would I bother talking? "Okay, kiss me," I say.

He grins. "Oh, trouble..." He leans in to kiss my cheek.

"You realize he's going to tease you now, yes?" Morpheus murmurs, his warmth a blanket against my back that sends tingles down my spine. "And I don't mean with words."

Maliki's smile widens. "Definitely not entirely with words, anyway," he says, then kisses my chin.

I frown. "This was not the kind of kissing I anticipated, Maliki."

"Then perhaps you should share what's on your mind, beautiful girl," he drawls. "Otherwise..." He kisses my throat and then my shoulder. "Morpheus, would you mind helping me out on my quest?"

"Not at all," he replies, his hand skimming up my side to the strap on my shoulder.

I'm wearing another one of those golden dress things. The silk is surprisingly comfortable to sleep in. But really, I wore it because Maliki seemed to like it when he first arrived. And I wanted to entice him to react in a fashion similar to before.

It seems it's working now.

Sort of.

I think.

I…

Morpheus drags the strap down my arm, causing the fabric of my dress to glide along with it. He doesn't stop until he's exposed my breast, which causes Maliki to murmur, "Thank you, Morpheus," before lowering his mouth to my exposed flesh.

Only, he doesn't kiss my nipple.

He just licks and nibbles around it instead.

All while Morpheus returns his palm to my side to draw lazy circles against my hip bone with his thumb.

I shiver between them, my thighs tensing with an unspoken need.

A need that Maliki heightens when the stubble on his chin brushes my aroused nipple. It's a tender caress. A *teasing* touch.

And I suddenly understand what he meant by *teasing* me without words.

"Maliki…" I grab his shoulder, then his neck, and try to guide him where I want him. But he's stronger than me and merely chuckles against my stiff peak before lifting his head up and meeting my gaze.

"Yes, Sera? Have something you want to say?"

"Maybe something you want to ask for?" Morpheus adds, his voice a low rumble of sound that leaves me trembling against him. "I'm certain Maliki will be accommodating to any request you would like to voice,

little dreamer. Just as I'll fulfill any fantasy you may desire."
He kisses me right below my ear, then skims his teeth
against my pulse.

I dig my nails into Maliki's neck, my back arching to
give him better access to my breasts.

But he doesn't do what I want, what I *need*.

"Words, trouble," he murmurs. "Give me your words."

"Yes, Serapina," Morpheus adds, his lips at my ear
again. "This is a lesson in communication. If you want
something, you voice it. Because soon, you won't be able to
consent. So we need to know what your limits are before
you lose your mind with lust."

"How do I know what to ask for when I haven't done
anything?" I counter, unable to mask the frustration in my
tone. They want me to *communicate*, but I have no idea what
to say. "I just want you to teach me."

Maliki pulls back, his gaze going to Morpheus. "Our
girl wants a lesson."

"Indeed," Morpheus replies. "Is there any topic that's
of particular interest to you, Enforcer?"

Maliki considers him for a moment before going onto
his elbow and staring down at me. "Have you played with
his knot yet, trouble?"

I swallow and shake my head. "No. Not really."
Because I don't think the dream counts. And I didn't really
get to explore him much in that fantasy; it ended too early.

"Do you want to play with his knot?" Maliki presses.

"Yes," I answer without hesitation. I feel like I've been
waiting for eons to actually touch Morpheus. To stroke
him. To *kiss* him. To everything with him.

I… I want the same things with Maliki.

And maybe Hades, too.

If Hades even wants me.

A pang touches my heart, but I shove that thought

from my mind, determined to focus on Maliki and Morpheus. They're here with me now and finally want to touch me after two days of holding back.

Which has me wondering, *What's changed? Why now?*

"Tell us what you're thinking about, trouble," Maliki says, his golden eyes searching my face. "Talk to us."

"Yes, little dreamer. We want to hear your mind," Morpheus adds against my ear, his palm giving my hip a squeeze. "We can't properly please you unless you communicate."

Communicate seems to be the word of the day.

But I suppose they're right.

I want to trust them, to be with them, to… to explore whatever this is between us.

I've seen how Alina's mate-circle works, have envied her lifestyle and dynamic. And it seems I might have a similar one forming around me.

If I embrace it.

If I trust fate.

Swallowing, I look up at Maliki and say, "You've barely touched me these last few days. I don't understand what's changed or why. And… and I'm thinking about Hades, too." It's a lot to admit. But why should I hold back? If they're going to judge me for my thoughts, then they're not the males for me, right?

Stars, when did I start thinking about a mate-circle and what I want from them? I wonder. *When did this become my life?*

"We've held back because we needed to know if Demeter is a risk," Morpheus says, his thumb drawing circles again. "But Hades confirmed that she's locked up and can't touch you."

My brow furrows as I try to glance back at him. "You talked to Hades?"

He shifts to let me roll to my back and goes up onto his

elbow like Maliki, the pair of them staring down at me. "Yes," Morpheus confirms. "While you slept."

"Oh." I swallow. "So he returned... and left again?"

"No, he's still here," Morpheus informs me softly. "He's working on something in the maze right now."

I'm not sure why, but his words make me feel a little lighter. Like a weight has lifted from my chest. Only, I don't understand why I haven't seen Hades yet.

Is he avoiding me? I wonder.

Or perhaps he doesn't want to see me with Morpheus and Maliki.

I know he doesn't want to share. He's made that clear. Yet he allowed them entry into the labyrinth. That has to mean something, right?

"Do you want to talk to him?" Morpheus offers.

"Only if he wants to talk to me," I reply without thinking, then wince. "I mean... if he's, er, not avoiding me? Us?" Thorns, I feel foolish. Why am I even questioning these things? "Never mind."

Morpheus arches a brow. "No, Serapina. No *never mind* anything. If you want to talk to Hades, he'll want to talk to you. He would never avoid you, little dreamer. He would, however, give you time to process everything."

"I can speak for myself, Morpheus," a deep voice says, causing my gaze to shift to the doorway where Hades is standing.

His gaze runs over Maliki's shirtless state before coming to rest on my breasts for just a beat before rising to my face.

"What my cousin says is true—I would never avoid you, Serapina," he tells me. "You're my mate. But I won't pressure you into being around me, either."

I sit up and look at him. *Really* look at him.

He's wearing one of his dark suits, the fabric pristine.

But there are shadows beneath his eyes that suggest he's not rested in days. His hair is messy like he's run his fingers through it several times, perhaps even tugged on it. And his jaw is dusted with overgrown stubble, not unlike Maliki's chin at the moment.

However, where Maliki just looks relaxed, Hades appears to be disheveled in a way that tugs at my heart.

I'm not sure when I started caring about the God of Death's comfort, but I'm not shying away from the instinct. Things between us are confusing. Strained, even. Yet I feel a pull to him that's undeniable, especially now.

He's done everything I've asked.

And he's apologized in his own way.

While I may not agree with some of his choices, I understand them.

Though, I wonder how he's feeling about me, knowing that I'm... I'm not his version of Persephone.

"Do you want me to stay?" Hades asks, his dark eyes holding mine. "Or would you like to be alone with Morpheus and Maliki?"

I stare at him, uncertain of how to answer that.

Do I want him to stay? Yes. Yes, I think I do. But not if it's going to make him uncomfortable.

Which means I have to... to *choose* between disappointing him by asking him to remain or disappointing Morpheus and Maliki by requesting time alone with Hades.

And I... I don't want to make that choice.

It's not fair to any of them. I—

"Sera was just requesting a lesson," Maliki says, interrupting my inner turmoil. "Seems she's quite curious to learn more about knots. Do you want to provide the demonstration, or do you prefer to watch?"

I hold my breath, afraid that Hades is going to deny both options. Or worse, look *pained* by the decision.

Yet all I see in his gaze is heat as he says, "I'll watch."

My heart stops in my chest. Not because I'm scared or because I'm overwhelmed by the concept of Hades observing my "lesson," but because I can't believe he made the choice so quickly. Does that mean he actually wants to watch? Or—

"But I also want to *instruct*," Hades adds, his focus shifting to Morpheus.

And I'm not breathing again, too.

I glance at Morpheus, noting the way his gaze narrows slightly, the two Alphas seeming to have a silent conversation with their eyes alone.

After a beat, Morpheus nods.

Then he looks at me. "Are you okay with this, Serapina? Hades telling you what to do to me?"

I swallow. "I, er, yes." The stammering irritates me. I've never really been with a man before, let alone three, but I don't want to be a meek participant, either.

I want to be strong.

Worthy of their attention.

"Teach me." The two words leave me with more confidence, and I direct them at Hades. It's my way of accepting him as the *instructor* while also letting Maliki and Morpheus know that I'm serious about learning. "Tell me what to do."

HADES

Fuck.

Teaching Serapina how to pleasure a knot certainly wasn't on my agenda for today. I was in the middle of re-manifesting the heart of the maze. I wanted to add some life, which isn't my specialty at all, but I was trying to create a surprise for my mate.

Instead, I felt her call—her *need*—and ended up misting back to the cabin to check on her.

Which is when I overheard her conversation with Maliki and Morpheus, their discussion on the importance of communication pleasing me.

I was about to return to my task when I heard her say she was thinking about me. At first, it felt wrong to eavesdrop, and I fully expected to be punished for it—by hearing her speak her negative thoughts aloud.

However, the dynamic shifted when she expressed concern that I might be *avoiding* her.

If anything, I was giving her space to process, just like Morpheus said.

But at that point, I couldn't remain in the hallway any longer. I needed to speak for myself.

And now... now I'm going to prove that I can learn how to share—not just to her, but to myself as well.

Even if it goes against every instinct I possess, I mentally mutter.

Stepping through the threshold, I slip out of my jacket and walk over to drape it across the back of a nearby chair.

Serapina's eyes are on me as I unfasten my cuff links, causing me to want to exaggerate my movements. I set them on the table beside the chair, then undo the cuffs of my dress shirt to slowly roll the fabric to my elbows.

All while my mate observes me.

Her attention is a welcome caress, her open interest causing my knot to throb in response. But I don't allow her to see my intrigue as I face her, instead looking down as I complete my task and only meeting her gaze as I reach up to unfasten and pull off my tie.

"Undress," I tell her, the demand leaving my lips with ease.

Serapina swallows, her lashes fluttering a little as her inner Omega peeks at me from within. She's trying to be bold, which just makes her that much more alluring.

Because Persephone was never like this in the bedroom. She always submitted.

But Serapina... *Fuck.* She holds my gaze as she tugs the other strap of her gown down, providing me with an unfettered view of her chest. I allow her to see my approval as I glance down, pleased that she's obeying me. But even more pleased that she's confidently doing so.

I sit down in the chair that I draped my jacket over and smile when Serapina goes up onto her knees in the center of the bed. It's a beautiful sight, my mate kneeling with her hands on her hips. And an even more alluring view as she gathers the fabric of her gold negligee around her hips.

My lips part as she pulls the dress upward to remove it from over her head, leaving my female completely naked whilst kneeling.

"Fuck, Sera," Maliki groans, his gaze roaming over her with open admiration.

"She's truly stunning, isn't she?" Morpheus comments as he leans back into the pillows and tucks an arm behind his head. I suspect he's doing that to keep himself from touching her. He knows I want to lead this lesson, and he's ensuring I remain in charge by holding himself back.

"Fucking exquisite," Maliki replies.

A pretty blush spreads across Serapina's chest, but she doesn't look down or away from me. Instead, she holds my gaze like she's waiting for me to compliment her, too.

No, not *waiting* so much as *demanding* that I share my thoughts. Tell her how I feel. Give her some indication of my approval.

But I'm not sure how to reply with words. She's a Goddess. The most gorgeous creature in all the dimensions. And I can't believe she's mine.

So rather than speak, I push away from the chair and walk over to where she's kneeling on the bed.

She swallows as I stare down at her, my heart suddenly in my hand as I reach out to brush my knuckles down her cheek. "Are you ready to begin, darling?" I ask her softly, my thumb tracing her jaw.

Serapina nods. "Yes, my lord."

My touch lingers, part of me not wanting to release her ever again. She's the first person I've allowed myself to caress since I lost Persephone. The first being I've actually wanted to indulge. The first woman to bring me to my knees in well over two thousand years.

She has no idea what power she holds over me and my instincts, how my beast longs to worship her in every way imaginable.

But she's right to want to *learn*.

There's so much that she doesn't understand. So much for her to experience.

However, I still can't bring myself to step away from her. Instead, I find myself leaning toward her. My knee on the mattress, my palm cupping her cheek, my forehead meeting hers...

It's a tender moment.

A second of submission on my part.

A deep-seated need to simply shower her with my gentleness.

No one else will ever witness this side of me. *No one except her and the males in this room.*

I can't even be bothered by their presence, not while holding my mate.

They're here to please her, too. Which means they understand my gesture more than anyone else ever could.

An exhale escapes Serapina, her subtle shudder telling me this hold is impacting her just as much as it's impacting me.

Maybe even more so.

Because this is about our souls. Our hearts. *Our beings.*

We're rekindling something here that's been long forgotten, or perhaps awakening a new bond.

This is all so convoluted. But resurrections have never been a straightforward process.

And nothing about Persephone's initial disappearance could be considered *normal*. Yet she's kneeling before me in a brand-new state, one I think I may be falling for in an entirely new way.

It brings up my previous reflection where I wondered if it's wrong to crave her like I do, all while knowing she's not the Persephone I once adored.

Does it matter? This is fate. This is who we are. This is my *Omega.*

I want to taste her.

To know her.

To be with her.

My heart skips a beat in my chest, the organ seeming to only exist for her. This Omega. *My mate.*

I know she's waiting for a demand, but there isn't one I can give. Not like this. Not right now. Because I'm too consumed by a need I can't explain or define. A need that overrules reason and thought and compels me to lean forward. *To kiss her.*

I don't fight the urge. I merely give in to it.

And press my lips to hers.

The way she sighs against me says it was the right way to show my approval. She didn't need words; she needed actions, a knowledge her body proves by melting into mine as I deepen the kiss with my tongue.

Fuck, she tastes like the sweetest sin.

A temptation I shouldn't allow myself to explore.

Yet I'm a slave to her being, lost to her existence, consumed by her soul.

My Serapina.

The resurrected form of my mate.

My everything.

The one I'm meant to be with for eternity.

My true heart.

The Omega I have to share because that's what she desires. And I want to give her the world.

But more than that, I want to protect her.

Which I know Maliki and Morpheus will help me do. It's unnatural to rely on anyone other than myself, yet I can't deny the relief I feel knowing Serapina will always be safe with us.

Unlike Persephone, a dark part of me whispers. *I failed her.*

And I started by failing Serapina, too.

However, I'm going to make it up to her. It's a vow I whisper with my tongue against hers, a promise I solidify by clasping my palm around the back of her neck, and a benediction my soul whispers to hers as I hold her close.

I'll be better, Serapina. I'll be everything you need and more.

Which means I need to prove I can do this. *Prove I can share.*

It hurts, but I slowly ease away from Serapina, my mouth hovering against hers for a lingering moment before I press my lips to her ear.

"I want you to be my good girl and take off Morpheus's pants," I whisper to her. "Then you're going to do the same to Maliki. After that, you're going to touch them, Serapina. With both your hands and your tongue."

She shudders against me, her nipples so hard I can feel them through my dress shirt.

"If this becomes too much, though, I want you to say my name, okay?" I add softly, my eyes meeting Morpheus's before looking at Maliki. I know they can hear me, and they'll understand the importance of what I'm doing. "Tell me you understand, Serapina."

"I understand," she breathes.

"Very good, darling," I murmur, pressing a kiss to her skittering pulse. "And if for some reason you can't speak, I want you to hold up two fingers." I grab her hand to create the action I mean and hold it up for her to see as I ease back from her. "Understood?"

"I understand," she echoes, swallowing.

Smiling, I cup her cheek again and lean in to brush my mouth against hers. "Good girl," I praise her. "Now go free Morpheus's knot and Maliki's cock. I want to watch you pleasure them."

Her pupils dilate as I pull away, her lips deliciously swollen. But not nearly as swollen as they're about to be. Because she has two mates to please, and I know they're going to enjoy testing her limits.

I hold her gaze while walking backward to my chair, then I sit and lift one leg to balance my ankle on my opposite knee.

Serapina stares at me for a long moment, causing me to arch a brow. "Is there a problem, darling?" I ask her.

She licks her lips and shakes her head. "No, my lord."

My lips twitch. The formal address is one I usually hate, but not from her. It feels purposeful right now, like she's using it as a way to communicate her comfort level. My name is her safe word. She might not know what that means, but it's implied. So she's using a title instead.

"Then get to work," I tell her, a hint of command in my tone. "I expect eagerness, Serapina. And obedience."

A pretty flush blossoms across her cheeks, followed by a hint of resolve. She wants to please me. But more important than that, she wants to be strong. Courageous. *Adventurous*. I can see the determination flashing through her features as she rotates toward Morpheus.

He's the picture of ease, relaxing against the pillows with both hands tucked behind his head now, and shirtless. All he has on is a pair of gray sweats, just like Maliki, making Serapina's task somewhat simple. It's a good initial assignment because what'll come next won't be so easy for her to do.

The three of us will be exceptionally demanding; that much is clear.

Though, I suspect Morpheus and Maliki will both ease Serapina into their particular tastes. I've already seen the evidence of that with my best friend. And given how soft Morpheus has been toward her, I expect the same from him.

He proves me right as he stares up at her with an expression of pure adoration, his blue-green eyes capturing and holding hers in a look of encouragement that has Serapina smiling shyly back at him. She reaches for his pants and unties the top before giving them a good tug.

His hips lift to make it easier for her, and his lips curl. "Eagerness noted and approved," he says, looking at her while speaking to me.

Or I assume that comment was for me since he used the same term I uttered seconds ago.

"Obedience, too," he adds, confirming he's talking to me and not her.

"Hmm," I hum noncommittally, wanting to see how much bolder our Omega can be.

She finishes pulling off Morpheus's pants, then glances over at me with a haughty little look before moving on to Maliki.

I don't let her see my responding smile, instead only revealing it when she's focused on my enforcer. She's trying to prove something to me. Or maybe to herself.

Regardless, I'm amused.

And equally intrigued.

Because this is so new. So refreshing. *So alluring.*

It's almost like she wants to test my limits along with her own, only in an entirely different way. I don't think she's aware that she's doing it. Fuck, it's probably not even intentional. Yet here we are.

Maliki lifts his hips just like Morpheus did, only he grabs Serapina the moment she's finished removing his pants and yanks her in for a long kiss.

It's a break in protocol.

One I know he's doing on purpose to piss me off.

But I don't say anything. I just watch as he devours our mate, then arch a brow at him when he pulls away from her. The look he gives me in return dares me to say something.

I don't.

Because that's just how we play.

He enjoys pushing my boundaries almost as much as I enjoy watching him seduce and fuck.

It's a give-and-take between us that creates an intriguing dynamic, one that has secured our lifelong friendship.

"Since Maliki is being impatient, I want you to touch Morpheus first," I say, punishing my best friend in my own way.

But, in truth, I'm also rewarding him.

Delayed gratification gets him off.

And I'm fairly certain he'll also be aroused by Morpheus coming down Serapina's throat.

"The key is to tease," I tell Serapina. "I think your mates have done a good job of introducing you to the concept, but if you want to return the favor, I suggest kneeling between Morpheus's legs and running your nails up his thighs. Then lean down and gently kiss his knot."

My cousin arches a brow at me, then looks at Serapina with an open invitation in his eyes. "Do whatever comes naturally, sweetheart," he tells her.

It's on the tip of my tongue to remind him that I'm leading this lesson, but Serapina touches his thighs to spread his lower limbs and moves to kneel between his legs, just like I instructed.

A purr escapes my chest, my approval highlighting the sound and causing her to glance at me.

I gift her with a little smile, telling her without words that I appreciate her listening to me, then nod for her to continue.

She swallows and faces Morpheus again, then leans down to kiss him just like I told her to.

Morpheus bites off a curse, his upper body tensing as he clearly fights the urge to reach for her.

Because the little vixen gave him an open-mouthed kiss, not a closed one, leaving a damp spot behind on his flesh.

My lips twitch at her subtle disobedience. Though, I suppose I didn't give her specific instructions on *how* to kiss him.

"Do that again," I tell her. "With more tongue."

She looks at me, then bends over to lick him from base to head, all while staring up at him.

"*Fuck*," Morpheus growls.

"You told her to do whatever comes naturally to her," Maliki points out. "I think we have our answer." Approval radiates from my best friend.

It's an approval I echo.

Although, I don't let her hear it in my voice as I say, "Wrap your palm around his knot and give him a squeeze, Serapina."

She does as I demand but licks him again as well.

"If you're so intent on tasting him, darling, then wrap your mouth around the head of his cock and *suck*."

Her responding shiver is the only indication that she heard the light censure in my tone.

"You said you wanted eagerness, *my lord*," Maliki points

out as Serapina takes Morpheus's dick into her mouth and hollows her cheeks. "She's following your instructions beautifully."

"Indeed," I murmur, narrowing my gaze as Serapina takes more of Morpheus into her mouth.

My cousin releases another curse, his abdomen flexing as he once again fights the urge to touch her.

"Why don't you help her, Maliki?" I suggest, an idea forming in my mind. "Fist your hand in her hair and see how much of Morpheus she can take."

My enforcer meets my gaze, a wicked smile playing over his lips. "You want me to help her blow him?"

I arch a brow, cautioning him not to push me.

But all he does is say, "All right."

He moves to kneel beside Serapina.

Then takes hold of her head.

Pulls her off of Morpheus's cock.

And kisses her.

MALIKI

I'm purposely pushing Hades, as I need to know his boundaries here.

He wants to be in charge. Fine. I've played that game thousands of times with him.

But this is his mate.

And Morpheus is involved, too.

That creates an unclear landscape, one I want to understand before I truly indulge in this experience. Because I need to ensure Sera's safety and happiness.

If Hades loses his fucking mind, she'll be caught in the middle. I won't let that happen. I'll take the brunt of his ire while Morpheus mists her to safety.

So I break Hades's rules and kiss Sera.

Not gently. Not sweetly. But hard. With tongue. Devouring her. *Claiming* her. And leave her panting when

I'm done. Then I wrap my palm around her neck and guide her back down to Morpheus's dick. "Part those lips for him, trouble," I tell her. "And relax your throat."

I focus on her for a moment, ensuring she does what I request, then look directly at Hades as I push her to take more of Morpheus into her mouth.

He holds my gaze, his nostrils flaring.

But I don't see anger or a need for retribution in his features.

Instead, all I find is *heat*.

It's a heat that burns hotter when Morpheus groans.

I glance down to find Sera massaging his knot while using her mouth to suck. "Shadows, mystery. It's like you were made for this."

"She was," Hades says, his tone lacking the arousal I saw simmering in his dark eyes. But a glance back at him confirms it's absolutely still there; he just sounds indifferent.

And when I feel Sera attempt to take even more of Morpheus, I think I understand why.

Hades is trying to goad Sera into pushing her boundaries by pretending that this bores him.

Arse, I nearly say aloud.

But I can't ignore how much Morpheus is benefiting from this. He looks ready to fall apart beneath Sera's touch, and she's only just started on him.

His muscles are all tightened, his jaw clenching as he forcefully keeps his hands locked behind his head.

The restraint is palpable.

And I imagine it's made even more intense by him being an Alpha. He's not used to bowing to anyone, let alone another Mythos Fae.

Yet he's trying to let Hades lead.

Though, it seems Sera is really the one in charge here.

Because she's swallowing even more of Morpheus now, all while fondling his knot.

"Fuck, little dreamer," he groans, his blue-green eyes smoldering with need. "The way you're squeezing me..." His back bows off the bed, the tattoos along his arms bulging as he fights his own urges.

I can tell he wants to touch her. To take over. To *lead*.

And something about that restraint makes this so much hotter.

I'm guiding Sera, Hades is managing the room, and Morpheus is simply being forced to enjoy the gift of our girl's talented touch.

"It should be her mouth you're complimenting," Hades says, pushing away from his chair to saunter over to the bed. "Is she using enough tongue?"

Morpheus makes a low sound in the back of his throat that I think is supposed to be a laugh but comes out strangled.

"Or do you prefer teeth?" Hades asks conversationally.

The God of Dreams looks at him. "I prefer whatever Serapina wants to do to my cock."

Hades grunts at that. "I suppose we know why I'm the better instructor, then." He sits on the bed and places his hand over mine on Sera's head. "Open your mouth a little more, darling. I want to see how much of Morpheus you can take."

He starts to apply pressure, but I stop him by pushing back. "Take a deep breath first, Sera," I interject, my eyes on Hades.

Hades's dark eyebrow inches upward, challenging me.

However, I don't back down.

It's his job to lead. And it's my job to protect. We each have our roles here, and he has to remember that if this is going to work.

He studies me for a moment before he dips his chin in subtle acknowledgment. "Maliki is right, Serapina. Inhale for us and be prepared to hold your breath for a bit while we test your limits."

Her eyes widen, causing me to add, "Remember your safe motion, Sera. If this becomes too much, just hold up two fingers and we'll stop."

Although, we won't let it get to that point. It's our job to ensure her comfort and security. But she doesn't know that yet. We have to build trust, and safe words are the best way to accomplish that.

"Inhale," Hades repeats, his dominant tone causing Sera to obey almost instantly.

I don't say anything, just focus on Sera's expression and the stiffness in her body. She's uncomfortable, which almost has me telling Hades to back off.

But her shoulders suddenly tighten like she's emboldening herself. Then she starts to take more of Morpheus into her mouth without us applying pressure.

Hades smiles, clearly pleased, and I stop pushing up against his hand and allow him to take over again.

Morpheus releases a groan that has Sera looking up at him, her pupils dilating at the sight of his muscles flexing.

"Very good," Hades praises her. "But don't forget to keep fondling his knot. That part of an Alpha's cock is extremely sensitive, especially when it's an Omega touching him there."

Morpheus makes a sound of agreement.

And Sera's nostrils flare.

She readjusts her grip on Morpheus while pushing herself to take more. There's a flash of alarm in her features when she realizes he's so deep that she can't breathe, but a glance up at his reaction has her relaxing.

"Mmm, that's it, darling," Hades murmurs. "Can you take any more?"

She responds by attempting to, then freezes and tries to pull back up.

"Shh," he hushes her when she starts to panic. "You're safe. Just relax for a little bit, then we'll let you breathe."

Sera doesn't immediately listen, her body strung tight like she's about to fight.

But then she seems to steel her resolve and forces more of Morpheus into her mouth.

Hades moves his hand away from mine to the back of her neck, his thumb instantly finding her pulse. "You're taking him so well, Serapina," he tells her. "Now pull back slowly for me, but don't release him entirely."

Her throat appears to be moving like she's trying to swallow, then she follows his guidance, and I remove my palm from her head and instead draw my fingers down her arm. "I'm envious of Morpheus right now, trouble," I inform her. "I think you've just made one of his fantasies a reality."

"If you only knew," Morpheus says, his voice strained. "Fuck, she's still sucking even though I know she wants to breathe."

"Because she's allowing her instincts to rule her movements," Hades says, pride in his voice. "Just as an Omega should."

Sera shivers, the reaction one I feel beneath my fingertips as I continue to stroke her arm.

"Now, if you need a break to catch your breath, I recommend pulling back to just the tip and swirling your tongue around the head while you discreetly inhale," Hades goes on. "But don't forget to keep massaging his knot. Yes, Serapina. Just like that."

She shivers again, clearly enjoying his praise.

"Tell her how you feel, Morpheus," he adds, the command in his tone clear.

"Like I'm about to explode," the God of Dreams replies with a groan. "Fuck, Serapina, you're making it difficult not to touch you."

Hades smiles. "You hear that, darling? Morpheus wants to thread his fingers through your hair and force you to take him deep again."

"Not what I said," Morpheus grits out. "But not wrong either."

"Do you want him to touch you, Serapina?" Hades asks as he leans down to brush his lips against her ear. "Before you answer, I need you to know that saying yes will move us into the next phase of your lesson."

She looks at Morpheus, then tries to look at Hades.

He waits.

But she doesn't speak.

Instead, she moves back down Morpheus's shaft, causing the man to hiss in response.

"Hmm, I'm accepting that as an affirmative answer," Hades says, his grip loosening on her nape as he starts tracing her delicate spine. "Morpheus..." He doesn't finish the comment but gives the other Alpha a meaningful look.

Morpheus frees one of his hands and reaches for Sera, but he doesn't force her down on his cock. He simply brushes her cheek with his knuckles, his reverence palpable.

It elicits another tremble from our Omega, her arms pebbling with goose bumps beneath my touch. I lean in to kiss her shoulder as Hades continues his journey down her back to her ass. When he reaches deeper, Sera jumps.

"Shh," he hushes her again. "I already warned you that the next lesson will be about multitasking. You have multiple mates to pleasure, Omega. That means learning how to divide your focus and… accepting us in your many holes."

The way her body stiffens, coupled with his words, tells me he just emphasized his meaning by sliding a finger inside her.

"Easy, Serapina," he murmurs. "Remember that you're the one in charge here. If we go too far, you tell us with a signal."

I press my lips to her shoulder again, then kiss my way up to her ear. "Trust us to make this good for you, trouble," I whisper. "We won't hurt you."

"Quite the opposite, actually," Hades adds, his hands obviously punctuating his point as a garbled moan escapes Sera.

"*Fuck*, that felt good," Morpheus says, his touch sliding up into her hair. "Make her do that again."

Hades doesn't reply verbally, but the sound Sera releases confirms he listened to Morpheus's request. I grin and place a kiss just below her ear. "Good girl, mystery. Keep making Morpheus feel good."

"Oh, this isn't just about my cousin." Hades's tone is deep, his words drawing my attention to him. "I said I wanted to watch her pleasure both of you, didn't I?"

Sera gasps around Morpheus, her cheeks blossoming with color.

"Hades," I warn.

"She knows how to make this stop, Maliki," he returns. "However, the way she's squeezing my fingers right now tells me she wants more, not less."

Her eyes practically roll into the back of her head as Morpheus pushes himself into her mouth, his control seeming to snap. But I watch him rein himself back in with a sharp inhale, his muscles tense as he gentles his hold on Sera's hair.

Only, she's having none of it.

She swallows him deep while squeezing his knot, then moans once more at Hades's ministrations below.

"Look at you, darling Goddess, taking my fingers while sucking Morpheus's cock," he says, his free hand running up the back of her thigh to caress her ass. "But I want you to satisfy Maliki, too. He's been so patient, eating your pussy and introducing you to ecstasy with his tongue. I think it's your turn to please him, hmm?"

Fuck. His words are somehow making me harder than I already am.

"As I said, this is about multitasking," he continues. "I want to watch Maliki take this sweet virgin cunt while Morpheus fucks your mouth. But I don't want you to come, darling. Not yet."

She shudders at his words, or maybe from the way he's touching her.

"Because if you're a really good girl, I'll reward you after they fill you with their seed." He leans forward to place a kiss between her shoulder blades. "What do you think, Serapina darling? Do you want to feel Maliki inside you? Driving deeper than my fingers are right now? *Fucking* you with abandon?"

"You can say no, Sera," I remind her, wanting to ensure that she knows she's the one who is really in charge here. "If you're not ready, just hold up two fingers, okay?"

She doesn't.

Instead, she grips Morpheus's knot harder with one hand and grasps his hip with the other, like she's trying to anchor herself in place.

"If you felt how harshly she just clenched her pussy, Maliki, you would know she wants this," Hades says, his eyes meeting mine. "But I expect you to make this good for her. It's her first time. And you're the least likely of the three of us to hurt her."

I arch a brow. "Since when have I been known as a gentle lover?" He's watched me more than enough times to know that I'm the opposite.

"You'll be easier for her to take than me or Morpheus," he replies. "You'll also make sure she enjoys it. Otherwise, I'll kill you."

I huff at that. "Your threat isn't why I'll make her enjoy it."

"I know."

"Telling her she's not allowed to come basically ensures I'll force her to climax all over my cock," I go on, pretending like I didn't hear his response. "I'll fuck her so good she won't need either of your knots."

He smiles. "We'll see, won't we?"

"Only if she agrees," I counter.

He pulls his hand out from between her legs to show me his soaked skin.

"Her slick is all the agreement I need, Maliki," he murmurs before sucking each finger clean. "Get down there and taste her for yourself if you don't believe me. But our mate wants your cock. So either you give her what she desires, or I'm going to take her virginity with my knot."

SERA

Oh. My. Stars.

I have never felt more alive than I do right now. Everything inside me burns. My veins. My chest. *That space between my thighs…*

Hades's touch sent me to a new place of existence, his fingers stroking my inner walls awakening an insatiable creature inside me. One that causes me to push my rump into the air, like I'm begging Maliki to take me.

It's insanity.

It's intense.

It's a fantasy come to life.

Except I only ever experienced this sort of thing with Hades in my dreams. Not three males. Yet he's sharing me with Morpheus and Maliki.

I don't even know how to comprehend this madness. This shift. *This exquisite paradise.*

I'm naked.

Morpheus is naked.

Maliki is naked.

And Hades is fully clothed.

I don't know why, but that fact makes everything even hotter.

Morpheus's grip tightens in my hair, reminding me that it's his cock in my mouth. Not that I forgot. His knot is throbbing beneath my hand, the bulbous muscle a brand against my palm.

Hades just threatened to take my virginity with his own knot, which I don't fully understand. But I'm curious about how it would work since that part seems to be at the base of the shaft.

I squeeze Morpheus a little, wondering if the bulb moves.

He responds by tugging on my hair. "Not yet, little dreamer," he says.

Part of me wants to pull off of his cock and ask him what he means. However, I don't want to stop laving him with my tongue and mouth.

He tastes good. Like sin and decadence, if those two things even have a taste. I'm not sure. But he keeps leaking precum—a term I learned from Hades, once upon a dream—into my mouth, and I'm addicted to the flavor.

I want more.

I want to swallow him whole.

I want to feel him come undone.

However, it's Maliki who seizes my focus as his lips brush my shoulder.

"Do you want this, trouble?" he asks, the words a low rumble that elicits a tremble in its wake. "I know we gave you a safety sign, Sera, but I need your consent before I do this."

Morpheus's grip on my hair lessens, his gaze meeting mine as he coaxes me upward. I release him with a pop, causing his lips to curl. "That hungry look in your eyes is going to exist inside my mind for eternity, little dreamer."

Rather than let me go, he sits up and pulls me in for an unexpected kiss, one that leaves me quivering in his lap.

Because wow.

Wow.

He's kissing me like I'm his. And maybe I am.

Three mates. Is that even possible?

Do I want to question it?

No. No, I do not.

Instead, I allow my tongue to glide against Morpheus's, noting how similar this is to the dream we shared. Only it's better because I know this is real. This is truly him. *We're here. We exist. And right now, I'm his…*

He guides me closer until I'm fully straddling him, my heat up against his wet shaft, the intimate kiss sending shock waves through my body.

By the time he releases me, I'm panting.

"Oh, you're very ready, aren't you, little dreamer?" he murmurs, his eyes burning into mine. "I can feel you pulsing against my knot, begging for a cock to fill your sweet little cunt." He tilts his head, sending his silver hair to the side. "But I think Hades is right—Maliki should be first. He won't be as harsh for your first time."

Maliki makes a noise of disagreement. "I won't exactly go easy on her either."

"None of us will," Morpheus says as he cups my cheek. "Though, I don't think she minds." He leans in to kiss me again, causing me to tremble against him.

Because he's right.

I don't mind.

Not at all.

I just want more of this experience. More of them. *More sensation.*

I press into his hot shaft and shudder when he grabs my hip to stop me from going further. His opposite hand remains on my face as he pushes me away. "Give Maliki your consent, Serapina, and he'll fulfill your every desire."

A breath escapes me, one that feels heavy and light at the same time.

I feel enslaved to these males, to their hands, their mouths, their *needs*.

Or maybe it's my own.

I... I don't know. But as Morpheus nudges me toward Maliki, I give in to the movement and reach for his broad shoulders. Maliki catches me easily, pulling me into him in an instant and capturing my mouth with his own. I'm not even sure how my body moved the way it did, like I flew or misted between them. However, I'm suddenly straddling Maliki and not Morpheus, and a familiar vibration thrums between my thighs.

His tattoos.

Oh, stars…

"Tell me to fuck you, trouble," he says against my mouth. "Tell me you want this."

His words are similar to the question he asked before, the one I couldn't answer. But he's giving me a chance now, a way to tell him what I desire.

I'm overwhelmed. Overheated. Overcome.

However, I feel safe with him. With *them*. Which might be insane. Or maybe it's just fate.

Regardless, I want to embrace this. "I want you," I whisper, swallowing as I lean back enough to meet his gaze. "I trust you."

His golden eyes burn into mine. "Shadows, mystery," he breathes.

And then he's devouring me with his mouth, his tongue setting a pace I am forced to match.

Because this is Maliki. My protector. *My… my someone.*

I feel connected to him. Like I've chosen him somehow. Or perhaps he's chosen me.

I don't care. What matters is that this feels right, and I don't want it to end.

I'm lost to his touch, his heat, his *lips.*

He's kissing me like it's the only way he knows how to survive.

I cling to him, my body alight from within as he lays me out on the bed and settles between my thighs.

There's nothing gentle about this. It's all feral energy. All *need.* And I revel in his movements, my legs wrapping around his hips.

"Reach between us, trouble," he says. "Put my cock where you want it."

Stars, the way those words make me feel is paramount to any other experience in my life. I'm lost to Maliki. To Morpheus. To Hades.

I just… I just want this moment to never end.

"Now, Serapina," Hades says, causing me to quiver.

There's something about his dominance that undoes me. But it's more than that right now. His words feel like *permission.* Like he's testing his own boundaries with mine. Ensuring we can be a unit.

I don't know how I know that. How I suddenly seem to understand it. However, it feels right. *All of this is right.*

Swallowing, I draw my palm down Maliki's muscular back to his side and then slip my hand between us, just like he instructed.

And boldly grab his shaft.

Definitely right, my mind echoes as a sense of completeness overcomes me.

This is where I'm meant to be. Where I *want* to be.

Beneath Maliki.

Staring up into his gold eyes.

While positioning him at my entrance.

"Take me," I tell him.

It's bold. It's crazy. It might even be nonsensical.

But I'm beyond thinking. All I want to do is feel.

And feel I do as he thrusts into me without pause.

A gasp escapes me at the intrusion, pain shooting through every inch of my being and causing my eyes to widen. "*Maliki.*"

However, before he can even reply, his tattoos begin to *writhe.*

And oh. *Ohhh.* "*Oh, stars...*" I arch into him, the sensations confusing. It hurts. Yet it feels *so good*, too. Like my insides are alive with electricity. Humming. *Convulsing.*

His name escapes me again on a moan, my toes curling as I squeeze his hips with my legs.

He's not even moving, just using his shadows to massage me from deep within.

There's some place inside that pulses in response, the foreign feeling shooting off messages to my nerve endings that leave me quivering beneath him.

"I... I..." I don't know what I want to say. How to articulate what he's doing. It's too much. It's not enough. It's going to make me *explode.*

Just like I did when he pressed his cock to my clit...

"Maliki," Hades says, a warning in his voice.

"I already told you—Sera's my boss now." He punctuates his words with a punch of his hips that makes me see stars. "And my girl wants to come." He starts moving, his rhythmic thrusts combining with the vibrations to create a delirious cadence that causes me to nearly black out with lust.

All I can do is feel.

Indulge.

Exist.

Because Maliki is driving me wild with his claim, his cock hot and throbbing inside me in a way I can't even begin to comprehend.

I try to keep up, my body moving with his as I chase a high unlike any I've ever known.

It's there, on the cusp of my vision, dark and light and *volatile.*

When I reach it, I detonate, the sensations rippling through me with an echo of insanity. I'm screaming. I'm humming. I'm *floating.*

Someone growls.

Someone else purrs.

And Maliki groans. "Fuck, her pussy is strangling my cock."

"Whose fault is that?" I hear Hades ask through the haze of my mind.

"Mine, and I'm not fucking sorry," Maliki says, the words sharp as he continues to move inside me.

But then the world tilts, and I find myself on all fours, my nails digging into the mattress as Maliki bands an arm around my stomach to hold me up on my knees. "Open your mouth for Morpheus," he says, his lips somehow against my ear.

I feel Maliki's chest against my back, his body sweaty with lust. Just like mine.

And his cock is deep inside my lower half, buried against that place that makes me quiver.

"Part your lips, sweet girl," Maliki adds. "Suck Morpheus off while I fuck you from behind."

Thorns, I'm going to lose my mind, I think as I somehow follow Maliki's order to open my mouth. Morpheus is already there, the head of his cock pushing over my tongue in an instant.

I feel his hand in my hair, helping to guide me down over his shaft.

Maliki's arm tightens around my core as someone takes my hand to place it on Morpheus's hip. My other palm leaves the bed to wrap around his knot. And a fresh wave of heat washes over me when I realize it was Hades who moved me into this position.

"Multitasking is vital when you have multiple mates," he says, his lips right against my ear. "Now let them use you, darling. When they're done, I'll clean you up."

That fresh wave of heat turns *molten*.

I'm pretty sure I stop breathing.

Not that it matters, as Morpheus thrusts into my throat.

He uses his grip in my hair to take my mouth the way he desires, pushing even deeper as Maliki moves with abandon below.

I feel so full.

So taken.

So claimed.

It's madness. It's beautiful. *It's us.*

I dig my nails into Morpheus's hip, holding on as he uses me. All while gripping his knot and massaging it the way I learned he liked earlier.

But Maliki isn't one to be ignored, his tattoos beginning to twist in a new motion below.

I squeeze around him, my body reacting to his sensual caress and building into a crescendo just like before.

Fae… He's going to make me come again. Even more intensely than before. *What if I black out while Morpheus is in my mouth?*

Surely he'll take care of me. I hope. Maybe.

But the way he's taking me now is in a manner that suggests he's as lost to this experience as I am. He's staring down at me, though, his blue-green irises swirling like twin flames.

It's hypnotic.

Gorgeous.

Erotic.

I can see his pleasure mounting in time with mine, yet I sense him pull back to let me breathe, his priority to care for me overriding his own need.

That's not going to work for me, I realize. *I don't want him to go easy on me.*

I want to be able to take whatever he needs to give and then some.

Which I demonstrate by driving right back down on his shaft, sucking him deep and hollowing my cheeks to a point that makes him curse.

"*Serapina*," he growls.

But Hades chuckles beside us as he stretches out on the bed. "Beautifully eager," he praises. "Make him come down that pretty throat, mate. I want to watch you swallow every drop of his seed."

I can't believe he just said that. That he's here. That he's *encouraging* this.

Maybe this is a dream.

Thorns, I hope not…

Maliki propels forward, hitting me so deep that I gasp. Only for Morpheus to drive into my throat and cut off my air.

Panic overtakes me for half a beat before sensation ripples up from below, causing my eyes to roll back into my head.

I don't know what I was thinking or doing or… or *anything*. I'm simply here. Being taken. Driven to a new high. Existing in the most insanely hot fantasy of my being.

"Fuck, Serapina," Morpheus grits out. "That way you're touching my knot..."

Touching is a kind term. I was digging my nails into it by accident. But it seems as though Morpheus *liked* that, so I do it again and earn a low hiss from the God of Dreams.

Hades hums his approval.

And Maliki... Maliki tightens his hold around my middle while bathing my back in his heat. "Make Morpheus come, trouble," he says against my ear. "I want to watch him explode down your throat, then make you climax while you *drink*."

My body convulses in response to his words, fear choking me as arousal tightens in my belly.

It's a confusing mix of horror and excitement.

One I embrace as I scrape my nails along Morpheus's tender skin and use my lips to massage his shaft while sucking him deep again.

I can feel his orgasm building beneath my tongue, his veins seeming to pound in my mouth.

He pulls on my hair as the muscles in his neck bulge. Then he growls my name and pushes himself into my throat, cutting off my airway and leaving me paralyzed as he begins to come.

I don't know what to do, this sensation completely new.

So I... I *swallow.*

Because how else can I react?

He's going to drown me otherwise.

But oh, *oh, stars,* he tastes good.

It's that same sin and decadence from earlier, the precum overflowing with abundance as he properly explodes in my mouth.

I gulp him down, just like Maliki and Hades instructed me to, *drinking* his seed as he groans through his release.

Except, he's not the only one making sounds. Maliki is

growling, too. Pumping his hips against mine. Heightening the erotic swirls of his tattoos. And reaching between us to thrum my clit with his thumb.

I jolt when I realize that sensation caused by his shadows is reverberating there, too. Against my sensitive nub. *From his hand.*

"Oh," I attempt to say, but the sound is drowned out by Morpheus's ecstasy, his cock still sliding between my lips as he continues to come.

I haven't taken a breath in... in a while. I can feel the burn in my lungs. The terror threatening to build in my mind.

But then nothing matters as I'm thrust headfirst into a dark oblivion, Maliki's ministrations overtaking all reason and realistic expectation.

I think I scream.

Maybe... maybe I gargle.

I don't really know. I just know I'm flying. *Soaring.* And Maliki is coming inside me, too.

His pleasure rumbles against my back, my name leaving his lips. Something pierces my shoulder. Teeth, I think. *Maliki's bite.*

I don't know what it means.

I don't know if he's just stifling his own ecstasy.

Or marking me.

I deliriously hope for the latter but assume the former.

Whatever it is, it doesn't truly matter. Because all I can do right now is feel. Exist. Bathe in the euphoric afterglow of being taken by two men.

Down my throat.

Between my thighs.

So thoroughly *fucked* that I have no idea how to speak or think or do anything more than swallow. Vibrate. *And accept this fate.*

The world peeks in and out of existence.

Breath fills my lungs.

Life pulses between my legs.

Words are whispered into my ear.

Words from the God of Death.

Maybe he's resurrecting me.

I nearly giggle at the concept.

But I feel his arms around me, his purr a beacon I curl into. I'm only vaguely aware that he seems to be shirtless now.

It doesn't matter. That rhythmic sound is soothing all my hurts. Lulling me into a state of serenity. Protecting me.

I yawn.

He chuckles.

And we settle into something warm. Something wet. Something equally as tranquil as his purr.

"Rest, Serapina," he murmurs against my ear. "I'll take care of you while you sleep. And when you wake, we'll start anew."

I don't fully understand what he means by that, but I think I nod.

Then I nuzzle into his chest, indulging in his crisp morning scent. Sigh. And let his purr quiet everything else.

My mind.

The erratic beating of my heart.

My painful inhales.

My world.

My being.

For just a moment, I lose myself to his familiarity. And allow myself... *to dream again.*

MORPHEUS

"You haven't tried to kill me yet," I say as my cousin walks in with a towel against his wet hair. "I consider that to be a sign this might actually work between us."

He snorts. "You're not the one who fucked Serapina and marked her." His dark gaze cuts to Maliki, who is lying naked in the bed with me, his arms around our freshly bathed mate.

"I warned you that if I joined the mate-circle, my focus would be on her. Not you. As for marking her…" He trails off, his gold eyes drifting down to our sleeping female. She hasn't stirred since her magnificent climax, her body replete from our ministrations.

Fuck, she's stunning, I think, somehow even more attracted to her now than ever before. Maybe because I watched the Goddess inside her bloom during our bedroom play.

325

Or perhaps I'm just falling that much more in adoration with her.

"I'm not sorry," Maliki murmurs, his palm trailing up her arm to pause at the indents his teeth left on her shoulder. It's not healing, suggesting it is more than just a marking—it's a *claim*.

Which is interesting, as... "I didn't realize Corpse Fae claimed their mates with a bite."

He smiles. "I'm more than just a Corpse Fae."

"Clearly," I reply, amused.

Hades simply grunts, obviously not as entertained by this development.

"Are you going to punish me, my lord?" Maliki asks conversationally, the formal title one that has Hades's jaw clenching in response.

It's an intriguing physical reaction, considering he seemed to like Serapina referring to him as such. But Maliki is obviously doing it now to irritate him.

"I should," Hades informs his enforcer. "But I told you to ensure my wife's satisfaction, and, well." He looks down at the sleeping beauty. "You succeeded."

"You also instructed her not to come," Maliki points out. "So you'd better not be planning on punishing her for disobeying your order."

Hades huffs at that. "I don't think I could ever punish Serapina. Fuck, I'm not even sure I knew how to properly punish Persephone."

I arch a brow, surprised he just admitted that aloud. "This labyrinth says otherwise, Hades."

"I'm trying to fix it," he mutters.

"I know." I can feel his magic all over the maze, shifting form and re-creating the walls with more life. Though, it's not something he can truly manifest. He needs our mate to help him.

However, Serapina is still mostly human.

Mostly, because, well, a human would not have survived what Maliki and I just did to her. But she's not exactly an Omega yet, either. She's existing in a strange hybrid state, one I hope will be fixed once she goes into heat.

"When she wakes, she'll be ready to run," Hades says, changing the subject slightly. "And I suspect she's going to want all three of us to chase her."

I study him. "Are you going to allow that?"

He stares back at me. "I let her fondle your knot."

"You did." My gaze drops to where his hands have balled into fists. "Which took significant restraint."

"Yes," he agrees, his fingers flexing as he tries to forcefully relax.

Which, naturally, doesn't work.

"It's okay to feel possessive," I tell him, my eyes slowly returning to his smoldering irises. "That's part of who we are, Hades."

"Yet you somehow seem to be completely at ease," he mutters.

"I've mastered my instincts over several millennia, Cousin," I remind him. "Knowing I'm fulfilling my mate's wishes… helps."

Hades nods like he understands. Or maybe he's choosing to see that point of view. Perhaps it'll help him.

Regardless, his effort is noted.

"I want to finish what I was doing in the maze," he says, looking down at her again. "I'll return when she wakes."

He doesn't wait for us to respond, simply mists from the room.

Maliki chuckles under his breath, then focuses on our resting mate. "Can you see what she's dreaming about?"

I run my fingers through her hair. "She's currently floating in a lagoon with two moons shining overhead." It's the same place I found her in the other night when I joined her in the water. "Want me to wake her?"

He shakes his head. "I just want to make sure she's safe."

"She's secure in my dream world. Whatever Hades did to fix the barrier seems to be holding, but I'm definitely keeping a mental eye on our mate."

Maliki leans in to kiss her cheek, then settles onto the pillow beside her. "Good. Wake me if anything changes." The words are a sign of trust, his faith in me to guard our female a compliment of sorts.

However, his shadows seep out of his skin to wrap around Serapina's sleeping form, his natural inclination to protect her overriding his commentary.

Though, I wonder if he even realizes he's doing it, because he's already falling asleep. I sense him in my dream world, searching for Serapina.

With a smile, I link them, showing him the lagoon and encouraging him to go play. He casts a smile upward, one I see on his face in bed, too, and I leave him to play with our Omega in the land of imagination.

It doesn't take long for Serapina to release a soft moan, her fantasy trickling into reality as she clenches her thighs and rolls toward Maliki.

"Hmm," I hum, settling against her back as she presses her breasts against Maliki's arm. "You keep sleeping, little dreamer. And I'll make sure you get where you need to go."

She pushes her ass against my groin like she understands what I said.

Maybe she did.

Or perhaps this is just my Omega reacting the way she should.

I trace my fingers up the side of her thigh to her hip and kiss the back of her head. Then I linger, inhaling deeply as the scent of her infiltrates my lungs.

She smells like decadent chocolate, her natural fragrance encouraging me to lick, nibble, and bite. But I hold myself back and simply continue skimming my hand upward.

Serapina shivers.

Then her sweet little rump pushes back into me again as another moan escapes her.

I smile into her hair, my palm curling around her hip. Maliki turns toward her in his sleep, his cock hard and ready against her lower belly.

"Well, that looks fun," I say against her ear. "I wonder, is he inside you right now? Fucking you to oblivion?" Because her hips are certainly moving in a manner that suggests she's enjoying his erotic vibrations.

And the way his tattoos are swirling all over her implies the same.

Yet she keeps pressing back against me like she's inviting me to play, too.

"Such an eager Omega," I whisper, kissing her neck and then her shoulder. "You want all your mates to pleasure you, don't you, little dreamer?"

Her lips part on a pant, her nipples beading as I admire the view of her writhing between me and Maliki in her sleep.

"Fuck, sweetheart, you have no idea how often I've fantasized about this—playing with you while you dream." My hand slides to her belly, the back of it brushing Maliki's hard cock as I glide my touch downward. He releases a subtle growl, no doubt sensing my presence. But he doesn't wake. He stays in the dream with Serapina, just as he should, while I allow my fingers to slip downward.

However, I pause just before I reach her cunt.

And curl my hand into a fist.

Because we haven't discussed her boundaries in a sleep state yet.

This might be my kink, but I don't know if it's hers.

Swallowing, I force my hand to return to her hip and bury my head in her neck. "The restraint I have to show around you is borderline painful," I admit. "But I'll suffer another eternity of agony if it means pleasing you, Serapina."

She's mine to cherish. *For always.* And I refuse to hurt her faith in me.

So I hold her while she begins to pant.

Kiss the back of her head as she seeks friction against Maliki.

Bite back a growl when her ass meets my knot.

Then I purr when I feel her come apart between us, her dream having sent her body into a feverish climax that causes her eyes to open in shock.

Maliki is right there with her, his golden orbs heavy with lust as he stares at her and then at me. But as Serapina begins to truly awaken, her lips part on a gasp, drawing our focus back to her.

She studies Maliki for a moment before looking back at me.

I smile. "Hello, gorgeous Omega," I say, recognizing the dilation of her pupils. "Ready to test your mates?"

She swallows. "I… I don't know."

I arch a brow. "You don't know?"

"I feel strange."

"Like you're about to combust even though you just came whilst asleep?" I suggest.

She shudders. "That was real?"

"The sensations, yes," I murmur. "How you got there, though, was a dream. I did my best to respect your boundaries, which was rather hard with your delicious ass pressed up against my knot."

Her eyes widen and she rotates toward me, her gaze running over my naked body to my throbbing cock. "Oh," she breathes. "*Oh.*"

"Yes, you made noises similar to that while you slept." I reach out to tuck her hair behind her ear. "It took significant effort on my part not to reach between your legs and help you along."

She stares at me. "You didn't touch me?"

I shake my head. "Only held your hip, little dreamer. And kissed you a few times on the neck and head."

"Nice show of restraint," Maliki interjects.

"Consent is important," I reply, my words for him and for Serapina. "I would love to fuck you while you dream, sweetheart, but only with your permission."

Her lips part, her pupils seeming to throb. "Yes," she tells me. However, a frown follows her affirmation. "But not right now."

She sits up, the movement so sudden that she sways a little.

Except, before I can reach for her to steady her, she's already moved up onto her knees.

And then she faces us both.

Her nose crinkles. "I still feel weird."

"Like you want to run?" I guess.

"Maybe?" Her brow furrows. "I... I don't understand."

Maliki goes up onto his elbows, his long legs crossing at the ankles. "Do you feel antsy?" he asks.

"A little."

"Aroused?" he presses. "Ready to fuck again?"

Her cheeks turn a pretty shade of pink. "Maybe."

He smirks. "'Maybe' isn't good enough, trouble. Or did you forget your lesson on communication?"

"We could remind her," I suggest, glancing at him.

He meets my gaze. "We could. We should." He looks back at her, a threat lingering in his tone as he adds, "*We will.*"

She scrambles off the bed, her eyes widening. "Not yet."

"Why not?" he asks.

"Because…" She trails off and looks around. "Because I'm not ready."

His eyebrow wings upward. "To be fucked?"

She shakes her head. "Not yet." She takes a step backward. "I just… I need a few minutes?"

"Only a few minutes?" he counters, clearly having fun playing this game with her. Because he can see as well as I can that she's already starting the chase. That's why she's inching toward the door. "Or would you like a longer head start?"

"And maybe some clothes or shoes?" I offer, manifesting some for her that she stumbles over as she reaches for the knob.

She gapes down at the stretchy black pants and tank top, as well as the running shoes and socks.

Without looking at us, she bends to scoop them up.

Then darts out of the room.

Maliki considers the doorway for a moment before glancing at me. "Will she do this every time she goes into heat?" he asks conversationally. "Or is this a one-time experience?"

I shrug. "Depends on her mood, I think. But typically, it's an initial chase that leads to a claim. However, if she likes it, then this may become a normal occurrence in our lives."

"Hmm, I think I might enjoy that." His thoughtful tone holds a deep note of interest, one that echoes through me as well.

Only, neither of us moves.

We lounge in the bed, giving our Omega time to collect herself. To dress. *To run.*

It's clear in her scent that her heat cycle has officially begun. She's not lost to lust yet, though. That'll come in time.

First, she runs.

Once she's caught, she'll set her rules. Provide her choices. Give us boundaries to play within. Tell us if we can claim her. Rut her. Breed her.

And after that… *we fuck.*

For days.

Maybe a week.

But only if we *win* her.

Which requires pursuing her.

I listen for the tell that she's ready—the slamming of the front door.

Then I roll off the bed to find some clothes. Maliki follows me into the closet, taking his cues from me, and gets dressed.

Hades arrives the moment we reenter the bedroom, fully dressed in another one of his fancy suits.

He looks over my slacks and dress shirt, then takes in Maliki's choice of sweatpants and tennis shoes.

"I'm giving her five more minutes to run and hide," he tells us, a clock manifesting on the wall. "The moment the countdown ends, *we hunt.*"

SERA

I HAVE NO IDEA WHAT I'M DOING.

Everything feels unreal.

This labyrinth.

What just happened with Morpheus and Maliki.

And Hades, I think, remembering his presence. His dominance. *His demands.*

I... I don't understand these sensations. This world. *This pang in my lower belly.*

Maliki met me in the lagoon, but all of that feels like it happened hours ago. Yet it was just in my mind, a *dream*, one I woke up to... *as I came.*

I spin around, noting the somewhat familiar walls. I saw them when I first arrived. Examined them over the last few days. But there's something different about them now.

Vines, I think. *There are... vines.*

They're crawling all over the etched skulls, giving the path before me *life*.

I pause, staring at them. Wondering why they exist.

How they exist. *Hades*, I realize, sensing his touch. His manifestation.

He tried to change his design.

Why?

I whirl again, staring back at the skull-shaped cabin. Somehow, I know he's returned. It's… it's bizarre. Like I'm linked to him in a way that I haven't felt before.

Part of me longs to return to him. To Morpheus. To Maliki.

Except my steps take me in the opposite direction, a foreign side of me needing to *run*.

It's an intrinsic need that rings alarm bells in my mind. I… I know Hades said this would happen, that he built this labyrinth for this very reason. However, each step I take causes my stomach to churn that much more violently.

It doesn't feel good.

Or exciting.

Or right.

Only there's something strangely familiar about the wrongness flooding my being. Like I've experienced this pull before…

In my dream about Demeter? I wonder, frowning.

No.

It's similar, yet not.

Is this just a response to my Omega soul? Being confused by my desire since I'm used to human needs, not Omega needs?

Maybe.

But that doesn't explain the familiar wrongness.

My legs continue to move, taking me deeper into the maze, while my mind spins with caution. The urge to scream fills my lungs. Although, my lips don't part. It's like my body isn't fully under my control.

Which I've felt before, I realize. *But when?*

A vision of another corridor flickers through my mind, like it's being pushed to me from some repressed memory.

I chase it while my feet continue to pound against the hard ground.

Except suddenly it's softer.

Littered with petals and grass.

What? I nearly stumble as my brain tries to force my legs to cease running. Yet all I do is sprint harder. *What is happening to me?*

I look down and note the cement beneath my feet. However, I *feel* the plushness of a courtyard.

No.

Not a courtyard.

A hallway lined with fire lilies.

I smell their sweet perfume, loving the way they burn for me. Just like Hades...

I blink, the image gone in a flash and replaced by my eerie surroundings. Skulls etched into cement. Cobblestones. *Blossoming flowers.*

I shake my head, so confused by the juxtaposition between two realities.

Or is it a memory....? My lips curl down at the possibility. *What am I remembering?*

I search my surroundings, noting how they continue to fade in and out of another time. Another place. *Another experience.*

My heart beats hard in my chest, the sensation one I recognize. It propels me back to a moment when I was running against my will. Trying to stop. *Screaming inside with no outlet.*

I swallow, the terror of that day rolling through me in a foreign caress. Yet the memory of it is palpable. Like I know that moment better than any other.

Except it's gone in a flash, replaced by my chilling

surroundings once more as Pip flies into my path. His blue eyes are wide, his hands thrown upward to stop me.

I halt, suddenly in control of my body, and he gestures for me to turn around, a pleading look on his face. "What's happening to me?" I ask him, my voice a rasp of sound. "Why do I feel so strange, Pip?"

He points again at the path I've just run down, urgency in his features.

Until he begins to fade away into another vision. One of a frolicking beast. No. A... a... *deer*. Only this is no ordinary deer. It has antlers, a majestic black tail, and the markings of a standard animal. But its mouth is moving, and words are leaving its lips. Not sounds. *Words*.

It's talking to me.

Only, I can't hear what it's saying.

I try to read its lips, to understand the words.

Delos, I breathe in my mind, suddenly aware of his name. *A gift from Diana.*

My lashes flutter, the knowledge unexpected and the origin unknown.

Except...

Except it's not *entirely* unknown, is it?

Persephone, I realize in the next beat.

But the image of Delos vanishes into a very panicked Pip. He's still telling me to turn around. However, my feet refuse my mind all over again. I want to listen. I want to *obey*.

The world fades once more into a lush green garden, the bushes around me too tall to see around. It's beautiful, the flowers blossoming, the sun shining overhead.

Everything stills inside me, my lungs seeming to work for the first time in *eons*.

I close my eyes for one blissful second, indulging in the

beauty of life. The glory of *existing*. It's an allure I can't deny, a call I long to answer.

"Come home," a soft voice whispers into my ear. "I miss you, sweetheart…"

I shiver, the nickname one that was recently uttered in a very different voice.

A masculine one.

Morpheus.

My world turns, and I'm back in the maze, the thought of him seeming to return me to the present.

Where Pip is whirling around in front of me like a pissed-off tornado.

Though, he's not alone now. Athena, the owl I've only briefly met, is hovering above him, her wings spread wide as she flaps them at me.

Air rushes over my being, forcing me back several paces.

Agony ripples up my legs, the sensation stirred by my need to push *forward*, not go *backward*.

But another burst of energy from Athena's feathers shoves me in the direction of the cabin. Or where I think it is, anyway.

A yelp escapes me as jaws close around my thighs. However, a quick glance downward shows the familiar heads of Howl and Mort, their teeth gentle despite being huge and aggressively holding on to my legs.

They start to walk backward, causing me to stumble along with them. Only for a flourish of mist to whip around us all, stirring us up into a magical cyclone.

Another scream tries to escape me, but I'm lost. Flying. *Suddenly alone…*

All the familiars are gone.

Even Pip.

And I'm... I'm in that dark space again. The one where I have no body. No corporeal form. No *anything*.

Just my thoughts.

No, no, no!

I am *not* going to fall into this vapid nothingness again.

I refuse.

I shove against the mental constraints, locking into my imagination and *envisioning* a door.

It opens to reveal that maze of bushes again. Fire lilies. *Delos...*

But instead of staring straight at him, he's looking at a dark-haired woman with big brown eyes set in an oval-shaped face. She's stunning. Petite. And commanding the life around her.

Except she appears to be moving against her will, being dragged down the lively corridor by an invisible force. Her lips are parting on a scream she can't release. And Delos is desperately trying to grab her with his jaws, to tug her back.

But an arrow sails from out of the darkness ahead, spearing the beast right in the heart.

Which leaves the woman shaking with rage and despair. She looks at her beast, her eyes filling with tears, and suddenly I feel her torment. Her heartbreak. *Her fear.*

Because I am her and she is me.

Persephone...

Her nails claw into the ground, her legs kicking as she's suddenly on her back and being dragged across the earth.

But everything heals in her wake, leaving no signs of a struggle. Even Delos seems to evaporate into nothing.

As though neither of them was ever there.

"This is for your own good, child," a voice says, one I know too well by now. The same voice that whispered for me to come home. The same voice that told me I deserved this fate. The same one that dragged me off into a garden for thorns only knows how long.

Demeter.

Her desires whirl around me, her nurturing intentions a palpable presence that almost coaxes me to her side.

Only, I've seen the truth.

There are good Alphas in this world, I think, the words ones I can hear myself saying out loud in an accented tone. One that's similar to Hades's. *The God of Death is a good Alpha, Mama.*

I've never spoken those statements aloud, and yet I have.

As Persephone.

Her mind brushes mine. Her memories. Her experiences. *Her plights.*

The Omegas, I think, feeling them all around me. *Hearing* their pain. Their cries. *Their dreams burning away into ash…*

This is the place of rebirth. Resurrection. A plane created by Demeter using her gifts…

And the ones Persephone inherited through her mating.

It's all so clear to me now. So present. *So real.*

Yet, I know this isn't happening right now. I'm not truly in this world.

I'm in Hades's maze.

With my intended mates.

I close my eyes once more, picturing that world. The one I was running within when the strangeness overcame me. The place where my Alphas are waiting. Where my enforcer provides protection. *Where my body still exists…*

Sensations overwhelm me, ones I finally recognize.

A chill underlined in smoky wisps.

The scent of a crisp morning.

Sinful touches that inspire dark desires.

The combination causes me to fly once more, only it's

not a cyclone of foreign energy rotating around me this time. It's the caress and embrace of my future. My males. *My intended mates.*

But it's so much more than that.

I feel our maze.

Our familiars.

Our lives.

It's encased in a cold coffin of death. However, inside, we thrive.

The walls are frigid, the floor even chillier.

Yet vines can grow here.

Roots are possible.

Life will begin anew.

I can create. Hades can resurrect. Maliki can protect. And Morpheus can inspire.

It's an incredible marriage of circumstance and fate.

A world I want to be part of.

A bond I'll never leave willingly.

Something screeches in my ear, the agonizing sound going straight to my heart. But it doesn't pierce the shield around my vital organ. Instead, it withers away.

Because I'm safe here.

With my mates.

Surrounded by their warmth.

Their affection.

Their strength.

Demeter can't touch me.

It's a fact that becomes true as I open my eyes and find Maliki holding me, his gold eyes intense. Morpheus is beside him, his hand on my arm.

And Hades's palm is around my throat, his body seeming to cradle mine along with Maliki's.

It's like they caught me falling from the sky and formed a nest around me on the ground.

"Sera," Maliki breathes.

I stare at him, my lips parting to say his name.

But the gravity of everything I've just experienced whips around me once more, and all I can do is *scream*.

Because it's too much.

Too intense.

Too hot.

A combination of convoluted experiences.

I can't breathe.

I can't think.

Except my brain is on fire with the past. The present. *The now.*

My limbs shake.

My lungs burn.

My heart races.

I try to tell them I remember, that I know where the Omegas are, that we have to help them. Yet all I can do is whimper. Cry. *And beg.*

Because my world is upside down.

My body is being turned inside out.

And I register with a delirious thought that my heat has finally begun. It's the only explanation for what's happening to me right now.

Which means I'm about to be mindless. Hopeless. *Entirely at their mercy.*

Hades purrs, like he's excited by the prospect. However, in a grounding moment, I realize none of them are trying to fuck me. Or knot me. Or claim me.

They're simply comforting me.

Because Morpheus is purring, too. And Maliki's tattoos are vibrating.

"You're safe," Hades whispers against my ear. "Just focus on your breathing, all right? Inhale and exhale."

"Don't close your eyes, Serapina," Morpheus says

when my eyes begin to droop. "Look at me, sweetheart. Stay here with us."

I stare at him and then at Maliki.

Hades is the only one I can't see since he seems to have me and Maliki on his lap somehow.

Rather than ask questions or try to figure out how I've ended up in this nest of limbs, I just do what they suggested and *breathe*.

It's easier than thinking.

Easier than *remembering*.

But as soon as my heart stops thudding in my ear, I clear my throat.

Because *easy* isn't always *right*.

I need to tell them what's happened. What I know. *What I saw*.

"Persephone didn't betray you," I say, my voice a rasp of sound.

However, I know Hades heard me because he stiffens beneath me.

"She tried to crawl her way back to you," I go on. "Delos was there to help. But Demeter was too strong." My voice grows more powerful with each word, my reality mingling with my past, my soul oddly at ease as the truth finally reveals itself in my mind.

I feel miraculously whole.

Strangely vulnerable.

And exceptionally furious.

"I remember everything," I say, straightening my spine as I sit up more fully. "And I think I know how to find the other Omegas."

The Netherworld Fae Trilogy Concludes with
Knotted Myths...

Continue the series with *Knotted Myths*…

I remember everything now.
Every sordid deed.
Every lie.
Every manipulation.

My soul was deceived by the one Alpha I should have been able to trust.
Locked inside a mortal shell.
And anchored to a plane of nonexistence.

I'm determined to free the innocent Mythos Fae tangled up in this ancient web.
Only, I have to figure out how to free my inner Omega first.
Which is proving trickier than I could ever have imagined.

The three dominant fae in my life are determined to help me.
Protect me.
Mate me.

But surviving means working as a mate-circle, something that doesn't feel possible.
Maliki and Morpheus no longer trust Hades's motives.
And Hades isn't a team player.

If we can't find a path forward, we may be forever bound by the myths of our past.
Or I might be forced to make a choice.
One that will break my heart.
And destroy my soul…

Author's Note: *Knotted Myths* is the conclusion to the Netherworld Fae trilogy. It's a Hades & Persephone "why choose" retelling with Omegaverse vibes. Because knotting is always a good time…

LEXI C. FOSS

USA Today Bestselling Author Lexi C. Foss loves to play in
dark worlds, especially the ones that bite. She lives in
North Carolina with her family. When not writing, she's
busy crossing items off her travel bucket list, or chasing
eclipses around the globe. She's quirky, consumes way too
much coffee, and loves to swim.

Want access to the most up-to-date information for all of
Lexi's books? Sign-up for her newsletter here.

Lexi also likes to hang out with readers on Facebook in her
exclusive readers group - Join Here.

Where To Find Lexi:
www.LexiCFoss.com